HELL'S GATE

PARANORMAL ARCHAEOLOGY DIVISION
BOOK 1

ERNEST DEMPSEY

138 PUBLISHING

JOIN THE ADVENTURE

Visit ernestdempsey.net to get a free copy of the not-sold-in-stores short story, RED GOLD.

You'll also get access to exclusive content not available anywhere else.

While you're at it, swing by the official Ernest Dempsey fan page on Facebook at https://facebook.com/ErnestDempsey to join the community of travelers, adventurers, historians, and dreamers. There are exclusive contests, giveaways, and more!

Lastly, if you enjoy pictures of exotic locations, food, and travel adventures, check out my feed @ernestdempsey on the Instagram app.

What are you waiting for? Join the adventure today!

PROLOGUE

1959, TIWANAKU, BOLIVIA

Edmund Kiss leaned on his wooden cane as he stared at the Puerta del Sol; the Gate to the Sun. The warm summer sunshine beat down on his beige jacket and pants. A wide-brim hat shaded his face and ears, as well as portions of his neck. Knowing he would burn easily at this high elevation, the rest of his skin was covered. At his age, he didn't have time for such an inconvenience as sunburn. He knew he wasn't long for this world, but there was still enough time to change everything—to get back all he'd lost, reestablish his name, and create a legacy that would last until the end of time.

Just standing here again—before these ancient ruins—was a small victory for the old man. He'd been in this very place over thirty years before, contemplating the meaning of the bizarre Gate to the Sun.

As far as anyone knew, the ancient civilization of Tiwanaku was built at the highest elevation of any identified early structures. Kiss believed it was created over seventeen thousand years ago, though most experts have thoroughly discredited that hypothesis, along with the World Ice Theory.

Through the years, he'd been bullied and shamed out of every scientific community he could think of, even some that he didn't know existed. The outcry against his so-called ludicrous theories had been harsh, but nothing hurt him more than the evidence that all but eradicated most of his work.

They called it pseudoarchaeology, a science without basis or the remotest fragment of fact. That was the worst title someone like him could endure. "Pseudoarchaeology," he spat. "We'll see."

His voice cracked, but there was only one person near him to hear it. His assistant, a local named Paolo, stood next to him wearing a traditional Andean outfit that Kiss had seen many of the men in the area wearing. It comprised of a long-sleeve white shirt, dark vest, and matching dark pants. On his head, Paolo wore a wide-brim straw hat.

The Bolivian turned to Kiss with questions in his eyes. "I'm not sure about this, Herr Kiss," Paolo confessed. Fear caused his voice to tremble, and his accent thickened.

Kiss nodded. "I know, *Paolito*. I know. But it is our destiny, my young apprentice. We both need this. You for your family, and me... well, I have endured enough. This experiment will prove my theories correct, and it will make you famous enough to buy your family a decent home, food, and everything you could ever want."

The mention of food caused Paolo's stomach to grumble. He was hungry, but only had a few traditional Bolivian *cuñapés* in his bag. The small baked bread rolls wouldn't do much to fill his belly, but they were better than nothing, which was what he'd seen Kiss eat over the last thirty-six hours. The old man was a machine and seemed to exist on nothing but coffee, but Paolo knew his employer had to have eaten something—he'd just never seen it.

Paolo nodded as he considered the vision Kiss painted for him, a vision of a better life for his wife and children. They lived in squalor, in nothing but a wooden hut with dirt floors. This man had shown up from a foreign country with enough money to pay for two weeks' worth of work—a small fortune to Paolo—but the promise of much more wealth to come was what had lured the young man to the side of the mysterious Edmund Kiss.

"So, all I have to do is walk through the gate?" Paolo asked. Uncertainty still shook his voice.

"That's it," Kiss confirmed. His raspy response ended with several coughs, and for a second Paolo thought he saw a smattering of blood on the old man's wrinkled, freckled hand.

Paolo swallowed back his fear. "The legends say that—"

"I know what they say," Kiss snapped. His voice boomed for the first time since Paolo met the old man, and the young Bolivian shuddered at the near-demonic response. He cringed and took an involuntary step away from the German.

Kiss sighed. "*Lo siento,*" he said, apologizing in Spanish. "I know the local legends, Paolo. One claims that to walk through the gate is to invite instant death by the gods. Another piece of lore suggests that it will transport you to another place, another world perhaps, maybe even to the home of the gods themselves."

"Yes, Herr Kiss. Among others."

"You speak of the realm of demons, yes?"

Paolo nodded reluctantly.

"I don't believe that one, Paolo. You must not, either. Those are old fairy tales, told to keep children away from the ruins. Nothing more, I assure you."

He noted the doubt still gushing from the man's eyes and nodded. "It's fine, Paolo. I'll do it. Don't worry. Perhaps I'll still share the glory and riches with you." Kiss stiffened and clutched the satchel under his arm tighter.

He took a feeble step forward, leaning on his cane as little as possible without falling over. With the first step, the old man's ankle twisted and he nearly fell. Paolo surged forward and caught him under the right arm. He hoisted Kiss upright and shook his head.

"No, you are already too weak. The air up here is thin, and you're already struggling. I will do it."

Kiss grinned devilishly. The young man had bought it.

"Here," Kiss muttered as he unhooked the satchel from his shoulder. "Take this."

"What is it?" Paolo asked. He eyed the satchel with curious skepticism.

"There is a special crystal inside that I carry wherever I go. It will protect you, just in case some of those old legends are true." He flashed a friendly smirk and then winked. "It's for good luck."

Paolo nodded and took the satchel. He started to open it to see this mysterious crystal, but Kiss reached out and snatched the younger man's wrist with a surprisingly strong grip.

Kiss squeezed so hard that Paolo winced from the pain. "No," Kiss ordered. "Do not open it. It is a sacred crystal and must be kept covered at all times."

Paolo frowned at the explanation. "Where did you get it?"

Kiss sighed. "Never mind, Paolo. I can see you're not the man for this job. I wonder if I might find someone in the village with more courage. Perhaps I missed my guess with you. It's just that..." He pretended to be distraught about the whole thing, adding drama to the moment. "Well, it's just that...I have more money for you. Another two weeks' worth of pay. But if you're not up for it, no worry. You go on back to town, and I'll find another person who wants to make some money."

"No," Paolo refuted. "I can do it. I just wanted to see this crystal, that's all. I'll do it." His pay had just doubled. His eyes were wide with hope as he realized he was about to earn a month's salary for just walking through some ancient stone doorway.

The Bolivian tucked the satchel under his arm and took a step forward, no longer hindered by the superstitions that had racked his fears since arriving at the ruins. This place was full of rumors, legends, and myths that kept the locals at a safe distance. When they did visit, it was mostly for honoring ancient rituals; rites that had long since died with those who'd created them so many centuries before. Occasionally, a local like Paolo would show tourists around. He'd done it before for extra money, and since he could speak competent English, he'd done well.

He neared the stone gate and paused, his torso wavering over his waist. He stared at the monolith towering over him. A crack ran through the upper right corner of the stone, a reminder of how it had looked when the first explorers rediscovered it in the nineteenth century. The monolith had been lying on its back when the new visitors arrived, and a portion of the gate had cracked through. Historians and archaeologists worked to restore the ancient doorway so it would look more as it had when it was first erected. The crack, however, remained.

Emboldened by the promise of financial stability for his family, Paolo steeled his nerves and stepped forward.

Kiss watched with rapt intensity as his guide moved closer to the doorway. He had no idea what would happen, but he needed to find out. Was this simply a symbolic door the ancients of Tiwanaku put here for ceremonies? Or was there a deeper purpose, a more mysterious reason behind it?

Paolo slowed as his feet neared the edge of the threshold. The bright sun beat down on his face as he inclined his head to look up at the stone gate once more. He blinked back the searing sunshine and lowered his head. He frowned as he realized that the satchel under his arm had become warmer, much warmer. Not only that; it seemed to vibrate.

He turned toward Kiss. He was still standing in place, watching with curiosity.

"I think something is wrong with your crystal," Paolo said. "It feels hot. And I think it's vibrating."

Kiss quickly shook off the insinuation. "It's fine, Paolo. Now, please. We really need to get back to town. Could you hurry? Just step through the door. This is the easiest money you will ever make in your life."

Paolo knew the man was right. All he had to do was take a few steps through some ancient stone doorway and his family would be provided for better than they had ever been. He'd still work, of course, which would bring in extra money. Maybe he could pay to get a real floor, or even a different place to live, a better place for his wife and kids.

The visions of a better future squelched any doubts that lingered in his mind. He turned back to the doorway and stepped forward.

Kiss watched, stiffening his spine as Paolo stepped into the doorway.

A loud ringing abruptly filled his ears. He winced at the painful sound, but that didn't keep him from seeing the most incredible but terrifying sight he'd ever witnessed in his life.

A bright light appeared in the doorway where Paolo had been standing. The bluish-white sphere had consumed the Bolivian in an instant. Kiss swallowed, but didn't dare look away as the ball of light remained suspended in the air several feet above the ground.

The ringing waned and the sphere pulsed slowly, then the cadence picked up. The orb swelled with each pulse until it occupied the entire doorway.

Kiss bent over his cane and narrowed his eyes. There were people in the ball of light, but none he recognized. The images blinked for a moment before being replaced by another, then another, over and over again. Most of the people he saw were dressed like the natives of centuries past. One appeared to be a chief donning a massive headdress that looked like a jaguar. Another was covered in feathers.

Then, suddenly, the orb pulsed one last time and vanished.

Kiss stared absently at the gate. After nearly a minute, he stepped forward. "Paolo?" he said. "Where are you?"

Silence.

"Paolo? Are you there?" Kiss took another wary step toward the gate. He pushed back his fears. What did he have to be afraid of? He knew he would be dead within a year—if he died sooner, would it matter?

He clenched his jaw and shuffled ahead until he reached the opening to the gate. He looked up at the top and around at the sides of the doorframe, reaching out his free hand and touched the smooth stone. Kiss sighed and stepped into the doorway. He looked around the backside to see if his guide was hiding behind the monolith, but there was no sign of him.

Paolo had vanished. And Kiss's only sample of the strange element had disappeared with him.

1

ATHENS

Neil ran harder than he ever had in his life, ducking around small trees planted along the curb and weaving through the endless stream of pedestrians in the Athens old city district known as Plaka.

Cafés bursting with dinner patrons and drunken revelers lined the sidewalks, making it nearly impossible to walk without stepping onto the street. Luckily for Neil, this section of the district was pedestrian only. He'd often thought that all Athenian streets should be pedestrian only, considering how narrow so many of them were. He'd seen more than a few busted side mirrors on the tiny cars driven by the locals, and he wasn't the least bit surprised.

For a moment, he thought he might have lost the men who were chasing him, but an angry shout from behind interrupted those few seconds of respite.

Neil knew not to look back; he had to keep pushing forward. These men were dangerous—no, more than that—but he couldn't think of a word that adequately described the absolute fear they could instill in a person's mind, the sickening things he'd witnessed, and the soul-tearing experiences of the last two months.

He put those thoughts to the back of his mind as he fled with the artifact safely zipped into the inner pocket of his jacket.

The metal object wasn't large, but he felt the weight of it was slowing him down; like a ship's anchor dragging along the sea bottom. Neil knew that was his imagination in overdrive, but it felt like a reality.

He shoulder-barged into a man wearing a tight black Nirvana T-shirt, spun, and kept running. The guy shouted obscenities in Greek, but Neil ignored him as he sprinted down the street.

He twisted to the left, narrowly avoiding a young couple pushing a stroller. As he spun, he caught a glimpse of the illuminated Acropolis, dominated by the Parthenon perched at the top. The darkening sky to the east provided a dramatic backdrop to the ancient temple site.

Neil wished he had time to appreciate it, soak in the ancient history, but below the view, on the street behind him, were four men hell-bent on ripping him to pieces.

They were gaining, and it appeared the henchmen weren't in the least fatigued. Neil, however, gasped for every breath, pushing hard against the burning in his legs. He was in excellent shape, but these hunters seemed almost superhuman.

Suddenly, the crowds of people and seemingly endless rows of sidewalk cafés gave way to a quiet, darker section of the street. The businesses here were closed, save for a hookah lounge on the right with its few patrons and the occasional bar.

Neil's abrupt confusion sketched across his face. He'd gone from what was obviously a popular area for the locals, into what appeared to be a seedy location, in a matter of seconds.

He took the time to turn and look back. The blond man was still leading the pack of wolves at his heels, all of them muscular and graced with chiseled facial features. The leader was perhaps an inch shorter than the rest and had a slighter build. He knew they'd been special ops in the past, most of them the product of German elite forces training, but they pursued him with inhuman intensity.

He cut to the right at the next intersection and found himself on another equally sketchy street, the windows and doors secured with black iron bars, and graffiti adorned the exterior walls.

This street rose at a slight incline. He couldn't recall being in this area before. The sound of a metro train over the rise gave him hope. If he could get to the nearest station, he could blend in with the crowd, get on a train, and escape. Once he was back in the UK, he'd be safe.

Neil heard the footsteps behind him closing in. He and his pursuers were the street's only occupants, a fact that reassured his previous assertion that it wasn't a place for tourists to hang out, rather a spot for underground criminal activity to thrive.

He was nearing the top of the hill when a man stepped out in front of him. He had his hands in the pockets of tanned khakis and a pair of expensive loafers on his feet. His shirt, a navy-blue Polo, was tucked in. The white belt was a bit much, but it stood out and contrasted the rest of the outfit.

Three more men, dressed much like those chasing Neil, emerged to stand behind the man.

Neil felt his legs give out as he staggered to a stop, mere yards from the casually dressed man.

"In a hurry, Neil?" the man asked. His blond hair shook as he spoke, and his crystalline-blue eyes pierced Neil's soul.

"You could say that," Neil answered, giving the man no sense of control over the situation, even though that's exactly what the guy had.

"Oh, Neil," the man mused, "did you really think you could steal one of my priceless artifacts and get away with it?"

"Thought had occurred to me."

"And do what with it?" The man splayed his hands out wide as if the street itself might answer the question. "Were you going to sell it? I can tell you: No one is going to pay much for that trinket."

"Then why do you want it so bad? I thought you said it was priceless."

"It is to me," the man said. His face darkened as he took a step forward, almost as if the streetlights bowed before him.

Neil heard the men charge up behind him. Within a second, they were on him. Two grabbed his arms from either side while another punched him in the kidneys, dropping him to his knees. Neil's kneecaps screamed in pain as they smashed into the pavement, but he only let out a grimace.

Neil repeated his question. "Why is it so important, Buri? If it's just a trinket, why did you call it priceless?" Neil knew he was a dead man now. Nothing short of a miracle would get him out of this, and he was out of those.

The man named Buri stepped forward and plucked the artifact from the palm of one of his henchmen. He inspected both sides of the dark gray metal, analyzing the inscriptions of a language long dead. The characters carved into the artifact looked like runes, something that might have been connected to the ancient tribes of Norsemen who first emerged from Scandinavia so long ago.

A piece of gold flashed on Buri's right ring finger. Neil saw the ring he'd seen so many times since joining this operation. He'd recognized part of it, a symbol that should have died off at the end of World War II, but here it was, rearing its ugly head again.

During his time undercover with the black-market artifacts dealer, Neil learned that Buri had inherited it from a family member, probably two generations removed. The man was too young to be the direct heir, probably a grandson. Neil figured him to be in his early forties.

"I'm glad to see you haven't damaged it," Buri said dryly. "That would have been a shame, although I doubt there's much you could have done to it." He shook the disc up and down in front of Neil's face. "Do you know what this is?"

Neil struggled against the men holding his arms like a wild animal caught in a hunter's snare. "It's an artifact. Nothing more. A piece of history that belongs in a museum." Neil spat the words, but he knew that they were hollow, unconvincing.

Buri snorted and shook his head. "Try again, Neil. If that's your real name. Which agency are you with? I'd guess MI6, but this isn't really their thing, now is it?"

"More people know what you're up to than you think," Neil sneered. "You can kill me, but there will be more coming for you. You won't get away with this."

The leader in the Polo chuckled wickedly and then stood up straight once more. "This is a piece of an ancient machine, technology that was lost a long time ago." His German accent melted around the English words. "Once we have all the pieces, we will be able to unlock the door."

"Door? What door? What are you talking about?" Neil continued to pull against the tight grip on his arms and wrists. He needed to keep Buri talking.

Buri grinned and leaned forward again. His expensive cologne wafted through the warm summer night and into Neil's nostrils. It made him cough; the scent sickened him. It was tacky and cloying, over refined, as were many of the perfumes and colognes wealthy, powerful types like Buri preferred.

"That is none of your concern, Neil. I can see that we will need to be more careful with our recruiting process in the future. We mustn't be so quick to allow new members into the fold."

Buri turned to the man nearest him. "Kill him. Be quick about it. Dump his body in the train gap over there. Make it look like suicide."

The henchman next to Buri gave a curt nod and stepped toward the prisoner. Buri turned and began to walk away, but Neil would have none of it.

"That's it?" Neil shouted, doing his best to draw the attention of anyone in the vicinity. "Can't do it yourself, so you have to have your goons do your dirty work?"

Buri wouldn't be goaded into some bravado-filled shouting match. To him, a mole was the worst kind of problem. Someone had screwed up, someone on the inside, and he needed to figure out who that was. He knew who had brought Neil to him. It was one of his trusted lieutenants, and there would be questions that needed answers.

"Did you hear me, Buri?" Neil yelled. His training kicked in and he twisted his right wrist as he slipped his right foot back, effectively drawing both men holding him toward his front.

The unexpected maneuver threw them off balance and the two guards toppled forward over his back. One of them hit the side of his head on the pavement and grasped at his skull, his vision blurred.

The other rolled over, recovering instantly, and now Neil was on his feet again—surrounded by Buri's men.

One was still on the ground, but there were still six ready to pounce. None of them had their weapons out, and Neil could only assume that was because shooting him would draw attention, plus the men had been ordered to make it look like suicide. Difficult to do that with a body full of bullet holes.

"Come on then," Neil said to the men as he spun around in a circle, meeting each and every eye. It was like looking into the eyes of dead men. Their cold, vapid stares displayed a vacancy of conscience he'd never seen, even in his line of work.

The men closed in on him as one. He'd been outnumbered before in a fight, but had survived because his opponents didn't understand how to attack simultaneously, as a unit. These men made no such mistake.

Neil knew how to handle it, though.

He did as he'd been trained: pick one target and attack with as much violence as he could muster.

One of the men was slightly shorter than the others, if only by an inch. His build was also slighter, though there wasn't an ounce of fat on him. He was lean muscle all over and would be quicker than the rest, unless Neil missed his guess. At the moment, he'd take a speedier enemy over a stronger one. Once in the grasp of the others, he doubted he could get away again.

Neil surged at his target. As he guessed, the blond man with the pointy nose and narrow jaw dipped right and countered with an elbow to Neil's back. Another tried to grab the prisoner, but Neil saw it coming and twisted out of the way, stumbling away from the circle of death.

The men adjusted and formed a half circle around him and once more closed in. Neil had bought himself a moment, though, and he lunged at the initial target again. He threw technique and strategy out the window, opting for brute force. He knew he was stronger than the one man. He'd deal with the other five after, although the one who'd hit his head was back on his feet again, albeit a touch dizzy.

Neil called on an old technique he'd learned back when he played semiprofessional rugby in England. He lowered his shoulder and drove it into the ribs of his target, plowing through him with devastating force. Neil heard something crack and knew it wasn't his collarbone, so it had to be a rib. The man didn't scream in pain as he was driven backward and onto the ground. The back of his skull hit the pavement with a sickening smack, and his eyes stared blankly into the darkening sky overhead.

Without hesitating, Neil rolled over the top of the dead man, planted his hands on the ground, and pushed hard. He extended his legs and hit the recovering henchman in the neck with the heel of his right shoe, crushing his larynx.

Neil whipped his legs around, landed on his knees, then sprang up again. Two men were down, leaving five more. He noted Buri had stopped in his tracks and was now watching the melee as he stood alone at the corner.

With two men down, the half circle tightened as they approached again; though this time the henchmen were more cautious.

"Have to take me all together, eh?" Neil spat, wiping the side of his face with the back of his right hand. "None of you man enough to do it on your own?"

The men surrounded him once more, and Neil turned, spinning in place as if waiting for a dance partner to make their choice as to who would tango first.

"Stop," Buri commanded. Neil hadn't noticed the man shift his position. Now he was behind two of the men in the circle. He stood there casually, as if he had nothing better to do, but there was an intensity to his gaze. "Let him come to me."

Neil's eyelids narrowed. His brow wrinkled in confusion. "You won't fight me," Neil said. "You may not know much about me, but you know I'm good."

"I know everything about you, Neil. I know you're from Newcastle. That accent is unmistakable. While I may not know who sent you, I know someone did. And I'm about to send them—and the mole in our organization—a message."

Rage burned inside Neil as he listened to the man's words. He'd watched Buri do horrific things to people, not directly but through his henchmen—men like those surrounding Neil at this very moment. Most victims were scooped up in big trafficking rings, the largest percentage coming from Asia. Neil knew many were from North Korea, but the Chinese also made up a big part of the population.

Neil thought of them and the things they'd been through. He recalled the dungeons under this very city, the laboratory that was designed to inflict pain as much as it was to test the bounds of the human mind and body. He'd seen such images from World War II, after the Allies had emerged victorious. To think that those kinds of things could still be going on was beyond disturbing, and it fueled Neil's urge to kill the man in the Polo, at whatever cost.

He could deal with the other five after Buri was dead.

Neil stepped forward carefully, easing past the men who had moved to the side to let him through. He raised his hands into a fighting stance and waited.

Buri motioned him forward, still not taking up a defensive position or looking at all like he wanted to fight. He looked more like a middle-aged man waiting to tee off at a golf course.

"Fine," Neil said.

He moved quickly toward his target, his jaw clenched. He faked a jab, then faked a roundhouse punch, hoping to hit with a real jab as a third move.

Buri, however, was too fast. He didn't flinch at the first two fakes, then as Neil snapped his fist forward, Buri twisted, grabbed Neil's wrist, and flung him forward in one quick maneuver.

Neil felt his weight surge forward. He tried to recover, but momentum dictated everything now. The last thing he saw was Buri spinning around with something shiny in his hand.

The artifact smacked into Neil's temple with a thud, and the world blurred in his vision. He staggered to a stop, only able to keep his legs under him with the greatest effort he could exert. His hands hung limp at his side as he wobbled in all directions.

"You see?" Buri said, stepping up to his opponent. He clapped his hand on the back of Neil's neck and forced the British agent to look him in the eyes. It didn't matter if he could see clearly or not. "No one can stop us, Neil. No one. And when we open the door, our power will be unlimited."

Buri stepped behind Neil with the deftness of an assassin. He wrapped his forearm around the man's head and pulled on his neck with the other hand. An audible pop escaped Neil's neck, and his legs gave out. He fell to the pavement at Buri's feet.

Buri looked down at the dead agent without concern. "Now, as I instructed before, dispose of the body and make it look like suicide. Toss it onto the train tracks. And do not disappoint me again."

He turned and walked by the two men on the ground who were still trying to recover from their injuries. Buri never looked back as he walked around the corner and disappeared into the night.

2

ATHENS

Detective Dimitris Frangos stood over the body, showing no sign of the disgust his brain seemed so eager to vent. He'd seen more dead bodies in his line of work than most people would see in two lifetimes, but this was the first he'd seen in this condition.

It wasn't the dismembered pieces that were unusual; he'd seen a suicide-by-metro-rail before. Those hell-bent on killing themselves would typically walk onto a track or jump from a platform mere seconds before a train came along.

This victim—that's what he was calling it despite his department calling it a suicide—had chosen a different route. He'd gone to the trouble of climbing a steel fence that was meant to prevent this sort of thing, at least in part, then jumped to the tracks thirty feet below.

The coroner claimed his neck was broken when he landed on his head. There were two primary wounds, one on the right temple and the other a deeper injury to the top of his skull, just above the right ear. The initial hypothesis was that the man jumped, struck his head on one of the rails, broke his neck, and died instantly. But that didn't explain the wound to his temple, at least not in Dimitris' mind. And it certainly wasn't a sound explanation for why this man jumped to his death-by-train when the next metro wasn't due to arrive for another five minutes. Again, he embraced the facts. Most suicides-by-train were well planned, the victims not wishing to linger long on the tracks—the wheels made certain, with devastating effect, there was no coming back.

The victim also had no identification on him; another anomaly to this case that most of his peers seemed happy to write up and file away.

A cell phone was the only thing in the dead man's possession at the time of his death. The forensics team had not been able to unlock the device, but Dimitris knew people on the force who could handle that, though he only trusted one of them.

Corruption was rampant in Greece—as in most countries—but particularly in Athens where high-ranking officials had been called out for years over bribery and embezzlement and working under-the-table contracts as far back as the 2004 Olympics; a venture that essentially bankrupted the nation and caused more than a ripple across the economies of Europe.

Despite the corruption at the top, Greece remained a relatively safe place. Murders and other violent crimes were rare, with most of the crime on the streets committed by pickpockets lifting money or identification from tourists, and even that wasn't rampant. They rarely preyed on the locals of Athens, and usually operated on the metro trains. Dimitris often walked through different parts of the city late at night, and he never felt unsafe. During one such walk a few weeks ago, he concluded that it was ordinary people who were blessed with integrity, whereas politicians had very little. Perhaps it was like that everywhere.

Dimitris knew this wasn't the work of pickpockets. Either it was suicide, as his colleagues claimed, or it was murder and the killer tried to cover his or her tracks by dumping the body over the fence. That would be a difficult task for one person. He didn't know anyone on the force who could lift that much weight by themselves, and there were some large guys in his department. Most were ex-basketball players, some of them in the professional leagues in Greece.

Dimitris wasn't one of them. He enjoyed watching the sport, but football was his game. His frame was just shy of six feet, which didn't lend itself well to basketball, but he'd been one heck of a striker on the pitch.

His eyes wandered to the victim's arm, which had been severed by the train. The metro driver hadn't seen the man on the tracks until it was too late.

Dimitris was hoping the phone, encased in a plastic bag, might ring and provide him with a connection to either the killer or someone who knew the man's identity. As yet, no such luck. It appeared he would have to elicit help to get the device unlocked. Maybe then he would get some information. At the very least, he'd get a phone number and a few of the most recent contacts. From there, he could get the investigation off the ground.

As the thought sped through his mind, the crew taking care of the body lifted the corpse by the legs and began sliding it into a black bag.

The man's head rolled to the side, the neck limp and powerless to resist any movement. The packing guys often displayed a lack of empathy, except when there were onlookers, in which case they would show the utmost respect for the body.

In this instance, Dimitris was glad for their carelessness. It gave him an idea.

"Hold on," he said, waving to the two men as they loaded the body bag onto a gurney. "Wait a moment."

The two men looked up from their grisly task and saw the detective hurrying toward them.

"I'm sorry to bother you," he said. "One moment before you load the victim into the van."

The men shrugged and stepped back from the wheeled stretcher.

Dimitris reached into his jacket pocket and found the blue nitrile gloves he'd brought along. He usually carried a pair with him to crime scenes, preferring to bring his own than use the ones issued by the department. Call it a touch of paranoia, but he preferred to do things himself—less chance of screwing something up that way, and if he did, he knew who to blame.

He slipped a glove onto his right hand and unzipped the body bag. The victim's swollen face appeared, the eyes closed in eternal slumber. Dimitris nodded and then slipped the second glove onto his left hand. He removed the phone from the plastic bag and swiped up from the bottom, initiating the face recognition software.

The two men from the coroner's office were appalled by the detective's intentions, but they said nothing.

After holding the phone over the dead man's face for a moment, Dimitris looked at the screen. The words on the device told him the face wasn't recognized. He grunted in disappointment.

"Is...is that the victim's phone?" one of the men asked. He had a thick head of black hair that dangled below the tops of his ears as he spoke.

"Yes, it is."

The man licked his lips and frowned. "Well, if you're trying to open it, the man's eyes would have to be...open."

"Ah," Dimitris said in a matter-of-fact tone. "Very good."

He reached over with his left hand and, to the chagrin of the two bagmen, pried the eyes open with his thumb and forefinger. Then he held the phone over the man's face again and swiped up to open the software.

This time, when Dimitris checked, it was on the home screen and displayed a collection of apps.

"That did it," he said. "Thank you, gentlemen. That will be all."

Dimitris turned and walked away. The two men stared after him, wondering if he was going to close the dead man's eyes. When Dimitris was several yards away, they figured he wasn't returning and did the deed themselves, then zipped up the bag again.

Dimitris wandered over to his car and eased into the front seat. He stared at the device, noting the red oblong indicator in the top left. The numbers were still running, like a clock in a football match.

The dead man had made a recording, and it was still active. Dimitris scrunched his face and narrowed his eyes as he looked at the screen, trying to decide if he should open the recording app or not. He glanced over at the two men who were now loading the body onto the ambulance and waved nonchalantly.

The men seemed to pay no attention as they went about their task.

Dimitris pressed the red oval with his gloved index finger and the recording app bloomed to life. He pressed the stop button and then saved the recording under the title Last Words.

Then he went into the settings and changed the display lock to *Never* so the device wouldn't shut off. He knew he couldn't change the victim's pin without the previous one. There were channels he could navigate to take care of that issue, but he wasn't sure he wanted anyone else to know what he was doing. This one had to be kept quiet.

He closed the door of his car, hit play on the recording, and listened.

3

ATLANTA

Tara Watson stared at her husband, waiting for him to break. The intensity of her gaze alone nearly caused him to crack. What had he done to deserve this?

Alex Simms did his best to hold her stare, but the searing pain in his mouth was too much to bear. He could feel the tears welling in the corners of his eyes, and knew he'd lost.

"Ah!" he gasped and reached for the cup of Thai tea sitting next to his plate of pad Thai.

He wrapped his lips around the straw and drew the cool, creamy liquid into his mouth, instantly soothing the burning heat.

"I told you you couldn't do Thai hot," Tara said, leaning back with a satisfied, gloating look on her face. She draped her wrists over her crossed legs and sat there looking smug while he drained the contents of the cup.

Alex nodded. "Yeah, yeah. You were right. That's...way...too...hot," he said between gulps. The straw gurgled, signaling the cup was empty, but the peppery flames in his mouth were barely stifled.

"I need more," he said. Reaching over, he snatched her drink before she could stop him.

She shook her head, laughing. "Maybe we should do something a little less spicy for you next time."

Alex nodded eagerly as he drained the contents of the second cup. "Yeah," he agreed after setting the cup down. "I think I'm going to take a break from Thai for a while."

"Maybe we'll do Moroccan tomorrow."

The momentary relief on his face turned to horror. "Seriously? That food is just as spicy."

She bellowed a loud laugh and nearly fell out of her seat. "I know. I'm just messing with you, honey."

She stood up and walked over to his side of the table, bent down, and planted a kiss on his forehead.

"I don't know how you eat that stuff. It could melt steel."

Tara grinned at him. "Or maybe you're just not meant to eat spicy stuff. Not everyone can handle Thai hot."

She let her fingers trace over his shoulders, then pulled away and walked over to the nearest computer.

Alex stared down at his mostly full plate and realized he was still hungry. He was not tempted to finish the pad Thai, though. He'd have to grab a burger or maybe something from one of the vending machines upstairs.

He watched as his wife leaned over one of the chairs in the lab to stare at the information scrolling across a computer screen. It was one of six such screens at that workstation. There were three other stations just like it, one in each corner of the cavernous laboratory.

This was their den; their lair, as they sometimes called it. The lab was located in the basement of the International Archaeological Agency in Atlanta and was where they spent most of their time, even sleeping there occasionally.

It was a good thing, too.

Their boss, Tommy Schultz, or his partner, Sean Wyatt, would often call on them for their expertise, or their uncanny ability to find information other people could not.

With state-of-the-art technology and the fastest quantum computers in the world, Alex and Tara—affectionately known as the kids—could dig up vital details in the time it would take others days to find, if ever.

Recent events, however, had changed everything.

A group of middle schoolers, who called themselves the Adventure Guild, had discovered a bizarre artifact in the mountains of western North Carolina. The artifact was crafted in the shape of a pyramid and was made from a substance that had never been discussed in any scientific circles, at least not that Tara and Alex had heard.

The strange substance was an element called Quantium. That was all they knew, but it was apparent that someone else knew the term, too. The middle schoolers found themselves in a heap of trouble, though through their wits and skills had outsmarted a group of bad men who had their sights set on the Quantium pyramid.

With the artifact safely returned to its home, the hope was that there would be no more trouble surrounding the new element. Before returning it to the temple, Alex and Tara had taken a tiny sample and put it in a glass case, sealing it airtight.

The sample was brought back to the lab for testing, but early indications were that even their high-powered systems couldn't properly analyze the mysterious element.

The confusing data that flowed over the computer screens indicated that Quantium's properties were unlike any other element. The atomic arrangement of protons, electrons, and neutrons differed from anything Alex and Tara had ever seen. The sample's atomic orbit was haphazard, the electrons swirled around in different directions, the same direction, and no direction—essentially sitting still—all at the same time. To say it was bizarre was an understatement.

"What's it doing now?" Alex asked as he picked at the noodles in his bowl of pad Thai. He appeared to be considering another go at the way-too-spicy dish. The faint trace of fire still smoldering on the back of his tongue, however, prevented any such foolhardy action.

"Same as before," Tara answered. She straightened and looked over her shoulder at her husband, who was still sifting through his food with a fork.

"And by that you mean it's still as completely haphazard as before. No pattern. No discernible systematic cycle."

"Exactly. It's really weird but very cool."

"You think we should run more tests on it?" Alex raised his hopes along with both eyebrows. He loved this kind of stuff.

"Maybe, but I have a feeling they will come back with the same results. This element doesn't obey the laws of classical physics, not entirely."

"Aptly named substance then, Quantium," he smirked.

"Definitely. But I have so many questions."

"That makes two of us."

"I mean, where did it come from?" She put her hands on her hips and chewed her bottom lip as she pondered the question. "No one has ever reported finding anything like this in nature."

"You think it's synthetic?"

"Maybe?" She answered the question with an uncertain one of her own.

Tara's phone began to vibrate on top of the metal table where she'd been eating. The device rattled and danced, startling Alex. He nearly fell over backward off his stool.

He looked at the phone. "It's Tommy."

"Can you get it?" she asked.

Alex nodded and picked up the phone, tapped the green answer button, and held the device to his ear. "What's up, Boss?"

"Code black," Tommy said sharply.

Alex's spine stiffened.

"Yes, sir," he said and ended the call.

"Code black," Alex snapped to his wife.

She was hunched over the desk again, staring at the computer monitor when she heard the words. Tara turned and looked over her shoulder at Alex. Seeing the stern look on his face, she nodded. She slid into the seat in front of the keyboard, swiped the mouse to the right, hit the escape key, and then pulled up a minimized window. It was nothing but a black screen with a blinking cursor. She tapped the code word into the command box and pressed enter. There was no look to her husband for confirmation.

A code black had to be taken seriously. Always. Especially considering what they were dealing with.

Immediately, the computer shut off. She turned and looked at the metal-and-glass container to her right. It was shrouded in wires that were connected to sensors and various analytical instruments within the case. Inside, a metal ball was suspended by several cables and hooked into several other wires.

The second Tara pressed the enter key, the case began lowering into the floor. It took less than three seconds for the containment unit to descend out of view. The moment the top of it disappeared, a thick floor tile slid into place, covering the hole almost seamlessly.

Once the case was out of sight, Tara and Alex knew that two six-inch steel plates would slide over it. Those plates were also topped with a lead panel. The containment unit would be safe from detection—and an air raid.

Alex picked up his fork again and began playing with his food. Tara returned to the table and continued where she had left off, nibbling on some panang curry with tofu and rice.

It wasn't long before Tara saw the reason for the code black. A man in a navy-blue suit and matching tie strolled down the corridor just beyond the glass windows that lined the inner wall of the laboratory. Four other men trailed behind him. Each of them wore dark blue jackets with bright maize letters on the back. These men had thicker chests and backs, indicating the bulletproof vests they wore beneath their windbreakers.

The group followed Tommy, their boss, as he calmly ambled down the corridor.

"FBI?" Tara asked as she forked some curry into her mouth.

Alex turned and looked out into the hall as the men marched to the door and stopped, waiting for Tommy to open it.

Tommy pressed the numbers on the keypad. The door unlocked with a loud click and then swung open. The man in the suit cut in front of Tommy and stormed into the lab. His shiny black shoes clicked on the hard floor.

"Sweep this entire room," the man said, pointing a finger around the perimeter.

The men in the windbreakers split up and began searching the lab. They flipped over papers, opened drawers, and checked display cases—the ones that weren't locked airtight.

"Please, Agent Brooks," Tommy insisted, "we have quite a few priceless items here that we are researching. Tell your men to be careful. I'd hate to have any of these artifacts damaged."

The man called Agent Brooks turned to face Tommy after staring at Tara and Alex for ten seconds. He whirled around on his heels like a man who'd been in the military most of his adult life. As he moved, the salt-and-pepper hair on his head didn't budge. It was frozen in a permanent quiff only a few inches long but pristinely swept to one side and up slightly to the right.

"Then give me the artifact," Brooks demanded, "and we'll be on our way."

Tommy sighed. His thick, dark brown hair jiggled slightly as his chin dropped to his chest. "I've already told you: We don't have an artifact like what you're describing. You can have a look around. You're not going to find some...what did you call it?"

"Quantium, Mr. Schultz. It's called Quantium. And you know exactly what I'm talking about." The man took a threatening step toward Tommy, narrowing the gap between them to only a foot.

Brooks was around the same height as Tommy, just a shade under six feet tall. Tommy was easily stronger than the wiry agent, but what the man lacked in size he certainly made up for in ability. His suit was taut, and it was easy to imagine the body of a mixed martial arts fighter inside it. Brooks was older than Tommy, too, probably in his mid-fifties, which was also not a good sign. If there was one thing Tommy knew, it was not to pick on guys who were a little older than him. In a brawl, experience counted for way more than most people gave it credit.

This wasn't a nightclub, though, and the two men weren't drunkenly arguing over a woman at the bar. Brooks was a federal agent, and without some kind of protection—the legal kind—Tommy and his crew were at the mercy of the authorities.

Tommy wished his friend Sean was there, but he was off on an assignment, transporting some artifacts for the Israeli government.

Sean would know how to work these guys over. He spoke their language, knew how to deal with them. He could get them out. But Sean wasn't there.

At least Tara and Alex had done their part in hiding the evidence. They were still sitting at the table eating, although it appeared Alex was only playing with his food.

To say Tommy was glad he'd set up a safety protocol for an event such as this was a massive understatement. He had a feeling when they brought back a sample of the Quantium that it could possibly draw the wrong kind of attention.

There was no way to know what kind of energy signatures that tiny sliver was putting out, and if there was part of the government tuned into that, they'd find it. Tommy wasn't sure if that's how Brooks learned of the element in the lab. Right now wasn't the time to ask. It was hidden in a place where these men wouldn't detect it.

Agent Brooks turned toward the young couple at the table. He laced his fingers behind his back and took a deliberate step toward them. "I assume that your boss here, Mr. Schultz, has instructed you to keep quiet and not tell me or—anyone else that may come asking —about the sample of Quantium you recently recovered."

Tara and Alex stared at him blankly, just as they'd practiced.

He went on. "My name is Todd Brooks. I'm with the FBI." He whipped out the badge from his suit's inside jacket pocket and held it out for them to inspect. He did it with a measure of bravado that spoke volumes to the level of ego this man drew from his position.

"Oh, nice to meet you," Alex said. He stuck out a hand to shake with the federal agent but received no return gesture. After a moment, he retreated and went back to looking clueless.

"I'm with a special branch of the Bureau," Brooks stated. "We investigate unnatural phenomenon and try to determine scientific explanations for such phenomena."

"You mean you cover stuff up from the public," Tommy said. He made no attempt to hide his irritation.

Brooks didn't bite at the bait and kept his focus on the married couple. Apparently, he'd pinned them for pliable; easy to work over to get what he wanted.

"Where is the element?" he asked, so bluntly that it genuinely caught Alex and Tara off guard.

Alex twisted his head and stared blankly into his wife's emerald eyes. "Element?"

She shrugged. Her eyebrows mimicked her shoulders, rising slightly then drooping again. "No clue." She turned to face the intruder and crossed her arms. "We aren't really in the business of working at the atomic level here, Agent Brooks. We work with artifacts. That's it."

"Oh, really?"

"Yeah, really."

Tara had always been the better poker player in the relationship. She could bluff with the best of them. At one point, Alex even suggested she enter the World Series of Poker just to give it a shot, but she wasn't interested.

Brooks inclined his head, eyeing her suspiciously. All the while, his men continued to scour the lab for any sign of this mythical element they claimed was here.

"Hey, be careful with that," Tommy snapped at one of the agents. The young blond man sported a military-style haircut. His head whipped around at the warning. "That is a very delicate artifact."

The man frowned. "It's a piece of stone."

"It's a piece of clay from a tablet that's over five thousand years old. So, do us all a favor and don't touch it. I assure you, the element isn't in that fragment."

The agent paled at the gravity of the information, and he gently set the clay shard back on the fabric surface where he'd found it. As he continued searching the room, he did so more delicately than before.

Tara's and Alex's eyes widened at the sight of something in the corridor beyond the interior wall. Tara didn't hide the smirk begging to creep across her face.

"What's got you so happy all of a sudden? You do realize that you're interfering with a government investigation. I could charge all three of you right now and take you in for further questioning."

"That's not how it works, Todd," a woman's voice said from the doorway.

Everyone in the room turned to face the entrance, wondering who would dare to cut into the conversation. Tommy knew who it was and released a wide smile. It was good to have friends in high places.

4

ATLANTA

"Emily?" Brooks said, suddenly confused and more than a touch concerned. "What are you doing here?"

"I was in the area," she said, leaning casually against the door's metal frame. Her arms were crossed over her chest, one finger tapping on a forearm. Her dark brown hair was loose for a change, swept back over her right ear and dangling over the left. She wore a black business suit. The skirt stopped just above her knees, showing off her powerful, slender calves.

Emily was known in the defense and justice communities as “the untouchable.” Many of the higher-ranking agency officials were jealous of the perceived power she wielded, but others knew she had a very difficult job. Those people became her allies, and she had fingers in every justice and defense department pot in Washington—and beyond.

"Oh?"

She rolled her shoulders. "I like to check in on my friends from time to time. You do know my main office is here in Atlanta, just a few blocks from here. Or maybe you weren't cleared for that information."

He shifted uneasily and cleared his throat. "What are you doing here, Emily? Covering up for your friends?" He fired the shot, but it did no damage.

"Absolutely, Todd. Now, if you don't mind, you're interfering with official Axis business."

Brooks snorted derisively. He detested Axis. They operated outside the boundaries and rules that the FBI and CIA had to watch so closely, though the latter tended to bend them more often than not. Confessions of CIA black sites made that painfully obvious.

But Axis answered to no one but the president, another person Brooks didn't care for. He hadn't liked the former leader, either. John Dawkins had declined to increase their funding despite multiple requests. He hadn't decreased their budget, either, but that didn't satisfy Brooks.

"One of these days, Emily, you're going to misstep, and when you do—"

"Are you threatening me, Todd? Because it feels a little like you're threatening me." She cocked her head to the side, and the loose strands of hair jiggled. The other agents in the lab stared at her with a mix of incredulity and fear.

Brooks said nothing, merely inclining his head slightly in a show of pride that would bow to no one.

"McCarthy's puppet, eh?" he said, referring to the current president of the United States. "Did Gwen send you down here?"

"Maybe. Maybe not." Emily's voice remained flat, emotionless. She'd seen pieces of work like him before. "Perhaps you'd like me to call her, and you can ask her yourself, seeing how you don't have her direct line."

The air was sucked out of the room. It was surprising that no one gasped at the barb.

Brooks bit his lip and stiffened his jacket. He calmed himself for a second. "Come on, men. Looks like we're out of our jurisdiction."

The other agents exchanged bewildered glances and then started for the door, filing out and passing by Emily as they left.

Brooks was the last to leave, but he stopped at Emily's side to offer one last parting shot. "I guess this is what happens when we let women run the show, huh?"

She arched one eyebrow and snorted a sincere laugh. "Unemployment is at an all-time low. The economy is strong. We're not at war with anyone. Stocks are through the roof. Yes, I'm sorry we girls aren't good at running 'the show' as you call it." Her air quotes further mocked him.

He swallowed hard and stormed out the door, tail tucked firmly between his legs.

The door closed behind him, and Emily strode toward Tommy and the kids. "I have to be honest, guys, I thought he was going to say something cheesy. Like 'This isn't the last you'll see of me.'"

"He's not out of the building yet," Tara quipped.

The group laughed, but it was short-lived.

"How did he find out about the sample?" Tommy wondered out loud.

Emily let out a sigh and put her hands on her hips. She stretched her back until she felt one of the vertebrae give a relieving crack. Then she floated over to one of the chairs and eased into it with professional grace.

"Todd is part of a secret arm of the government. Branch Seven has clearance that most of the others don't. Only a few people inside the justice and defense departments know about what they do. If I had to guess, I'd say they have some kind of sensors in place that detect anomalous activities like, say, an extraordinary energy signature."

No one said anything for a moment, but Tara was the first to jump back in.

"You mean, like...from satellites?"

"Possibly. Project Echelon has been around for decades, a system capable of tracking every single aircraft on the planet, from the largest jumbo jet to the smallest Piper Cub. It's anybody's guess what they're working with now. I have access to almost everything we do, but even I have my limitations. So does our president."

"How is that even possible?"

Emily offered a *bless-your-heart* smile. "The president doesn't know everything, either. Most of the time it's intentional, though there are circumstances when it isn't."

"Intentional?" Alex asked.

"The president must maintain a certain level of plausible deniability. It's part of the job, and they know that. Most of them would rather not know what's going on behind the veil."

Alex and Tara couldn't believe what they were hearing. They had so many questions, but they reined them in when it appeared Emily wasn't done talking.

"For a long time, Branch Seven dealt with UFO sightings, things of that nature. More recently, though, I've heard rumors they have taken up a new hobby." She let her words foreshadow the punchline.

"Let me guess. Archaeology?" Tommy offered.

"I wouldn't call it that so much as looting. Word is that they've been actively confiscating artifacts of a...peculiar nature, objects that appear to have unusual qualities, like that sliver of Quantium you managed to get from North Carolina."

Tara still had her doubts. "The only problem I have with all this is that we haven't detected powerful enough energy signatures coming from the sample. There are some, but they're inconsistent, all over the place. Is it possible that someone ratted us out?"

Alex chortled at the use of the mob term.

"I would say yes," Emily replied after a brief moment of thought. "But you run a tight operation here. How many agents are employed by IAA? A dozen or so?"

"That's correct, including me," Tommy said. "And most of them are in other parts of the world right now. I vet every one of them personally. I'd say the odds of one of them leaking this info to Seven are slim to none." He knew what Emily would suggest next and addressed it. "I'll certainly do some checking just to make sure."

"That would be wise," she agreed. "But I doubt your issue is from the inside. More likely, a cop on the scene in North Carolina must have seen or heard something. Seven likes to have its fingers in a lot of pies. They have informants all over the world, in places you couldn't imagine. The police are one of their largest information networks."

The words hung like a heavy fog in the room.

"None of that is why I'm here, though," Emily confessed.

The statement caused the others to perk up.

"No?" Tommy asked.

Emily shook her head, pulled a white folder from her jacket, and handed it to Tommy.

"Were you...keeping that in your jacket, under your armpit, this whole time?"

"I didn't want Todd to see it," she admitted with a smirk. "He would have asked questions, and the less he thinks I know the better."

"What is this?" Tommy asked, staring at the folder in his hands. He seemed almost afraid to open it. The surface was marked only with a single letter *P*. "What's the P for?"

"Paranormal," Emily said with a quirky wink.

"Is this something for us?" Tara asked, a hint of excitement quivering in her voice.

"It's a case, yes. It was put on my desk, but I don't have anyone available at the moment to look into it. And besides, it really falls into your new area of expertise. You'll find additional information in there," she added, pointing to the folder. "Someone is stealing artifacts. They hit museums mostly, but also a dig site in Southern Europe. We have word that there have been several artifacts taken so far. I need you two to look into it."

"Artifacts?" Alex asked. "All due respect, Ms. Starks, why are you being bothered with this kind of case? And why does that involve us?"

"The artifacts are of a, shall we say, peculiar nature. Let's just say your new division was made for this. And since you're civilians, no one will suspect you. Not being a part of the system can have its advantages now and then."

"I haven't heard anything about thefts from any museums or dig sites," Tommy countered. "And I'd like to think I would have, especially if it was dealing with something, you know, special."

"It's all in that brief," Emily said. "In short, our government works with others around the world to conceal things like this. They're of a...sensitive nature, so to speak. If word got out about some of the discoveries that have been made recently, there would be security issues. My agency doesn't deal directly with helping keep those sites secure. We have other things going on." There was no derision in her tone, merely a lack of emotion. "Frankly, I think this suits your new division perfectly."

"How long have you been sitting on this?" Tommy asked. "This doesn't sound like new information."

"It's not. I've known about the thefts for a couple of months. Until recently, it wasn't something I thought to be a serious concern. Someone was taking weird artifacts. It wasn't my problem. Like I said, we're all hands on deck right now. Every available Axis agent is on assignment somewhere in the world. All of them are deep undercover. This kind of thing isn't our kind of thing. Although the murder might not be *your* thing, either."

"Murder?" Tommy asked.

"Yes. That's why I'm here. This isn't just a case for missing artifacts. Two days ago, a man was found dead on a metro rail in Athens. Authorities are calling it a suicide—said he jumped over the fence of a bridge that crosses the rail line."

"That's a gruesome way to go."

"But Athens doesn't have a metro line," Alex argued. "It's a big campus, but—"

"Greece, not Georgia," Emily corrected patiently, but her eyes rolled ever so subtly.

"Oh, right."

"Turns out the dead man was a British agent. He was on the payroll with MI6, but they shared no information about the mission he was on in Greece—other than the recordings from his phone."

"Phone?" Tara asked.

"All that we can piece together, and by we I mean Greek and British investigators, is that he knew someone was after him and started recording on his phone in case he didn't make it out alive. I guess the killer didn't count on him doing that because his phone was still recording after his body was recovered. Most of the recordings were sounds of the train, the city, etcetera. But there are several minutes of interaction between the victim and his killer, a man he called Buri."

The name lingered in the air for a moment, like the waft of a delicate perfume as a woman walks by.

"Buri," Tommy stated, his mind searching for an answer to the unspoken question. "That's the name of an old Norse god."

"Correct," Emily said. "See..." she offered a perky smile, "I knew you'd jump on this one."

Tommy ignored the comment. He was thinking now, drawing more information from his memories of studying Norse mythology.

"Buri was...man before man, a primeval version of the original Scandinavians. He didn't have a father or mother. Seems like there was something about a cow licking salt in the shape of a man to create him."

"That's...something I can't unsee now," Emily remarked.

Tommy shook his head. "Why would someone go by that name? If this killer wanted to sound powerful, why not choose one of the other Norse gods, Odin, Thor...almost anyone else?"

"I'll leave that to the experts," Emily said and took a step back. "We have, thus far, been unable to dig up anything on a criminal named Buri, but he can't hide forever. Everything you need to know about the case and the murder is in that file. The Greek authorities will aid you in any way they can, as far as their jurisdiction allows. The British have been far more secretive about this, but they will also cooperate if needed. Tim over at MI6 owes me one. Actually, he owes me four or five, but who's counting!"

"Sounds cool," Tara chirped almost uncontrollably. "Our first assignment. And we're tracking down some thieves. Almost like cops."

"You're not cops," Tommy said, concern evident in his voice. He glared at Tara until her excitement tempered, and then he focused on Emily, dipping his head forward as he stared at her. "You're asking them to go into a murder investigation in a foreign country."

"Pretty much," Emily reinforced. "And I'm not able to give you any sort of clearance. In fact, this assignment is off the record. We don't know anything about a man who calls himself Buri, and unfortunately, we don't know anything about the organization the victim was trying to, or did, infiltrate. We do believe that there is a connection between the artifact thieves and the dead man in Athens, but most of that is based on the conversation from his phone. Several times, he and the killer mentioned the artifact. This Buri character said something about it being part of some kind of ancient tech and that it would open a door to unlimited power. Again, this is all...confidential. That folder you're holding didn't come from me."

Tommy considered her words. "Artifact from an ancient technology? Door to unlimited power?"

"I'm only relaying what I've been able to uncover so far. As soon as I can get you a copy of the audio, I'll send it your way. Look, I don't want to put you in danger. I'm going with my gut on this. Let the cops handle all the police stuff—I want you to stay out of the line of fire. But this case is also dealing with things that are outside the realm of police expertise. We need you to figure out what Buri is up to with the artifacts. Help the cops any way you can, but just watch your six."

"Well, you don't have to worry about us telling anyone," Tommy reassured. "And the kids will be careful," he said with a wink in Tara and Alex's direction.

"I know that," Emily said. "I know I can trust you, all of you. And you three, and Sean—wherever he is—you are the best. Track down the artifacts; figure out what they want those artifacts for. We considered that the thieves may simply want to sell them, possibly to sponsor some kind of terrorist cell."

"That doesn't sound like an efficient way to sponsor terrorism," Alex snorted. "Hardly a steady revenue stream, anyway."

"We came to the same conclusion. And the victim's audio recording disproves that notion." Her expression darkened. "Be careful. I know you've been training with Sean for the last few years and that you know how to handle yourselves. I also know that if it wasn't for you two, that whole incident in Japan might have turned out differently. I would say I hope we're simply dealing with some black-market relic dealers, but those types can be extremely dangerous. So, watch your backs. Of course, I can't force you to do it," she confessed. "And if you're going to pass, tell me and I'll refer it to the next agency with available resources."

"Who would that be?" Tommy asked.

She arched one eyebrow with a mischievous smirk.

"Todd?"

She nodded. "Obviously, I would rather sweep it under the rug than give it to him. I don't trust him as far as I could throw him."

"I don't know," Tommy quipped. "I'd bet you could heave him a few yards."

She smiled at the compliment. At least she took it as such.

"We'll do it," Tara said. This time, she made the statement in a calmer tone.

Alex nodded his assent. "Yeah. We're not scared of a couple of artifact thieves."

"Fear keeps you alive, kids," she said. "Don't try to push it away entirely. Embrace it. Let it keep you sharp. Just like in sports: When you underestimate your opponent, you get beat. When you have something, let me know and I'll call in the cavalry. Just be careful—wherever you go. Good luck."

She turned, and then paused at the door. She ducked her head back through the doorway and grinned. "By the way, thanks."

Tommy smirked and folded his arms across his chest. "You're welcome."

5

ATLANTA

"So, our contact is a cop named Dimitris Frangos, and he's going to pick us up at the airport when we arrive in Athens." Tara leaned back into the seat and closed her eyes. They'd been on the plane for two hours. Night had enshrouded the aircraft an hour after leaving Atlanta and the moon hung in the dark sky to the south, its pale glow shimmering off the Atlantic Ocean.

Alex took his eyes from the window and focused on his wife. Her dark auburn hair was pulled back behind one ear, and her bright emerald eyes were so green they almost looked fake.

She met his gaze and smiled. "What?"

"Just admiring the view," he quipped, trying to sound clever.

"You're so cheesy," she jabbed, causing his cheeks to redden slightly.

"Um, excuse me? I think what you meant to say was thank you," he corrected. "I have a beautiful wife."

She laughed at him and shook her head. "Yes, you're so sweet. And the view ain't bad from over here, either."

The color in his cheeks deepened.

"Anyway," she said, fighting off her own blush, "like I said, Detective Frangos is going to meet us at the airport and take us to where we're staying. Tommy hooked us up with a pretty sweet apartment for the week. It's right across the street from the Acropolis."

"Cool. Would be nice to have a local to show us around. I could get lost in such a vast city."

She grinned and shook her head. "You need to let loose a little, stop worrying so much. You know he's not going to send us halfway across the world without making sure we're taken care of. He doesn't just call us 'the kids' because we're younger than him. It's because he thinks of us like we *are* his kids."

"I know. And you're right. I do need to stop worrying so much." He rubbed his knees with his palms, as if the action might help lessen the anxiety.

In truth, it was mostly gone now that they had a place to stay. This trip had been pretty spur-of-the-moment. One minute they had been sitting around the lab investigating the wonders of a new element, the next they were on the IAA plane heading to Greece.

"I'm pretty excited," Tara confessed. "I've always wanted to go to Greece. Too bad we won't have time to check out any of the islands while we're there."

"You never know," Alex said with a shrug. "It sounds like our time here is indefinite. Or at least until Tommy calls us back. Didn't feel like he was going to do that anytime soon, though. We could be here a while."

Hope gleamed in Tara's eyes. "Well, I won't put up a fight if we have to stay a month. I will miss the lab, but this is just so exciting."

He could see that excitement bubbling up in her eyes. "Okay, well, take it easy. We have a lot of work to do and not a lot of places to start." He sifted through his copy of the reports regarding the suicide of the British intelligence agent. The two had already come to the same conclusion as the man who'd put the report together.

It was clear that the lead detective, Dimitris Frangos, didn't believe this was a simple open-and-shut case of suicide. He was convinced that the man had been murdered, and once he learned the victim was connected to a British intelligence agency, Dimitris had doubled his efforts to find answers.

"It's strange," Alex noted, reading one of the paragraphs halfway down the page. He reached over and grabbed his coffee from a cup holder, took a sip, and then replaced it. "The cop we're meeting doesn't believe it was suicide, either. But he claims there are no witnesses who've come forward to talk about what happened. Surely someone would have seen the victim jump, or be tossed, over the fence."

"You'd think. So, imagine the kind of killer that is brazen enough to pull off a murder like that. They'd have to be powerful, right? Ton of money, influence, that sort of thing."

"Yeah," he agreed. "That doesn't give us a name and a face."

"We already have the name, though it doesn't help us much."

"Right. Buri. The primeval Scandinavian man; the created being without a father or mother."

"Why would someone call themselves that?" Tara asked.

Alex's shoulders lifted and then drooped. "Maybe he thinks he's the father of all Vikings or something. Ooooh...or maybe he's a soccer player and just wants to be known by one name, like all those Brazilian and Portuguese players."

Tara laughed and shook her head.

"What? It's possible."

"Fine," she relented. "We're looking for a soccer player who goes by a single name but is also the first Scandinavian to do so." She offered another chuckle. "Should narrow it down. Seriously, though, there aren't any records of a Buri anywhere. I can't find any in the criminal database, the most wanted, nothing. Interpol has nada on this guy."

"You know what that means, right?"

"It means he's either really lucky or extremely powerful."

"With enough money and connections, you can disappear, too!" Alex said in his best game-show-host impression.

"I'm curious to take a look at security footage from the area that night. They may not have cameras everywhere, but surely they have some. Maybe we'll get lucky and get a look at this guy. Would sure make it easier to find him a second time."

"You think?" Alex joked.

She shook her head and rolled her eyes. "Anyway, I suspect we'll get there, ask a few questions, and then end up coming home with nothing. There are just too many variables, and let's face it: Everything Emily told us was pretty vague. It also sounds like she pretty much has zero expectations for this operation."

"Except that she called *us* the experts. That makes me think she believes we can figure this out—even though we don't have much to go on."

"Or that we'll have more to go on when we get there. Maybe this Dimitris guy can shed some additional light on the subject. I can see why Emily thinks this Buri character is somehow connected to the artifact thefts, though it's a thin connection at best."

"I was going to say...that one requires a bit of a leap," Alex said. "Maybe Em knows something we don't, but if that is the case, she would have said more."

"Yeah, so let's look at this again." She pulled up a map on her tablet and twisted it around so Alex could see the screen. "At first glance, the thefts appear to be pretty random. No pattern except that more of them tend to come from places that are known archaeological hotbeds: Egypt, Italy, Greece; you get the picture." The places that had been hit by the thieves were marked with three red pins.

"Athens," Tara tapped on the screen, "is currently the number one place to acquire illegal items of a rare or antique nature."

"Or ancient, in some cases."

"Right. So, it would make sense for someone who's a big player in the artifact black market to be in Athens."

"Agreed. We just need our little ruse to flush him out."

They'd agreed on a plan that both believed would work, though it was impossible to say with any certainty.

The idea was simple enough. Two of the IAA's young agents were going to be in Athens to open a new exhibit in one of the museums. It featured a rare artifact, a relic that was only available to the scientific community for private viewing and study.

The truth was that the artifact was nothing unusual at all—and it wasn't a real artifact.

The piece to be put on display was nothing more than a hunk of metal, knocked off of ingots at a local forge. Tommy had a friend who did metalwork in Atlanta and had requested a couple of pieces for this unusual mission.

His friend hadn't asked why, though the man wouldn't have been over the line if he had.

The unshaped chunk of iron was a placeholder, nothing more, and the public was never going to see it. Tommy had arranged for one of the wings of the famous Acropolis Museum to be used for the "exhibit." It wasn't like they had tons of spare room, but they didn't need one of the fancier spaces for this operation.

The curator had found it odd that Tommy actually requested a room that was a little off the beaten path, one most visitors would rarely visit on their tours of the museum. He explained that he didn't want to detract from people experiencing the more famous artifacts that Athens had to offer, and that they needed a place where the object could be put on display to be studied by some of the local experts in the field of anthropology and its subfield of archaeology.

Tommy went on to explain that he only wanted these experts—or their students—to examine the artifact for the time being. He believed the item to be from the early Iron Age or late Bronze Age, and possibly originating from the Athens area.

The head of the museum took Tommy's request with the same lack of skepticism Tommy usually met. He'd made a name for himself in the world of history and cultural study, and that reputation carried him a long way when it came to making unusual requests of museum or government officials. In short, Tommy usually got what he asked for. Now, if he tried to get VIP concert tickets or a luxury box for a sporting event—aside from the one the IAA had at the Mercedes Benz Dome in Atlanta—he'd probably hit a wall, such was the scope of his influence. Famous and yet not at the same time.

For this mission, he only needed academic clout.

The museum curator was happy to lease out a room at the end of the building on the second floor. It was out of the way of the usual flow of tourist traffic and featured a pair of fireproof doors that would keep anyone out if he wanted privacy for analysts and researchers, or if he just wanted the item secured.

It was the perfect setup for their ruse. Now, all Alex and Tara had to do was put out some bait and see if anyone took it.

Dimitris was key to this part of the mission. Tara and Alex didn't have many connections outside of Atlanta, but the Greek investigator supposedly had a guy who was connected to the underground world of black-market artifact dealers. Such a person roused suspicion in the two American agents, but they didn't have much choice.

They would have to trust Dimitris, and his guy, if they were going to have a chance at tracking down this Buri.

"So, I do have to wonder," Alex said, looking over his copies of the case file with tired eyes. "The three artifacts that were stolen...they all look the same. These carvings look like little men with wings or something.

"Three stones shaped the same, with the same symbols cut into the surface. I wish we could have run those through the scanner while we were at the lab. Could have pulled up the origin of those glyphs." He yawned and covered his mouth out of habit. Then Alex rubbed his eyes, giving the fatigue one last punch.

"I know, right? Well, I'm sure we can figure it out. It is interesting, though. The three stones all looking the same." Tara spoke as if talking to herself. "Strange Emily didn't mention that detail. I wonder why."

"Maybe she didn't notice. Or maybe she decided that interpreting ancient stone glyphs wasn't her specialty and so she chose to hand it off to the experts." He flashed a proud grin.

Tara thought about it for a moment. Her groggy brain swam in a sea of wild theories, visions of historical moments, and exhaustion. "Maybe," she relented.

"So, what do you think that means?"

"It means that whoever is behind this isn't just some two-bit black-market antiquities dealer. They have a big network. Maybe global."

"Which means they have their fingers in a bunch of jars. They'd have to have teams already in place to work that fast."

"I was thinking the same thing. At least regional teams. I would think it impossible to have someone in every country. But definitely continental."

It was Tara's turn to yawn, and she stretched out her arms just as he'd done a moment before.

He admired her, just as he had when they first met. She was finishing her degree at Kennesaw State, same as him. They were still in their twenties, although thirty was creeping in fast. But she never seemed to age to him. She still had the same youthful energy in her eyes that she had the day they were introduced. He had no idea they would end up working together, and on some of the incredible projects that had dropped in their lap.

They'd grown closer over the years after they were both hired by Tommy Schultz at the IAA. All that time together in the lab might have driven a weaker pair crazy, but he and Tara worked like a machine, each with different gears and parts that synchronized with the other.

"Yes. Still a big undertaking," she said, "but if you break it down to regional areas, it would take way less manpower to pull off something like that."

"True," he said, his eyes widening at the realization. "According to this file, the three thefts happened within the last forty-five days. That's pretty fast for that many heists."

"They would have had to plan extensively too, not so much for the theft at the dig site, but at the museums for sure. Those places are usually very secure. A thief would have to figure out escape routes, response times for local law enforcement, and a slew of other details before going in."

"Yep," Alex said and yawned again. He needed some sleep.

Tara closed her laptop and stretched her arms, then lay back in the seat and turned her head toward the window. "I'm going to try to get some sleep," she said. "You should, too. Big day tomorrow."

"I know," Alex said with a smile, once more admiring his wife from across the row. He was also grateful she was finally calling it a night. She'd always been able to stay up later than him, not that he cared. He thought it made her cool. "Just have a few things I want to take care of first."

He looked down at the file in his lap and pored over the paragraphs again, eyeing the image of the cop they were supposed to meet at the airport in Athens. "Dimitris Frangos," he muttered, so low that Tara didn't hear him.

Everything was happening so quickly. It was all a blur, and Alex was still trying to process it. He had no idea that morning when he woke up that he would be going to sleep on a plane headed to Greece. It was exciting and a little unnerving at the same time. They were plunging headlong into what was likely a dangerous situation, but as Tommy said, they were well trained. They'd been working with Sean for years now and could handle almost any scenario thrown their way. At least Alex hoped so.

He reached up and switched off the overhead light, stealing one last glance at his wife. Then he reclined his seat until it was flat. He lay out on the makeshift bed and pulled a pillow under his head, then tugged at a blanket until most of his body was covered.

Alex lay awake for several minutes, his mind racing with what the future held. There was no way to distill any single possibility from the infinite buffet that swirled in his head. One thought, however, continued to batter his anxious brain. Over and over again it struck at his core, racking him with a tension unlike he'd ever felt before.

The only thing he cared about, truly cared about in this world, was Tara. He hoped he could keep her safe, but he also knew that wasn't necessarily his job. She was a grown woman and made her own decisions. She was intelligent, cunning, and wouldn't run headlong into danger. Still, this entire operation might be one bad situation, and if it was, he didn't want anything to happen to her.

His eyelids grew heavy as he continued thinking about the

mission. *Tara can take care of herself*, he reminded himself. Deep down, Alex wished this would be the most boring operation they'd ever conducted.

With thoughts of museums and walking around a huge city, fatigue pulled at Alex, and soon he surrendered, falling into a deep sleep.

6

CRETE

Buri sat behind his desk, slumping slightly in the lush leather chair. The panoramic window behind him gave way to a view of the ocean, its waves rolling gently toward the shore before breaking into foamy white crests and splashing onto the pristine beach that curled around the lagoon. He'd visited magnificent beaches all over the world, but the clarity and shades of blue in the water and the contrasting white sand outside his window surpassed anywhere else on Earth.

Matching palm trees swayed on either side of the balcony. The mansion was only two-stories, but the view was spectacular. The mountains of Crete rose up to the right and beyond the backside of the huge house. Looking past the balcony, the ocean stretched as far as the eye could see; only interrupted by several islands scattered in the distance. There were more than two hundred such islands surrounding the Greek mainland, and Buri recalled thinking that it could take several lifetimes to explore them all thoroughly.

He'd discovered this plot of land during the massive economic upheaval of the mid-2000s and purchased it on the spot. Buri made the most of people's desperation and scooped up real estate on a couple of the islands, as well as several properties in Athens. He'd also picked up a warehouse at Piraeus Port, which had come in handy over the years. Getting antiquities in and out of Athens was easy enough if you greased the right palms, and Buri certainly knew how to do that.

He reached over to his right and picked up a glass of white wine from the little bistro table. He touched the rim of the glass with his lips and then drew in a long sip, savoring the sweetness of the wine.

"Greece makes excellent white wine," Buri said. He twisted his head slightly to engage the man in the seat to his right, on the other side of the desk. Two of his guards stood behind the man, his clothes tattered, his face bruised and swollen.

The guards had worked him over for at least thirty minutes before bringing him to the office.

Buri glanced at the man again with only the slightest regard. "Why did you do it, Paul?" he asked, as casually as he would have asked what the forecast would be that day.

Paul breathed heavily. Blood trickled from a gash over his right eye and another on his nose, which was crumpled and broken in two places. Both eyes were almost swollen shut. There were at least three teeth missing from the prisoner's mouth, though his lips, covered in blood from the beating they'd taken, remained sealed.

"I asked you a question, Paul," Buri demanded. "Why did you do it? Why did you allow a British agent into our midst?" His anger escalated, his voice growing louder with each word.

"I didn't know," Paul said, his German accent hinting at his Bavarian roots.

"You didn't know?" Buri didn't believe it.

"I swear. Everything checked out. I did all the usual background checks on him. They must have hidden his real identity and concealed any connection to MI6 or whoever he was working for."

"Oh, you think?" Buri asked, sardonically.

"You have to believe me. I would never do anything to jeopardize this organization or its mission. You know that. You know me, Buri. Please. You have to trust me."

Buri took a deep breath and then drew another sip of wine before he set the glass back down on the table.

"The mission?" He stood and looked down at the prisoner, then at the half-empty wine glass. "Do you know why the white wine is so much better than the red wine here in Greece?"

The beaten man tilted his head up and tried to look at Buri through the slits of his swollen eyelids. "What?"

"The red wine here. It's not great. I've only ever had a few that are any good. And those are usually the cheap ones."

The prisoner clearly didn't see where Buri was going with this. "I...suppose that's true."

"Of course it is. Every local knows it. But every now and then, one slips through the cracks, and you find a good one. That isn't the point, though." Buri stepped over to the iron railing and planted both hands on the metal. He leaned over and took in the surroundings, inhaling deeply the salty air as it wafted in on a gentle breeze. "Most people speculate that it was due to being ruled by the Ottoman Empire for so long. As a result, Greece was largely a Muslim nation, not permitted to create alcohol in any form. Then after they gained their independence, the Greek economy was in such shambles that few people could afford to put money into expanding production of wines. So, it would seem the Greeks decided to go all in on white-wine making and didn't really focus much of their energy on the reds. Of course, this is all theory or conjecture."

He turned and faced the prisoner again. Through the thick, swelling flesh of Paul's injuries, Buri noticed the confusion on the man's face.

"I suppose that makes sense, sir," Paul said.

"Of course it does, Paul. And you see, when you have a disruptive element in your midst, it makes things difficult. Operations become harder to manage. It's like fighting a war on multiple fronts, and very few armies in the history of the world have ever had much success with such campaigns." He took a menacing step closer to Paul and stared down at him with disdain. "You have brought in a disruptive element, Paul. In fact, *you* were a disruptive element. You have made things considerably more difficult for me and for everyone in this organization. Now, we will have to take additional precautions going forward. This will cost us time and money, neither of which I enjoy wasting."

"I know, sir. I'm sorry. I swear, it was an accident. A mistake. It won't happen again."

"No, I'm sure it won't, Paul. I know you've learned your lesson. It's a difficult one, certainly, but one you needed to learn. One that everyone in the organization needed to learn."

He waved his hand around dramatically, implying that the two guards were learning it at that very moment.

"Yes, sir," Paul said humbly. He gave a nod. "I should have been more careful." Then he inclined his head. "But I went through all the usual protocols. I swear it, sir. You have to understand, I would never do anything to jeopardize what we're trying to achieve."

Buri nodded and turned away, resting his hands on the balcony once more. He'd come a long way from where he began his life, back in then-communist Berlin. Back then, he had nothing...nothing except the meager handouts the government gave his family in exchange for their lives. That's what it felt like, anyway. His parents worked themselves to the bone in the factories of East Berlin, slaving for long hours every single day in a thankless job that the government provided. They had no say in where they went or what they could do for fun—other than the government-approved activities or vacations. That time in his life had forged an anger, a simmering resentment deep inside his heart. It festered and grew until it burned with a searing heat...until the day his grandfather gave him something—something from beyond the grave.

Buri absently ran an index finger over the ring on his opposite hand. It was an unconscious tick, though in part, it had started deliberately as a way to pay homage to the order, almost like a devout religious parishioner with a set of prayer beads.

In his childhood, he'd been known simply as Paul Weber. The transformation began the day he discovered his grandfather's secret, one that changed everything for him.

"What do you think our purpose is, Paul?" Buri asked in a hushed tone that barely rose above the wind.

"What?" Paul wondered, confused.

"Our purpose. What is it? What is our divine goal for this order, this organization?" He put his hands out wide as if to catch the sunlight and then spun around dramatically. "You talk about what we are trying to achieve, yet you can't answer the question." He leaned back and planted his palms on the railing again.

"You know I know the answer to that," Paul defended with a sneer. "I know all of our plans, all of our goals. I know what the endgame is. I believe in it. If you think I brought that traitor into our midst on purpose, just say it. Otherwise, do whatever it is you plan on doing because I honestly don't care. I've given you everything. I've always been loyal to the cause."

"That's true, I think," Buri said with a hint of laughter tickling the back of his throat. "You've been a good soldier, Paul. As loyal as anyone I can imagine."

"Thank you." There was relief in Paul's voice, as if he was seeing the end of this interrogation.

"And because you're so loyal, I expect you to do the honorable thing now."

Paul had lowered his head for a second, but it lifted instantly when he heard those words. "What?"

"You have put the entire order in jeopardy," Buri said. "Your brethren's lives are in danger because of your carelessness. My life is in danger because of it. There is only one way you can make this right, one way I can know you are trustworthy."

Buri stepped to the side, letting his fingers drag along the top of the railing. It was a subtle insinuation piled on top of what was essentially a command, an order for Paul to take his own life.

"What?" Paul asked again. "You can't be serious."

"Paul, I've used up the time of several of my men today to extract information from you. I feel like they did a good job. You clearly didn't intend to bring a mole into our midst. So, all is forgiven. However, we don't have a retirement plan. I can't simply send you back out into the world. Neither can I keep you around. You could screw up again, and next time..." He lowered his head in mock contemplation, nodding slowly. "Next time might not be so fortunate for the rest of us."

A tear formed in the slit that was the prisoner's right eye. It was impossible to tell if the welling was from physical pain or the knowledge that he was about to die.

"I will make sure you are buried with dignity and honor," Buri said, "just as any member of us should be."

Paul's head turned, almost involuntary, back and forth slowly in rejection of the proposal. "I...I can't do that."

"Of course you can. You know you're going to die. I can't let you walk out of here."

Paul continued to twist his head one way then the other.

"Denial isn't going to save you, Paul," Buri said. He spat the name with loathing. It reminded him of a past he'd worked hard to forget. "I'm giving you the chance to go out on your own terms, an honorable death to make amends for the mistake you made, an error that could have cost all of us everything. Think of the lives you put in danger, Paul. Your brothers trusted you, and you betrayed them with your folly."

"I didn't betray anyone," Paul seethed. "You can't do this. None of you can do this. It isn't right."

The guards didn't move. Paul bet everything that they weren't ready for what his mind told him to do next.

He'd sensed a growing relaxation between the two guards, though if the conversation intensified the tiniest bit more, they might be back on full alert.

But who was he kidding? These men never let their guard down. They were hardened to emotion, their feelings blunted through years of training...among other things.

Paul stood slowly; the guards tensed.

Buri held up a hand and nodded at the guards. They lowered their hands and retreated a step.

Paul felt them shift, and for a moment he felt a glimmer of hope.

Clearly, Buri was confident that he would do "the right thing" and off himself, jumping from the balcony to the jagged rocks of the cliffs below. He felt his heart pounding in his chest, thumping repeatedly, beating faster as the seconds ticked by. It swelled to a steady staccato as he resigned himself to what he had to do.

Buri smiled, almost as if the man was the gatekeeper to the realm of the dead, a ferryman ready to escort him over the River Styx.

Paul drew a deep breath and took a step forward. Then another. He quickened his pace as best he could. The muscles all over his body were tender from the beating he'd endured. His legs ached, but standing had helped get the blood flowing again, and as he moved the pain almost felt like relief—in a strange sort of way. He could feel something, and sometimes—when you have nothing left—you just need to feel *something*.

Paul surged across the balcony toward his target. Buri's eyes widened, as if suddenly seeing a train barreling toward him with no way to get off the tracks. Paul lowered his shoulder to tackle the man and drive him against the railing. He didn't have a plan, as such. It was spur of the moment, total spontaneity, but Paul knew it was his only chance. If he could knock Buri over the railing, he would—by rights—take control of the entire order as its new leader. He would make changes, too. There would be no more of this rule-by-threat-of-death business. He would be a good leader, one who trusted his men implicitly, not just when they succeeded in their tasks.

The prisoner's feet pounded the floor as he sped toward Buri. At the last second, the look of concern on the leader's face melted into a begrudging grin. It was a barely noticeable expression, lips only slightly turning at the corners, but Paul saw it, and he knew he'd been too hasty with his attack.

The pain in his ribs, face, head, and the rest of his body screamed out as he took the last step and launched himself toward his target, unable to slow down—much less come to a halt.

Paul knew he'd been tricked. He'd let his anger get the better of him, not that it mattered. Whether he killed himself or not, the result was always going to be the same. He was a dead man. He'd failed the leader of the order, and Buri didn't accept failure in any form.

Buri twisted his body slightly, slapped his hand onto Paul's back, and grabbed at the onrushing-man's shirt. It took little effort for Buri to fling the charging Paul over the waist-high railing. The man's momentum did most of the work.

As Paul sailed over the rail, he met Buri's eyes for a fleeting second. There was no emotion in them, no regret, no pain, no sadness. He may as well have been flipping a bug off his shirt.

Paul plummeted down; arms and legs flailing as if that might save him. The back of his head hit a jagged outcropping on the cliff, which caused the body to tumble rapidly, head over heels, down to the rocky shore.

Buri looked down at the dead man for a moment, regarding him as he would some carrion on the side of the road. Thirty seconds later, a huge surge from the ocean sent a tall wave crashing over the rocks. When the waters receded back to the folds of the sea, the rocks were devoid of the corpse. It would take only a few more waves before any signs of foul play were completely removed.

Buri knew the body would be washed out to sea, where it would receive a burial by way of the scavengers and predators interested in human meat. There would be nothing left. A proper fate for a traitor.

The leader turned and faced the two guards at the door. He thumbed the ring on his right hand, running his fingertips over the sword wrapped in a Nordic sheath. He felt the runes that encircled the carved image and thought for a moment, as if the runes might grant him some sort of power.

Not that he needed it. He had everything he needed, including a legion of super soldiers—men enhanced by supplements and training that weren't...approved by the civilized world. Buri's predecessors had accomplished much in the way of pushing the human body to its limits, but they'd failed in achieving true enhancement of the physique. Where they'd failed, he'd succeeded, using a combination of new nutrition and supplemental experiments to create soldiers who were stronger and faster than average.

He eyed the guards with distant pride. The men weren't superhuman. Not even close. They were mortal like anyone else, but their muscle density, bone structure, and supporting cartilage and ligaments were heartier than almost anyone on the planet.

Buri stopped rubbing the ring and folded his hands behind his back. "Find out who knows about this and bring them to me. Who is investigating Neil's death? I hear that it isn't a closed case just yet. That means someone is looking into the possibility of homicide."

The guards exchanged an askance glance and then looked back to their leader. "Dimitris Frangos. He's a detective in the Athens police department."

"Will he be a problem?" Buri asked.

"Possibly," the blond guard to the right answered. "Any cop looking into anything we do is not a good thing."

"Agreed," Buri nodded. "Bring him to me. Alive, if possible. Dead is just as good. I'll make a call and suggest a replacement; someone we know is on our side."

The guards nodded and left through the door, allowing Buri a moment to himself.

He turned and placed his palms on the railing again and leaned over, staring out at the crystal-blue sea. It was hard to find blue water like that in many places on the planet. His eyes drifted down to where the body had been, and then he traced an imaginary line out into the open water where he imagined the corpse would be now.

Paul wasn't the first one he'd sent to the locker, the old mythical place where Davy Jones raked in the souls of those who died at sea. Buri had used this balcony to rid himself of several other problems in the past. Not once had a body floated to the surface or washed up on some popular tourist beach.

He knew the dead man was lost to the sea. Now he had to make sure one last loose end was tied off.

7

ATHENS

Tara and Alex stepped off the private jet and onto the tarmac. They winced against the bright, searing sunshine. Alex fumbled for his sunglasses, unable to get them on his face quickly enough to block out the painful rays of the sun. The two had been in the plane for nearly twelve hours, and the bright ball in the sky nearly blinded them after so long without daylight.

After their eyes adjusted, they could see the figure of a man standing beside a midsize black Skoda Octavia hatchback around a hundred feet away.

He was shorter than Alex, probably by three or four inches, and was more around Tara's height. He was stocky with broad shoulders, the black hair on his head was thick, and the two imagined that if it got wet, it would have curled instantly.

The cop wore a white shirt tucked into his belt with the top two buttons undone. His gray slacks ran down to black shoes that were made more for comfort than style. His workaday ensemble was more business-street than business-casual.

The man waved to them with a thick, stubby-fingered hand, and the two made their way, unsteadily, across the tarmac. They were still a tad wobbly from being stuck in their seats for half a day.

The dry air filled their nostrils, and the two looked around in every direction, taking in the sights. Enormous mountains loomed in the distance all around. Looking closer, Tara and Alex could make out observatories atop a few of the peaks. Pale green trees dotted some of the hillsides and slopes leading up the mountains. In a few spots, thick forests ran unabated for hundreds or thousands of acres. It was a contradiction in appearances to say the least. Depending on where you looked, it could be perceived as a barren desert or a lush oasis.

That was Greece in a nutshell, a complex culture and environment that had been carved out of the rocky peninsula for thousands of years, always changing, always evolving.

Tara and Alex strode the last few yards across the airfield and stopped short of the detective. He extended a hand and shook Alex's first, then Tara's. His grip was as strong as his shoulders appeared to be, and he was all business with only a hint of "tourist welcome center."

"My name is Detective Dimitris Frangos. Thank you for coming on such short notice. I trust your flight was a good one?" He eyed the Gulfstream with both curiosity and suspicion.

"Yep. No issues on that end, other than I didn't sleep much," Tara answered first.

"No? I would think such an expensive plane like that would have comfortable beds."

"Oh, it's plenty comfortable," Alex added. "I think we're both just excited to be here."

The cop arched one eyebrow and scratched the hair behind his right ear. "Is this your first time to Greece?" His accent was thick, but he spoke perfect English. From what the couple had heard, that could be hit or miss depending on the individual. They were relieved that communications wouldn't be a barrier with their chaperone.

"Yes," Alex said. "This is our first time here. We're both pretty excited—about the food, the history, all of it. Although I'm afraid there won't be much time for sightseeing. We have an investigation to conduct."

"Perhaps we can arrange a few tours when the work is done...if it gets done."

Tara sensed the doubt in his comment and in his body language. She knew they could be stepping on the man's toes. He was a local cop, and they weren't. Sometimes, those types didn't like outsiders sticking their noses into official police business.

"Well, we will do all we can to support your investigation, Detective Frangos. We won't get in the way." Her words seemed to soothe his reluctance, so she kept going. "From what we've seen in the file, it doesn't sound like many of your peers are on board with your theory that this was a murder."

Her words warmed him to their company like a hearth in the dead of winter. His lips partially creased in a grin. "Too many of them are on the take, paid to look the other way with some of the corruption that goes on in Athens. Others are too afraid to say anything. It's a fear culture that's been cultivated in some of the departments, not all, but enough to cause some of the men and women not to question things that should be questioned."

"But not you?" Alex asked.

A gust of wind picked up and blew across the tarmac. Tara's ponytail whipped around behind her neck. The sound of the wind and the planes nearby made talking difficult to the point that each person was all but yelling.

"Please, let's get in my car and continue this in a quieter setting." Dimitris motioned to his hatchback. He noted the two bags each was carrying. "I have more than enough room in the back for you.

He helped the two Americans load their luggage in the rear of the car and then opened the doors for them to climb into the back, assuming the couple would prefer to ride together, though it clearly made him feel awkward—more like a cab driver than a cop with two consultants.

Alex ran his fingers along the rich, reddish-brown leather interior. "This is really nice," he said. "I've never been in a Skoda before."

Dimitris shut the door to his car and revved the engine. "Thank you. I try to keep it looking good. I don't have much, but I take pride in what I do have."

Alex didn't pursue that line of the conversation any further. He knew cops around the world weren't paid enough for what they did, but they were a government entity, supported by taxes, and that meant some of their money always ended up in the wrong hands, either deliberately or by other means. Corruption in government was a global problem.

"I will take you to your apartment so you can shower and change clothes if you need to. Then we will go to the scene of the crime. It's been cleaned up now and all the police tape is down, but it will give you context for what happened and why I believe this was a murder and not a suicide."

"Sounds good, Detective Frangos," Alex said.

"Please, call me Dimitris."

"Yes, sir," Tara said politely.

The man wheeled the car away from the hangar and out through a gate along the fence that wrapped around the Athens airport.

Once they were on the road, he sparked the discussion again. "So, you two work for the International Archaeological Agency, yes?"

"That is correct," Tara confirmed. "We're heading up a new division in the agency. Our job is to investigate some of the more bizarre things that happen surrounding artifacts and relics."

"Bizarre?"

"Unexplainable stuff—or things that defy science."

"So, you mean, like aliens?" Dimitris asked, trying to understand.

Alex laughed and shared a knowing glance with his wife. "Not exactly, although we don't rule that sort of thing out necessarily. There are lots of locations around the world that experience strange occurrences. Often, these revolve around a historically important site or artifacts."

"Ah, like the Bermuda Triangle."

"Exactly," Tara agreed. "In fact, that might be a good one to add to our list when we get home."

"I see. So, do you hunt for ghosts, too?"

Tara laughed out loud. "No. We don't believe in ghosts, Dimitris."

He grinned at her response, showing off a collection of crooked teeth that were slightly stained yellow from years of smoking. A packet of nicotine gum in his ashtray told them that he was trying to quit the habit, but a pack of cigarettes in the passenger seat revealed Dimitris' ongoing struggle.

"Are you two hungry? I imagine you could use some good coffee and something to eat?" The cop looked in the rearview mirror with eager eyes, almost as if he hoped they would say yes. It sounded like Dimitris was the hungry one. He must not have had breakfast yet, and the clock on the dashboard said it was already nine in the morning.

"Yeah, definitely." Tara said. "I've been wanting to try authentic Greek food for a long time. I know we have some places in the States that are good, but I'm curious to see the difference between the original and the Americanized version."

"Ah, yes," Dimitris said. "I can't say that I know what the difference is, but I will take you to one of my favorite morning places. I think you'll like it."

The two in the back seat looked out their windows in awe and a dose of fear as the driver navigated the narrow streets. The traffic lanes were poorly marked with faded white paint. Cars lined the sidewalks, crowding the already slim space between the moving vehicles. Most of the automobiles were compact cars. Many were tiny, two-door vehicles less than nine feet long.

It made sense that people chose to drive smaller cars in the crowded metropolis of Athens. With such little room between other drivers and even fewer minuscule parking spots available, maximizing space was critical to daily life. Motorcycles and scooters also filled the busy streets, cutting between cars and riding on the lines like Tara and Alex had seen riders do in Los Angeles. Such maneuvers weren't legal in all states, but apparently that wasn't an issue in Athens. In fact, traffic permeated the entire driving culture here.

It was confusing and congested. A four-wheeled mayhem pie.

"Just a heads-up," Dimitris said, noting his occupants' interest in their surroundings, "Athens is a safe city. Pickpockets? Yes. But very little violent crime. However, we are terrible drivers."

Alex and Tara laughed at that.

"What?" Alex said, still chuckling. "Terrible drivers?"

Dimitris looked into the mirror at Alex and raised one hand off the wheel. "We know this. We may be...second worst in Europe."

Tara frowned, half-laughing and half-curious. "Second? Who's the worst?"

Dimitris stared straight ahead and thought for a long moment. Then he shrugged. "Actually, we may be worst. It is what it is."

The two in the back seat were still laughing when the detective pulled up to an empty parking spot across the street from a café. There was a bakery to the left with a red awning, and the entrance to the Neos Kosmos metro station.

"That's the place over there," Dimitris said, pointing at the café with a blank awning stretched out over the front windows and covering a small porch. Two couples were sitting at the two tables on the little deck, looking out toward the plaza as they talked. A collection of tables, chairs, and black-and-white umbrellas dotted the plaza in front of the café.

"Awesome," Tara said and opened the door.

The men climbed out and Dimitris led the way over to the stand where a hostess was seating customers. Dimitris held up a thumb and two fingers and motioned to a table in the plaza as he spoke to her in Greek. The girl nodded and smiled, then said something to him as she turned to grab some menus.

"We can sit over there," Dimitris said, pointing to the same table he'd indicated before.

The group shuffled over to the proffered table and eased into the metal folding chairs. A cool breeze rolled through the streets and dusted the patrons with a tickling chill that was more than welcome on such a warm day.

A tall young man, probably in his mid-twenties, approached the table. His dark, wavy hair shook in the breeze as he approached. He wore a black apron around his waist, along with matching pants and a button-up shirt.

He greeted the three with a smile and said something in Greek. Dimitris informed the server that his guests didn't speak Greek, or that's what Tara and Alex assumed, because immediately after a quick correction, the server spoke English.

"Hello, welcome. My name is Michael; can I get you something to drink?"

"Coffee?" Alex asked.

"Would you like espresso or cappuccino freddo?"

Alex looked at Dimitris who nodded approvingly.

"Yes. Um, the freddo espresso, please."

"How sweet?" Michael asked, holding his hands behind his back with genuine patience. "Light, medium, or strong?"

"Let's go with medium," Alex asked.

"Iced or hot?"

"I had no idea there were so many options," Alex admitted. "Iced, please."

"I'll have what he's having," Tara laughed.

"Make that three," Dimitris said with a smile.

"Excellent," Michael said with a nod. He spun on his heels and strode across the sidewalk, up the steps, and vanished into the café.

"So, first time in Athens. I hope you will at least get to visit the Acropolis. Many tourists come here to see that. Quite a bit of history here in this city, though, if you want to see something else before you leave. Your apartment is across the street from the Acropolis. You'll have a full view of it from your porch and living room. You also have internet and some other amenities. I will take you there when we finish eating so you can leave your things and change." He reiterated the plan, which wasn't necessary, but it told the two Americans that this detective was thorough and systematic, a pro who didn't like to leave anything to chance. It made sense, at least on the surface, that he was the one who was questioning the suicide ruling.

"Sounds good, Dimitris," Alex said.

"We have to be honest, though, sir," Tara said, leaning in with a serious look on her face. "We're not cops. I know you know that, but we certainly don't want to get in your way regarding a murder investigation."

"I appreciate that," Dimitris said with a curt nod. His voice was sharp but not condescending. "However, there is more to the story than just a strange suicide and a phone recording."

The couple cast a sidelong glance at each other and then redirected their gaze back to the cop.

He tilted his torso forward, getting closer to the other two. When he spoke, he did so in a conspiratorial tone.

"I figured out where the dead man was staying."

Tara and Alex furrowed their brows at the same time, wondering what that could possibly mean for them.

Seeing the lightbulb still dim over their heads, Dimitris continued. "I went there, unofficially."

So, he didn't do everything by the book, Alex thought.

Dimitris went on. "I searched the apartment."

"And?" Tara begged, not about to question the cop's motives or means. She heard footsteps behind her along with the sound of ice jiggling in liquid-filled glasses.

The detective stiffened slightly, sitting upright as the waiter approached with three clear glasses of dark liquid with a light brown froth whipped at the top. He set the drinks down on the table, one per person, and then asked what else the visitors would like.

Dimitris ordered a series of items in Greek and then turned to the young couple. "Do you have any eating restrictions?"

"We don't really like seafood, except for sushi. Most of the time, we try to eat vegetarian, but beef and chicken are fine." Alex offered an apologetic smirk.

"No problem. Everything I ordered will work for you then." He turned to Michael the server and said a few more words. The tall waiter nodded and spun around, returning to the confines of the café.

Satisfied the server was out of earshot, Tara pressed the detective. "What were you saying about the dead man's place? You said you searched it?"

"That's right," Dimitris said, reaching over and picking up the glass mug by the handle. He brought it to his lips and took a long sip. He gave a satisfied sigh and then set it back down. "Please, try it." He motioned to their cups with his right hand.

They nodded eagerly and both took a couple of generous sips.

"So good," Alex commented.

"We do enjoy our freddo here. You get this in America?"

"No. Not like this. This is next-level espresso."

Dimitris smiled, happy that his guests were enjoying both the place he'd picked and its fare. "As I was saying, the dead man's apartment isn't far from here, actually."

"How did you find it?" Alex asked, genuinely curious. He also wondered why the detective chose a location near the victim's residence.

"Again, his phone. I looked through his apps and found he'd used Airbnb to book the apartment. Expensive for the amount of time he was here, but I guess cost wasn't an issue since he was working for his government. The apartment was small, but he was alone, so he didn't need much. Great view, though. Rooftop patio wraps around the unit. He also had a view of the Acropolis, though not as close as yours."

The couple listened to his detailed appraisal of the dead man's apartment, but they wondered where he was going with it. He could have just cut to the point.

"Anyway," Dimitris said, jumping off his train of thought, "the place was small. Didn't take long for me to look through all of it. At first, I didn't find anything of interest. I figured the man was secretive, being MI6 and all. Their chain of command had been less than honest about their agent's mission. I shouldn't have expected to find anything."

"But you did," Tara said, her eyes locked on the detective with an intensity of an NFL middle linebacker.

"Correct."

Michael returned carrying three plates. One contained flaky cheese pies; another looked similar, but specks of green peeking out of one side revealed it was spanakopita; the third plate was a Greek salad, full of cucumbers, tomatoes, feta, herbs, and some dressing.

"Please, help yourselves," Dimitris indicated with a nod.

The young Americans picked out a little from each plate and put it on their own, nibbling conservatively until Dimitris joined them, taking samples from every offering and devouring it hungrily.

"As I was saying," he continued, still chewing on a hunk of cheese pie, "yes, I found something." He pulled out a folded piece of paper and passed it to them across the table.

Alex and Tara exchanged a look, and then Tara picked up the paper as Alex was wiping a little grease off his fingers with a napkin.

She unfolded the page and looked at the scribbles on it. At first glance, it was confusing. The writing was in small print, easy enough to read, but the content was jumbled. Notes were in incoherent sentences. Some of the lines simply contained one word. Another odd notation ran along the right-hand side of the paper: a column of eleven lines filled with capital letters, varying from two to four as if composing acronyms for something. And then there were the drawings. The doodles occupied space on both sides of the sheet. Some of them were barely better than a child's attempt at sketches. There were both symbols and runes, and Tara and Alex immediately recognized the runes as Nordic in origin. One symbol struck Alex as odd, and he leaned closer to get a better look.

He narrowed his eyelids as he stared at the drawing.

"What?" Tara asked.

"That symbol," Alex said. "I've seen that before."

"Do you know what it is?" Dimitris asked, sounding hopeful through the mouthful of spanakopita. He picked up his coffee and sipped on it to wash down the food.

Alex worked his brain, searching the files in his mind for what he knew had to be there. He rubbed the bridge of his nose with two fingers until the answer came to him. When it did, his eyes widened. It was both a look of horror and fascination.

"What?" Tara pressed. "You're kind of scaring me."

"I'm kind of scaring myself," he said, blinking blankly at the sheet of paper. "That symbol was on the ring of every member of the Ahnenerbe."

Tara's eyes widened, but Dimitris was still in the dark.

Seeing their tour guide's confusion, Alex clarified. "The Ahnenerbe were basically the artifact hunters of the Nazi party."

8

ATHENS

Dimitris stared at Alex for a full minute, dumbfounded by the revelation. Finally he found his voice, "What?"

Alex nodded. "Yeah. I'm not sure why that...dead man...agent...drew this on here," he tapped the paper, "but that's definitely the ring of the Ahnenerbe. I wouldn't mistake it anywhere."

Tara nodded. She knew her husband was right. She'd heard of the group before but hadn't studied it as much as Alex.

"The Ahnenerbe were a think tank put together by Heinrich Himmler, but it was much more than that. Their overarching goal was to find artifacts and relics that could validate the German Aryan race as directly connected to the ancient Norsemen, more specifically, their deities. Himmler and his cronies scoured Europe and even went as far as South America in search of anything they could find that might prove the Germans were the true super race. Initially, their efforts were most likely to appease the masses, or anyone in Germany who might have doubted their cause. Later, though, it turned into an obsession for Himmler. It consumed him. Of course, the world knows about the atrocities that were committed at his command—the unspeakable experiments conducted on human subjects. To this day, we still don't know the extent to which those torturous experiments were exacted."

The table became silent. Even the cooling breeze died down a little, and conversations at the other tables seemed to fade.

"So," Dimitris quashed the silence with his gruff voice, "what was this MI6 agent doing drawing a picture of that ring?" He craned his neck to spy the emblem of the sword wrapped in a sort of upside-down bow, runes wrapping around it like a wreath.

Alex rolled his shoulders and picked up a piece of feta, popping it into his mouth. "This is definitely better than back home." He swallowed the cheese before going on. "I can't say for sure, but let's look at what we know. This guy's own agency didn't know what he was doing. At least none of the people you've contacted. And we have contacts of our own who corroborate what you know. Surely, he was answering to someone or reporting to someone back in London."

"Every stone I turn over turns out to be empty underneath."

"Right," Alex nodded. "Did you check the phone for contacts?"

"Of course I did," Dimitris said, sounding a touch more defensive than he planned. He calmed down quickly. "There weren't any. He'd deleted all the recent calls and texts, so there was nothing in there except the recording from the day he died."

"Curious."

"Secret mission," Tara said. "No known contacts. No one confessing to knowing anything back in London. What if..." She paused for a second, not sure if she wanted to jump off that cliff. "What if he was investigating a new version of the Ahnenerbe?"

The question hit Alex harder than Dimitris, who simply scoffed at the idea and picked one of the last two cheese pies. "Nazis? Here? In Greece? I mean, sure, we have some of the neo-Nazis, those types. But they're not archaeologists digging up or stealing artifacts to help them prove their superior Aryan lineage."

"Perhaps," Alex said. "But she could be right. These runes are clearly Nordic in origin. It's unlikely that the British agent would have ever seen these before except by random chance or—"

"Or if he'd seen them recently, say, with a group he was investigating deep undercover," Tara finished.

"Exactly."

"Okay," Dimitris said. "I'll go along with your theory. So, let's say we have a group of Nazis in Athens, and they're looking for artifacts that will...?"

"Prove their lineage to ancient Norse gods."

"Right. I can't exactly put that in my report."

"I see your problem," Alex admitted. "That said; it's the only thing I can think of at the moment. That emblem is definitely an Ahnenerbe symbol. It was on their rings, lapel pins, and even on some of their stationery for official communications between headquarters and their regional bases of operation."

"Who would be behind something like this, though?" Tara asked. "I know in the phone recording the victim mentioned the name *Buri* several times."

Alex turned to Dimitris. "Sort of a Nordic god; a primeval man who had no father or mother."

Dimitris nodded blankly, clearly not connecting all the dots yet.

"Right," Tara said. "The myth suggests he was created by a sacred cow licking some salt." The detective still drew a blank, and so she went on. "Anyway, doesn't matter. The point is that the Ahnenerbe were trying to find a link between them—or who they wanted to be—and the original Norsemen, as we mentioned before, but that wasn't the only thing they were trying to find."

Dimitris' right eyebrow lifted slightly. "Oh?"

"They were also after something else; a weapon of untold power."

"Weapon?"

"Yes," Tara nodded in confirmation. "Not just one, though. They were looking for anything that would give them an edge in the war, something that would make them the unchallenged power on the planet."

"Such as...the Ark of the Covenant?" Dimitris asked.

Tara smirked, and her green eyes gleamed in the warm sunlight. "Possibly. It's been well documented that they searched for the Holy

Grail and possibly the Ark—Indiana Jones notwithstanding—but they were grasping for anything along those lines, any relic that could make them invincible."

"But they never found anything?" The detective sounded hopeful.

"Not that we know of, though it's possible they did discover something that they didn't fully understand or couldn't control. They were, after all, running short on time as the Allies pushed closer to Berlin."

After listening intently and patiently, it was Alex's turn to jump in again. "I know that they discovered some interesting items in various places around Europe, but most of those 'discoveries' were frauds, or they required a huge leap to connect modern Germans to ancient Scandinavian tribes."

"You say they found fraudulent artifacts? How is that possible?" Dimitris looked baffled as he scooped a small pile of salad onto his plate.

"Well," Alex continued with a devilish grin, "that's why I used air quotes when I said the word *discoveries*. It was later learned that some of the artifacts that the Ahnenerbe found were actually planted by their own people in an attempt to rig the game. These fakes were made to look authentic and may have actually fooled a few naïve people who were too eager to believe in the connection between the Nazis and the ancient Aryan race. There were even a few planned expeditions that never got off the ground. One of them was set up by a man named Edmund Kiss. He believed that the ruins at Tiwanaku in Bolivia held some kind of secret power."

"Power?"

Alex lifted his shoulders and cocked his head to the side for a second. "Who knows? Nothing I've ever read or heard about that place suggests it has any sort of untapped powers, but there's no denying some of the odd details about it. Its location alone is pretty incredible, and why someone would have built there long ago is still a mystery, though best guesses are that the environment there was different all those centuries ago."

He paused for a second to take a bite of cheese pie and his eyes rolled back with delight. "That is so good," he said, then sipped his coffee before continuing.

"Tiwanaku features some fascinating glyphs: carvings of deities, animals, people, stuff like that. But the most interesting one looks like a person coming from space."

"How would they have known anything about space or spacemen?" Dimitris asked. "Are you saying they believed in aliens?"

"It's possible, but I think they considered beings from anywhere other than Earth to be more like gods than extraterrestrials. Still, it could be something else entirely. We simply don't know, but it's interesting to consider."

Dimitris chewed his food slowly as he pondered the answers he'd been given. "This Edmund Kiss you spoke of, what happened to him? Did he get arrested, sentenced with all the other Nazis? Or did he escape to Argentina like many of the others?"

"Actually," Alex said, "no one knows what happened to Kiss. He was stricken with a terminal illness some years after the war, but no one really knows what happened to him after the diagnosis. He may have moved away, tried to lie low as the pressure mounted to root out every known Nazi war criminal possible, but Kiss wasn't necessarily that. In cahoots with the Nazis, yes, but a criminal? Hard to say."

"He had no family? No friends?"

"Not that we know of. But I've only read about him in passing."

Tara chuckled. "You sure know a lot about the guy for just reading about it in passing."

Alex's face reddened, and he shrugged. "I guess. Things I find interesting typically stay in my brain longer."

"That's how it always is."

"True."

"So," Dimitris interrupted, "you think it's possible that we are dealing with a group of rogue Nazi treasure hunters, and this...Buri... is one of them?"

The couple exchanged another glance before Alex answered. "Yeah, possibly. I know it sounds crazy, but it would be reckless not to consider it. That symbol on this sheet of paper you said you found at the victim's apartment is either a really good forgery, wrought by the imagination of a crazy person, or it's something that this dead man saw, probably enough times that he dedicated the image to memory. That, or he has an eidetic memory."

"Okay. Good to know." Dimitris dusted off his hands and brushed a few flakes of crispy phyllo dough off his shirt. "So, we need to discuss your plan."

Tara and Alex nodded, their eyes locked on to his.

"I have made the arrangements with some of the cops I trust in my department. They will all be positioned around the museum for the next three nights. I had to use a few favors to get it done, but if it proves my murder theory correct, then we might be able to catch the person, or people, who did this. I have already let news of the exhibit leak to some of the more questionable people in the police department. I have my suspicions as to who might be working for less-reputable people. If I'm correct, we'll know soon."

"Informants on the police force?" Tara asked.

"Not all cops are bad. On the other side of that coin, not all are good, either. Taking bribes, leaking information to those who pay; it's all part of one of the oldest games in the book."

Neither of the Americans chose to correct his use of the idiom, though they both giggled internally at the thought of doing so.

"Do you think this Buri will be able to act so quickly?" Tara asked. "I mean, usually the best criminals do a lot of planning for their heists. Don't they?"

She didn't have much to go on in terms of police work, figuring out the minds of criminals or figuring out how to stop them, but she wasn't far off.

"Usually, yes. The good ones eliminate risk wherever they can. It's a business to them. Just like in the business world, you have good businesspeople and bad ones. The best try to eliminate potential problems before they occur or simply avoid going after prizes with too much risk. There are times, of course, where the risk is outweighed by a huge payout. Or the promise of it. The way this trap is laid will either lure Buri in or it won't. The setup is that the artifact will be in the exhibit for only three days and that for the first twenty-four hours, it won't be available for viewing as it goes through...analysis." He had to think of the word in English.

This was the first Tara and Alex had heard the exact details of the elaborate scheme, and they both looked dubious at the notion.

"Only three days?" Alex asked.

"That's the best we could do," Dimitris said. "But we made sure that any sources who go running back to Buri will tell him that it's supposedly a priceless artifact and one that has bizarre effects on water."

"Water?" Tara asked, nearly choking on a piece of spanakopita.

"Yes," Dimitris said with a proud grin. "That one was my idea."

"I don't mean to be rude, but why water?"

He raised a finger, still displaying the goofy grin. "Ah, you see, I hoped you would ask. Water is extremely precious. With it, you can create fuel. Why do you think astronomers are so consumed with finding water on Mars or on the moon? They know that if they can locate it, that place can become a launching pad for future space travel."

Tara nodded, her eyes wide with surprise at the man's assertion. "Good point."

"Yes. And here on Earth, water is also highly valuable. There are tales from many cultures about elementals—beings that were either made up of the elements of Earth, or people who could control elements with certain talismans or relics."

"Like the rings of Solomon," Alex said, using the often-debated topic as an example.

"I suppose," Dimitris said, rolling his shoulders. "But it would play into what these...Ahnenerbe," he struggled to say the word, "want."

"That's true," Tara agreed, thinking back on another element that was securely hidden in the vault of the IAA lab. She also considered the larger sample, the original that the middle school kids found in North Carolina. It was also safely hidden where it belonged. It was made from an element, and she suddenly began to wonder if there was any truth to the old stories about elementals. She shrugged off the fairy tales and focused on the conversation.

"We will have the museum covered in multiple shifts, and it will be under our surveillance for the entire span of the operation. If nothing happens, my team goes home and I look like an idiot. If we catch the killer, though, then perhaps we can find out who he truly is and what he's up to."

"Sounds good," Alex said nervously. "So, we're going to be on a three-day stakeout?"

"You two will be less than two blocks away at your apartment. If or when we catch this person, you will be notified immediately."

Alex considered mentioning that, aside from their knowledge they just shared, there was no real reason for them to be here. There had to be another reason, something that they didn't know about yet. But how did Emily know? Again, maybe she didn't. Was she passing the buck on this case? No, that wasn't her style. Emily's instincts were usually extremely honed in, and for her to think they should be in Athens for this ruse meant she believed their skills would be invaluable.

"Okay," Alex said, "when do we start?"

Dimitris grinned. "The seed has already been planted."

9

CRETE

Buri sat at his computer, staring at the images on the screen. The man over his shoulder was his trusted right hand, the one called Klaus.

"What do you think?" Klaus ventured, risking cutting into his employer's intense concentration.

Buri massaged his temples as he considered the prize. He'd been studying the layout of the Acropolis Museum for the last hour. The second Klaus came to him with the information, Buri immediately began scouring the internet as well as his extensive real-world network.

Most of his people hadn't heard about the rare artifact that was going to be on display for private groups of scientists and researchers. That left questions in Buri's mind. Too many questions.

Perhaps he was being paranoid. He knew that it was impossible for him hear or know about every single shard of pottery that was dug up from every corner of the world, but he wasn't trying to track ordinary artifacts. His eyes flitted away from the screen and scanned the room, noting the hoard of priceless treasures that occupied it.

Buri's vault was impressive to say the least. He'd designed the basement to house all of his ill-gotten items, not to show off to visitors, but simply for his private collection, though very few of those artifacts were there because of vanity. Every one of them served a purpose. Each object in his vault was the culmination of more work and research than he could ever imagine—because it wasn't just his efforts that produced them; his predecessors had done much of the heavy lifting.

When his grandfather died, Buri's father largely ignored the work of his own father, casting it into shadow for fear that the family would be scooped up by the zealous Nazi hunters that began scouring the planet after World War II ended.

Buri's father was savvy, intelligent in many ways, but his paranoia nearly cost them everything his father had worked on during the war. At least Buri was able to spend time with his grandfather up until he turned nine years of age. That time had been a priceless commodity.

Back then, Buri went by a different name, the moniker his family had bestowed upon him. He'd done his best to forget that name, to wipe it from his memory, but it would never leave, haunting him like an apparition, always there in the corners begging him to be less than anything important.

He wouldn't have it, though, and Buri clung to the last words his grandfather uttered to him on his deathbed.

Those words drifted through his mind, and for a moment he forgot his assistant was sitting next to him.

"Sir?" Klaus asked, wondering what his boss was thinking about. "Are you okay?"

"Yes, Klaus," Buri said. "I'm fine. I was just considering the possibility." He looked back into the chamber at the eleven glass cases that stood in the center of the room. Each one contained a white stand in the center, a strange stone perched on its top. On the face of each stone was carved another face, the body of an animal—perhaps a lion—and wings of a great bird.

Three more cases were arranged in a row opposite the eleven. Only one of the three cases contained an artifact. It was smaller than the other eleven, though it featured the same image. The two sister displays were curiously empty.

Beyond the display cases, a bookshelf lined the far wall. It contained tomes from fairy tales to modern fiction to mythologies of the ancient world. There were also a few reference works, such as encyclopedias and maps. Some of the volumes appeared old, with dusty or withering covers, the pages within almost brittle to the touch. Buri rarely handled them, though when he did, he used the utmost caution.

"Possibilities?" Klaus eyed his employer curiously.

"Hmm," Buri nodded. "We've recovered all but two of the artifacts," he said. "I'm not perfect, Klaus," he said with a grin. "I have daydreams the same as anyone else."

"You're thinking about what you might find on the other side of the door, aren't you?"

"Yes," he said with a solemn nod. "Our forefathers knew there was something on the other side, that there was a dimension apart from our own that was—most likely—far more technologically advanced than our own world. Power like nothing anyone on Earth has ever seen before."

Klaus had heard the speech before. It was one of the reasons he'd rallied to Buri's cause.

Originally, the Ahnenerbe had been a crackpot organization, built by a madman's lust for power. Buri knew his desire for power was not so dissimilar to that of Himmler's, but there was a difference between them. While Himmler had grasped at straws, reached to force evidence to prove what he wanted, he never achieved his goal. He'd largely disregarded the doorway as anything but ancient ruins, nothing but a pile of stones that had been left hundreds of years before by a civilization long since wiped out.

Himmler made brash claims about his discoveries and those of his organization, but the truth was that they never found anything of worth, except for one item. But that one thing they found that could have changed the course of the war, altered history, and brought Himmler fame and fortune, was the one piece of evidence the infamous SS commander had largely discredited. *Go figure.*

Buri turned his gaze to the wall directly in front of him. An enlarged copy of the document encased in glass hung just over the workstation. Buri didn't know who'd created it, but it was old; that much he knew for certain. The parchment was cracked and faded, the ink nearly evaporated to the point where it was difficult to read in some spots, but it was still clear enough that Buri had been able to surmise what it meant.

The copy of the parchment had been enhanced. It was easier to read and decipher, but Buri didn't need to look at it anymore. He'd committed the strange riddle to memory and knew exactly what he was looking for. His grandfather had taken copious notes and translated as much as he could.

The eleven with three are none without one. Scattered are they that open the gate. The power of the gods awaits he who walks through.

Buri and his new order of the Ahnenerbe had discovered several of the stones on their own, finding one of them nearly in his own backyard—on one of the northernmost islands in the Cyclades, the island of Andros. The others had been considerably farther away. Most had been held in museums with tight security, though one had been pilfered from a dig site before it could be delivered to a secure location. That had been a stroke of unexpected luck for Buri and his organization. Once word leaked that archaeologists had discovered an artifact that not only appeared to be of South American origin but also displayed strange effects on electronics, Buri knew that he was getting close.

With all but two of the artifacts secured, he was confident it wouldn't be long now. He reached up to his chest and ran a finger across the necklace under his shirt. It radiated a subtle warmth, but he didn't fear it. The circular medallion had been tested for dangerous forms of radiation but appeared to emit none. The power it possessed was of a different kind, an otherworldly kind.

Stealing from the dig site had been the easiest heist Buri had ever attempted. There was almost no security, save for a few guards. They had been easy enough to take down. One guard had even let Buri's men pass for a fee. No honor among thieves, indeed. Of course, it was a smart decision by the guard. They could be paid the equivalent of a week's wage to simply turn a blind eye and let the deadly team of thieves pass, or die protecting some old piece of junk.

Buri had set up an extensive network that encompassed the globe. Whenever a new artifact was found, he knew about it. Not much slipped past him in the fields of archaeology and anthropology. He was always at the forefront of any information, even before it was released to the public.

It had taken years and an exorbitant amount of money for him to establish such connections, but he'd done it, and now he was hooked in like no one else. His soldiers—as he called them—were positioned all over the globe, always watching and waiting to send him any news they were able to get their hands on regarding new discoveries.

Most of the time, the finds were not useful, not for what he wanted. Buri was clear in his goal, unlike his predecessor. Himmler had been hell-bent on proving the German connection to the Aryan race to further amplify the power the Nazis had established by brute force. The answer had been under his nose the entire time. They'd even been close to figuring out at least a small part of the equation. The famed Foo Fighters had caused tremendous chaos with Allied fighter pilots as they continued their raids on German strongholds. American and British pilots had no clue what they were seeing. Himmler himself wasn't entirely sure, but he knew he'd tapped into something, though he'd lost some of his best men in doing so.

In the end, those experiments had been lost, the documentation and details surrounding them left as invisible thoughts and ideas lingering in the haunted air of antiquated laboratories and fortresses.

Buri's mind drifted back to the moment, leaving the past behind to focus on the present and the decision that had to be made regarding this new exhibit.

"How did we not hear about this before?" Buri asked. "It's rare when something slips through our information network."

"True, it's rare," Klaus agreed, "but it does happen now and then, sir. We can't see and hear everything."

Buri didn't like that admission, but he knew it was true. There was simply too much ground to cover and not enough men to handle it.

"It's also possible that whoever discovered this was aware of the theft from the other dig site. With those stones popping up more and more frequently in seemingly random places, I would say whoever found it must have been exercising a bit of caution. They may be on to us." There was only a slight hint of warning in Klaus' voice.

"Anything is possible," Buri agreed. "Though, I doubt it. Word spreads quickly in the archaeology community. We can't let that get in the way of our mission. If this artifact is as it has been described, it's clear we need to investigate, even if it doesn't match the other one we have in the set of three. I suspect it's a fake or not the one we're looking for, though it could be that the glyph has been worn down over time and is unidentifiable. That might play to our advantage later on, perhaps as a decoy. Besides, we already know where the other two we need are located."

Klaus nodded. "Right." He paused. "Wait, we do?"

"Well, not exactly. But we know the general vicinity. The parchment says that the stones were distributed around the world so that mankind wouldn't consume itself with the power from the other realms."

"It also said that only the worthy should step through the gate and that only the worthy one will find all fourteen stones and return them to their place," Klaus added.

"Yes," Buri said with a nod. "And who is more worthy than me? I have sought these stones for years. It is no coincidence that they are appearing now, at the time we will emerge from the shadows and take our rightful places as gods among men. Ours will be a new nation, bred free of impurities, and the rest of the world will kneel at our feet."

Klaus gazed at his leader with pride radiating from his eyes. "Yes. And you will be at the head."

Buri shook his head in denial. "It isn't about me, my brother. You know that."

"I know it was you who brought us together. You revived the

cause. Until you came along, every single one of us was a lost sheep wandering in the wilderness without a shepherd. You have brought us hope, a chance at redemption, a chance to accomplish what our forefathers only dreamed."

"Yes, but I will not make the mistakes they made. They grew ambitious, prideful, vain. Their egos swelled until they couldn't see the right path. Then they were left with nothing but falsehoods that they tried to twist into truth, all along forgetting the true power that awaited them. This is about all of us. I'm merely the tool who brought it to the light for you and the others."

Buri thought of the order's membership. There were thousands now, all over the world. In the grand scheme, that didn't seem like many. There were over seven billion people on the planet, and a few thousand was less than a drop in a bucket. But from that small drop, a new empire would be forged. None would be able to stand before them—the super race.

"So, what are we going to do, sir?"

Buri brought his focus back to the computer monitor and the blueprints he'd pulled from the city. Getting access to such things was easy. All you had to do was cross the right palms with silver, and the world was yours. It was like that almost everywhere now. People were unsatisfied with their stations in life. They always wanted something more, something better or bigger. They believed money would solve those problems. Buri knew that most of the time that money would go to something stupid, or quickly consumed and forgotten, leaving the spender's pocket thirsty for more.

"We've been in there a hundred times," Buri said finally. "We know the layout like our own homes."

"Security is good there, though," Klaus countered.

Buri grumbled. "Yes, that's true. It's nothing we can't handle. Two of the guards are ours."

"They aren't on the schedule for this weekend, sir."

"Basil and Jerry?"

A nod confirmed the answer.

"I see." He pouted his lips in thought and thumbed his nose for a second. "You know, this will work out in our favor, not having those two on site. We can use this."

"How?" Klaus raised his eyebrows, not seeing the bigger picture.

"We get their security cards from them, uniforms, whatever we need to look like museum guards. We go in, take down the real guards, disable the systems, and take the artifact."

"A good plan."

"Thank you, Klaus," Buri said, slapping his comrade on the back. "Get in touch with the two guards. Tell them we're coming to Athens for a tour of the museum."

10

ATHENS

Alex and Tara watched the museum from under the shade of a collection of olive trees across the street. At least they assumed the trees were of the olive variety. They couldn't really tell, but it was as good a guess as they could muster. Olive trees seemed to be everywhere in Athens.

The olive tree on the upper plateau near the Parthenon was a famous one—called the *Moria*, or the mother of all olive trees—supposedly bestowed on Athens by the goddess Athena herself as a gift, dating back thousands of years.

Down through the ages, *Moria* had been nearly destroyed a number of times during various wars. For example, it was burned during the Persian invasion around 480 BC. Survivors of that incursion were able to salvage a cutting from the sacred tree and replant it. Throughout Greece's troubled history, each time the tree was damaged or nearly destroyed, it was saved by its people. The most recent offense to the *Moria* was when the Germans bombed the city during World War II. Once more, the citizens of Athens saved a cutting and were able to keep the tree alive.

The young American couple wanted to hike to the top of the Acropolis to visit the Parthenon and perhaps get a look at the legendary arbor, but for now, they were stuck watching the front entrance to the museum.

Every so often, they noticed a cop stroll by on patrol. All of them were dressed in plain clothes to keep a low profile. So far, Dimitris had been out of sight. He was running point and coordinating the entire operation, so that wasn't a big surprise.

"How long are we supposed to sit here?" Alex asked, crossing one leg over the other and propping a magazine on his knee.

"I don't know," Tara said. "I mean, Dimitris said we don't technically have to be here. The police are handling it."

"Yeah, but he said not to wander too far. He wants us to interrogate the thieves when they catch them."

"If they catch them."

Alex glanced askance at her, arching one eyebrow. "You don't think they will?"

"Hope so. I don't know about you, but I'm not going to sit on this bench for another"—she looked at her watch—"seventy-one hours. I can't believe we've only been sitting here one hour."

"No kidding. So, you think we can take a chance and run up to the Parthenon or no?"

She chuckled. "Probably not the best idea. Dimitris told us to stay close and stay ready. Remember?"

"I remember his suggestion was that we hang out in the apartment most of the time. No offense; it's a nice place and all, but there's way too much to do and see here to be stuck in an apartment for three days."

"I know," Tara sighed. "Maybe we'll get lucky and the thieves will come today."

"Well, Dimitris did say that their best opportunity would be when the delivery truck arrives. Which is in the next five minutes," Alex added as he glanced down at his watch.

Dimitris had informed the two that any heist attempt on the museum would be foolish. The room they'd chosen for the "artifact" was one of the most secure in the building, and there were no easy ways in or out of that particular wing. A thief would have to navigate through several hallways and other rooms, antechambers, and eventually, stairs or elevators just to get in and out.

Dimitris had also taken precautions against an inside job. He didn't fully trust two of the guards that were usually assigned to the museum, so he had them pulled and replaced with two of his own men.

That meant that the best chance for the thieves to secure the fake artifact would be to intercept it in transit. And Dimitris had leaked information about the transport truck to several sources; the exact route, the times of pick up and drop off, even the names of the drivers.

He'd opted not to use an armored truck as that would draw too much attention. Not to mention those vehicles were extremely difficult to navigate on the narrow, busy city streets. Instead, he went with a utility van overhauled to look like an ordinary van that a locksmith or plumber might use.

A car honked on the street, a common occurrence in this city. The noise snapped the two on the bench out of their haze.

"There it is now," Tara said, pointing up the street to the right.

Alex leaned forward and looked past her. A plain white van rumbled down the asphalt and came to a stop at a red light a couple of blocks away.

It was difficult to see the drivers from such a distance, but there were definitely two people in the front of the van. There were also two in the back, in the cargo area, but they were tucked behind the divider between the cab and the rear. Tara and Alex knew the guards were positioned in the back to act as the delivery boys for the museum. But if they were hit by the thieves prior to entering the building, those cops were more than capable of handling it, along with the two up front.

That didn't factor in those in the vehicles trailing behind the van. Dimitris had coordinated a further three unmarked cars to escort the white van to its destination. If anything happened, those guys would also be there for support.

Dimitris had taken every precaution; down to the smallest detail.

Now that the trap was set, they simply had to wait for their prey to take the bait.

Of course, all of this would be a massive waste of time if the thieves didn't bite. Resources in the police department were scarce, and Dimitris had gone out on a limb to arrange this operation. He was only partially doing it as a favor for Emily and the Americans. The bigger reason was that he believed the man named Buri was the one responsible for the murder of a British agent in his jurisdiction. Justice had to be served—no matter the cost. If it wasn't, this Buri could continue killing at will. He had to be taken off the streets.

Tara peered down the road at the white van as it sat at the red light. There were two cars in front of it and commuters surrounded it on all sides—compact cars, scooters, and motorcycles—as well as a couple of work trucks and vans.

Tourists were already flocking to the Acropolis, hoping to be at the temple's plateau before it got too hot later in the day. Perhaps they also thought they would beat the rush of other tourists if they got there early, but from the looks of it, everyone appeared to have the same idea.

People of dozens of nationalities strolled along the sidewalks, pointing up to the ancient temple site with wide eyes. They snapped pictures with their phones, others with expensive cameras.

Tara noticed one elderly couple staring up at the Acropolis, taking pictures of the Odeon of Herodes Atticus amphitheater. The ancient structure was perched on the side of the hill about a third of the way to the top, where the Parthenon overlooked the city. The amphitheater had been completed in AD 161 and was now used for special events such as concerts or musicals.

As the couple stared at the millennia-old structure, Tara noticed a young man in a hoodie walking toward them. His eyes were firmly locked on the old man's backside. Even from a block away, she could see that the man's passport was sticking out. The navy-blue top of the document immediately caused her to think the couple was American. Their outfits were ordinary, generic in design, with a flowery dress on the woman and a short-sleeved plaid button-up on the man, along with khaki shorts and some black Rockport shoes.

Tara couldn't believe what she was seeing as the kid in the hoodie sauntered up, bumped into the old man with his shoulder, said something—probably in the way of an apology—and continued walking. The maneuver was an old one, used by pickpockets since the dawn of time. It wasn't elegant, but it worked, as evidenced by the dark blue passport now in the young man's hands.

His pace picked up as he stalked toward where she and Alex were sitting. Alex, apparently oblivious to the theft, was looking over his *National Geographic*, reading an article about other famous places to see in Greece.

"Once this is over," he was saying, "maybe we could go up to the northern part of the country and check out Mount Olympus. What do you think?"

She wasn't paying attention, instead she kept her eyes locked on the young man in the hoodie as he neared their position. Behind him, the white van crossed through the intersection when the light turned green and then came to a stop at the next one, only one block away.

"Honey?" Alex asked.

"Yeah, sure," Tara answered vacantly. "Whatever you want to do."

The kid was only ten yards away. He hadn't even looked back at the elderly couple he'd just pilfered, and from the looks of it, the old man had no clue he'd just lost the most important document he could own in a foreign country.

The kid approached, apparently unaware he was being watched. Tara played it cool. It helped she was wearing sunglasses, a pair of chrome aviators that hid her eyes from others with their mirrored surface. She casually stretched out her arms as the young man neared, and then at the last second she turned her head the other way and kicked out her legs as if lounging on the park bench, unaware that the kid was about to pass by.

Her shin caught his ankle and he tripped, tumbling down to the sidewalk. He managed to catch himself with one hand, but his left elbow hit the concrete with a painful-sounding thud. There might have even been a slight crack, but the street was too noisy to hear it.

"Oh, my," Tara exclaimed, jumping up from the bench. "I am so sorry." She scrambled to help the young man up and descended on him faster than he or Alex would have thought possible.

"Here, let me help you up," she insisted. The stolen passport was lying next to her left foot and she pocketed it before the kid noticed.

Bending one knee, she grabbed his left hand and jerked it back. A surge of pain shot through his arm, and she knew that his elbow was, at the very least, badly bruised. More likely, he had fractured it.

"Ah!" he shouted in an angry tone. Then he said something in Greek that she didn't understand, though she had a feeling it was profanity.

"Oh, jeez, I'm so sorry. That sounded bad."

Then she leaned close, grabbed the kid's hood, and yanked it up a little so her lips were close to his ear. "I saw what you did," she said in a hushed tone that only he could hear. "You're lucky I don't make your nose a permanent part of the sidewalk right now. Quit stealing from innocent people. Get a job, or go to school, but stop taking other people's possessions, or I will find you again. You understand?"

The boy nodded sharply. He was probably seventeen or eighteen, but he might have been a year older than that.

"Good," she added. "Now, get out of here. You'll probably need to see a doctor for that arm."

She shoved him, and he stumbled to his feet, only daring to look back after he was a good fifteen yards away, tripping over his own feet and holding his left arm as he ran.

"What in the world?" Alex asked, staring at his wife in disbelief.

"He stole that gentleman's passport," Tara said, wagging the identification in front of him. "I'll be right back."

Alex watched, still with eyes wide, as she trotted up the street and handed the passport to the elderly man. She explained that he must have dropped it and should probably keep it in a safer place, also issuing a warning that there were pickpockets about.

The man, along with his wife, smiled and thanked her, and then

Tara returned to the park bench just as the white van passed through the intersection and approached the front of the museum.

"Look at you, being a Good Samaritan," Alex quipped with a toothy grin. "How did you even notice that?"

"I just happened to be looking in that direction at the van and saw that couple standing there. They weren't paying attention. Sort of like you," she winked.

"Ouch. I'll have you know I'm in the middle of some very important research."

"You mean like what sights we should see next, as in Mount Olympus?"

He swallowed and nodded. "Fair enough. Doesn't matter now. Show is about to start." He pointed at the van as it pulled up.

Two guards stepped away from the front doors of the building and toward the vehicle.

Then, everything seemed to move in slow motion.

Tara and Alex saw the guards making their way to the van, one languid step after another. They recognized two of the undercover cops standing in their positions just down the sidewalk in both directions. The men were watching the vehicle, not attempting to tear their eyes away from it, which probably made them stand out.

Two of the escort vehicles were a couple of cars back and proceeded to drive by and park beside the cars parked alongside the sidewalk, effectively double parking and inciting another series of loud honks and angry shouts. The third escort car parked behind the van, leaving enough of a gap so that the men in the back could swing open the doors and have room to exit the vehicle with their cargo.

All three of the escort cars' doors swung open. Two armed cops in plain clothes stepped out from the front of each and swept the area with their gaze to make sure they were in the clear.

"Something's wrong," Alex said.

"I know," Tara agreed, sensing it. "Is it me, or did time just seem to slow down?"

"It's not you," Alex confirmed. "And in my limited experience, that's when something is about to go down."

He stood up and fished the phone out of his pocket, ready to call Dimitris. As he looked out over the street to the museum, Alex realized they were way more out in the open than they had probably intended. Everything Sean taught him about combat, including long-range shooting, flooded his mind.

He spun his head around, twisting back and forth as he took in the dozens of excellent sniper positions around the museum. Someone could be positioned in the off-limits area of the Parthenon, where construction was ongoing in what was rumored to be perpetuity. Then there were the hundreds of trees and bushes. Even some of the balconies along the street could offer an excellent vantage point for a sniper.

His fingers swiped on the screen to open the contacts list, but a sudden movement out of the corner of his eye interrupted him. Alex looked up in time to see the doors to the back of the van swing open, just as a red MINI Cooper swerved to the right.

The car slammed into the rear doors as one of the guards stepped out, crushing the man's right leg. The van lurched forward from the impact, and the driver, who was in the process of stepping out, was knocked to the ground. He rolled to a stop, momentarily disoriented, then scrambled to his feet and drew a pistol from inside his windbreaker.

Two more red MINI Coopers sped up to the crash site. One smashed into the van's driver, flipping him up and over the hood, the roof, and the back hatch to finally hit the pavement with a thud. He didn't get up.

The four cops from the cars in front drew their weapons, but they were cut down by a series of rounds from an unseen shooter.

The sniper Alex feared.

He shoved his phone in his pocket and grabbed Tara, who'd stood up and was watching the attack unfold. He swung her behind the park bench for cover and then looked back toward the four cops. The first two were lying motionless on the asphalt. One was tucked in behind his vehicle, clutching his shoulder. The last one was peeking around the front of the car, trying to locate the shooter. Alex traced the man's eyes and located a cluster of trees in the Acropolis gardens that would have made a perfect sniper nest.

The third MINI Cooper sideswiped the escort vehicle to the rear of the van and nearly took out the driver. The man had been slower to get out of his car but faster to jump clear of the oncoming vehicle. He pulled out his weapon and opened fire, plunking three rounds into the hatch of the MINI.

Those were his final actions. No pop, no report or muffled click came from nearby. The bullet simply smashed through the man's forehead and exited through the back, dropping him to the ground.

Within seconds, the seemingly normal, busy morning street had turned into a war zone with multiple casualties.

Alex felt for the gun at his side, but it wasn't there. They'd left their weapons in the apartment at the request of Detective Frangos. It was with great reluctance they acquiesced, but they also understood the culture. Greece wasn't firearm friendly. Guns were outlawed except for special situations such as shooting or sportsman clubs, and of course the police and military.

"Yeah, we're unarmed," Tara said, noting her husband's unconscious check for his weapon. "What do we do?"

Alex watched in horror as the sniper gunned down the passenger in the third escort vehicle. It was unclear whether there was more than one sniper. Alex forced himself to kill all emotion and do what Sean taught them—analyze the situation and do it quickly.

11

ATHENS

Everything went to Hades in a hand basket in the blink of an eye.

One moment, the city street was relatively calm, save for the usual incessant honking and chaotic driving. The next, bullets were flying, cops were dying, and another was screaming in agony—his leg pinned to the back of the van, his torso hanging over the lip and into the cargo area.

Pedestrians panicked.

Men were yelling and women were screaming at the unexpected explosion of violence. They darted in all directions as they tried to flee from the carnage. Cars sped away and horns honked, sounding their desperation to get to safety. Farther up the street, cars began to turn down side streets in an attempt to funnel their way to somewhere, anywhere, else.

Alex assessed the situation just as Sean had trained him to do. The bullet that killed the cop from the third escort car came in at an angle. That meant the patch of trees and shrubs he'd noted before was likely hiding the only shooter.

"Call Dimitris," Alex said.

"What are you going to do?"

"I'm going to take out the sniper."

"With what? A rock from the Acropolis?"

He shrugged. "Maybe."

Then he spun around, vaulted over the fence that wrapped around the ancient grounds, and sprinted up the embankment toward a row of blocks that marked an old cistern.

Alex paused behind a stack of stones that were previously part of a wall of some kind. He caught his breath for a moment as he eyed the suspicious patch of greenery. He saw movement, subtle but definitely unusual.

He took a breath and was about to circle around behind the shooter when he sensed movement to his right.

Crap.

Tara leaped over the lower wall and joined him in the old cistern, barely out of breath.

"What are you doing?" he asked, perturbed.

"We're a team. I'm coming with you. If there's a sniper up here, I don't want you going after him alone."

He wanted to kiss her, but this wasn't the moment. She loved him, and he knew it.

"Fine," he nodded. "I'm going around behind the guy." He searched the ground around them and found a rock about the size of his palm, and then a second. He handed one to Tara. "Get as close as you can to that outcropping of bushes over there," he said and motioned to the area. "When I give the signal, throw that rock into the bushes and duck down."

"Okay...what's the signal?"

"I'll wave or something. Just watch me."

He was done talking. Alex vaulted over the three-foot wall and ran up the hill, careful to run on the balls of his feet to make as little noise as possible. He deftly avoided twigs and tall grass, afraid that the slightest snapping or brushing sounds would alert the sniper.

Every step Alex took, he feared the next bullet would be his. His imagination ran wild, filling him with the dread of what it would be like to be struck by a high-velocity round in the chest. If he was hit in the head, he wouldn't feel a thing. His body would probably take a few more unconscious steps before he hit the ground, dead, but he wouldn't know about it.

But the shot never came, and Alex found himself in a cluster of olive trees fifty feet below the pathway that passed in front of the amphitheater. He tucked in behind a tree that was too narrow to conceal his position, but it protected at least most of his body's center from potential bullets—he hoped.

He gripped the stone in his hand and looked back to where Tara still hid. She was watching him closely and holding her own rock, waiting for his signal.

Alex didn't dare nod at her for fear she might think that was the signal. He took a deep breath and then shifted out of his position, crouching low as he floated toward the thick cluster of shrubs. Forty feet from the upper perimeter of the undergrowth, he could hear the sniper fire another muffled shot. *Suppressor.* That explained why the reports were difficult to identify. Whether it was called a silencer or a suppressor—Alex knew people in law enforcement and the military who called it both—the attachment on this rifle was extremely efficient, keeping the sound of the shots to little more than that of a single kernel of popping...in a sock.

Through the foliage and branches, Alex could see the outline of the shooter as he drew closer to the gunman's position. The screaming of panicked citizens sounded farther away now, something Sean had said would happen in situations like this—if ever they got in this situation. He'd explained that specific senses heightened based on the need, and right now vision was taking over, along with the need for stealth.

When Alex was behind the thick stand of brush and olive trees, he stopped and crouched. He spotted a narrow opening in the thicket where the shooter must have entered to take up his position. Now Alex could see the man clearly. The opening was five feet high and a couple of feet wide. The gunman was in a pale green T-shirt and matching pants with tan tactical boots, like those Alex had seen on soldiers back in the States. The gunman was lying on his belly; the long rifle gripped with both hands and propped up on a tripod for stability.

Sirens whined in the distance, and Alex knew that if he didn't take out this sniper, the casualties could escalate quickly. The gunman was locked in on his scope, a fact Alex had counted on when deciding to flank the man.

Alex looked over at Tara, who was peeking over the wall. He gave a nod and flashed his right hand with the rock in it.

She nodded in return.

Alex crouched as she popped up from her hiding spot and flung the stone through the air. He never realized what a great arm she had; forgetting she'd played softball at Kennesaw State University during her undergraduate years.

The rock sailed through the air in a laser line toward the thicket.

Alex heard it clip a leaf on its way through, but that was the only obstruction the stone found on its way to the target.

He had intended for her to throw the rock as a distraction, then he could throw his own at the shooter's head, disorient the man, and then go in for the takedown. Any time you could get an edge over a skilled opponent, you had to try for it.

Instead, Tara's stone smacked the sniper in the temple with devastating accuracy. The man's grip loosened on the weapon and he slumped forward a moment before righting himself in a daze. He grasped at his head, wondering what had hit him.

Alex lingered no longer and dove into the thicket, brandishing his own rock over his shoulder—the need to throw it no longer present. He pounced on the gunman before the guy could even turn around. Alex brought the hard stone down onto the back of the man's skull once, twice, three times. The third blow rendered the man unconscious, or dead, Alex wasn't sure which, but he was down and that was what mattered.

Moving with deft expertise, Alex dismantled the rifle and pocketed two key components that rendered the weapon useless. Then he took the sidearm from the man's hip and tucked it into the back of his own pants, covering it with his shirt. Last, Alex checked the man's pockets and found a cell phone, a wad of euros, and a ferry ticket. He pocketed those items and, satisfied the sniper was out of commission with no chance of causing any more trouble, darted back through the opening in the thicket.

Alex sprinted back down the hill toward Tara, who was waiting impatiently.

The bitter smell of gun smoke drifted through the dry air. Car engines revved from down the street. Alex knew the thieves had probably already secured the decoy artifact. Reinforcements were still blocks away, how many he couldn't tell, but he guessed that few if any had arrived on the scene yet.

Alex and Tara needed to get back to the street or back to the apartment. The latter was probably safest, especially now that Alex was carrying what was likely an illegally obtained weapon.

But someone had to stop the thieves. This was their one chance to catch them and figure out what they'd been doing with the stolen relics, and for Dimitris it was his chance to possibly catch a killer. Then there was a strange absence of sound from the chaos below. The gunfire had ceased. Alex knew the small amount of time they had before had just shrank considerably.

Alex skidded to a stop at the edge of the cistern. "Come on," he urged, panting. "We can't let them get away."

Tara responded with a quick nod and hopped over the wall. They sprinted down the slope and reached the fence, climbed over it, and landed on the sidewalk amid what looked like an urban battlefield.

Wrecked cars with bent metal, broken glass, and ruptured tires littered the other side of the road. Windows were broken from the flurry of bullets that were flying during the gunfight.

Two of the MINI Coopers were already speeding away. The first smoked its tires as it slid through the next intersection, disappearing down the adjacent street. The second performed the same maneuver and vanished. The third car had the guard pinned to the van. It was only slightly damaged and still drivable.

It backed up quickly, whipping around so that the front was positioned to follow the other two. Then the driver glanced at Tara and Alex, who were staring, dumbfounded, at the vehicle.

The driver of the car stared at them for a second through the tinted windows. It was hard to see the detail of his face so identifying him would be impossible, other than to say he was a man with a short haircut. Even the color of the hair was difficult to discern through the tinting.

The moment seemed to last an hour, but in reality it was three seconds. He hammered the accelerator and squealed the tires. The car surged forward.

Alex reached back for the pistol he'd tucked in his belt, but it was gone. Tara rushed by him with the gun in her hand. She pumped her legs, running as fast as they would carry her. She held the gun at arm's length, trying to line up the driver in her sights.

She could have squeezed off multiple rounds, but there were still masses of people trying to escape the carnage, and the last of them were still visible down the block. She couldn't risk hitting them.

Instead, having seen where the first two cars went, she decided to try to intercept the driver at one of the next streets. Could she be so lucky?

She lowered the weapon and cut to the right, leaping onto the sidewalk in front of the museum.

"Where are you going?" Alex shouted, cupping his hands to his face.

Tara barely looked back over her shoulder as she shouted, "To cut them off!"

"Great," he sighed, throwing his hands up. He glanced to the right and briefly considered commandeering one of the police cars, but decided against it. In the city traffic—especially now that it was congested by panicked drivers—his wife had the right idea. On foot would be quicker, but which way was she going, and how did she know which way the getaway cars would go?

He knew the answer and made his decision.

Alex darted across the road, cut left, then cut right, chasing after Tara. She was fast, but he was slightly faster, and he pumped his legs with every ounce of energy he could muster to catch up to her fifty-yard head start.

He turned the corner and found a logjam on the next street. He'd narrowed the gap between him and his wife, but she was still more than twenty yards ahead of him and carrying the gun in her hand, which might have scared pretty much everyone she passed.

Hundreds of cars were stuck in gridlock. Only the red MINI Coopers were making progress as they plowed through café tables and knocked over trash cans as they sped along the sidewalk sending pedestrians diving for safety. The thieves paid no mind to people or vehicles as they clipped side mirrors and traded paint with nearly every car on the road.

It was like real-life bumper cars, without the fun.

Tara lowered her weapon as she maintained pursuit, closing in on the last MINI as it struggled to get to a clear street two blocks up. There, the traffic was flowing at a steady rate, and she knew that if the thieves reached that intersection, there would be no catching up to them.

Alex cut onto the road to run between the cars instead of trying to fight his way through the crowd. He was only fifteen yards behind his wife when someone in a tiny two-door opened their door and stepped out to see what was going on. Alex nearly barged into the man, but he'd expected that to happen at least once during his pursuit, and he was ready. He deftly jumped—in stride—and planted his right foot on the side of the little car. He pushed off hard, and flew toward the next car a few short feet away. The parkour maneuver worked to perfection as Alex flew over the driver's shoulder, landed his left foot on the opposite car, and leaped down over the door. He landed with a thud and lost his balance, toppling forward. He'd practiced that move a hundred times, though, and rolled to his feet without losing too much momentum.

The driver shouted something in Greek at Alex.

"Sorry!" Alex shouted back without looking.

He saw the three red cars up ahead and realized that if they reached the intersection two blocks away, they would be gone.

His chest swelled and shrank as he labored for breath, but he summoned every reserve of energy he had to push himself harder.

"The intersection ahead!" he shouted at Tara, who was now only ten yards away. "We can't let them get to the intersection!"

"I know!" she yelled back over her shoulder.

She swerved left, cutting in front of a green motorcycle, and then sped along the curb.

Alex followed and caught up to her at the next light.

Cars blocked the intersection, and many people were out of their vehicles, yelling what must have been obscenities at the drivers of the red MINI Coopers. If they were blessings, they were the harshest blessings ever uttered by mankind.

Tara twisted sideways to avoid knocking over pedestrians who were moving too slowly in their attempt to escape. "Out of the way!" she shouted. "Police! Move!" She figured the lie wouldn't hurt, especially as she was carrying an illegally obtained weapon. She hoped claiming to be a cop would put some minds at ease, but really, she just wanted them to get out of her way.

The getaway cars were halfway through the next street and were a single-file line of destruction; a scarlet snake slithering though the clogged street, leaving broken glass and twisted metal in its wake.

Alex was mere steps behind Tara as they pushed themselves to their limit. Their legs burned from the exertion, but they ignored the pain, digging even deeper.

The first getaway car reached the intersection and turned left, disappearing from view. The second was right behind and followed in its wake. The third was still within reach.

It ran up onto the curb to get by a motorcycle and a maintenance van, knocking over a table and two white chairs at a café. The table's center umbrella toppled over in dramatic slow motion before it crashed to the concrete.

Tara jumped over the table's legs five seconds later.

Alex weaved around it and leaped over one of the warped chairs.

The car was nearly to the end of the block.

Tara pounded the ground harder, giving the last of every ounce of energy she had. She reached out, only feet from the back of the escaping vehicle. The driver must have seen her because he stepped on the gas and the car lurched forward, scraping a city tree and narrowly avoiding crashing into it. Metal screeched on metal as he rubbed against the last two cars at the traffic lights.

Then, the light turned green and all the vehicles accelerated, desperate to get through the intersection.

The release was exactly what the getaway car needed. It sped away, whipping around the corner and leaving the two pursuers behind.

Tara and Alex reached the corner and watched as the last red MINI Cooper sped up the hill and around a curve. The two gasped for air for a long moment. Doubled over, they planted their hands on their knees as they tried to regain their breath.

"I...can't...believe...they got...away," she gasped, trying to talk between breaths.

Alex swallowed hard. "Yeah." Another couple of deep breaths. "I know."

She realized she was still holding the gun and that there might be people staring. She quickly stepped over to a waste bin and dropped the weapon into it, closing the lid with a clank.

Then a realization hit Alex. "Maybe not."

They trotted back up the sloped street, still too fatigued to run at full speed. When they reached the museum, the uniformed cops had arrived and were working to secure the perimeter. Two ambulances were parked at the scene and paramedics were attending to the injured. One of them was checking a dead undercover cop next to his car. The sight sent a rush of guilt-filled pain straight to the heart of the two Americans.

"Come on," Alex said, grabbing his wife by the elbow. "That sniper is our only lead."

She nodded, taking one last look at the grisly scene in front of the museum. They rounded the new police tape that was strung up across the street as one of the first responders did his best to urge people away from the area. It was still an active-shooter scenario as far as the police were concerned, and they wouldn't open up the road again until they were certain the attackers were either dead, departed, or arrested. With some of their own dead, it was easy to think the cops would be out for blood.

Alex and Tara skirted around the perimeter, wading through a few lingering onlookers holding up cell phones to broadcast the incident on their social media accounts, or perhaps simply share with friends. The people did this against the desperate pleas of the police. Apparently, once the cops showed up, people felt the threat was gone, which was not always the case.

"We'd better hurry," Tara hissed. "If that guy wakes up, he might start taking out people in the crowd."

Alex nodded, and his pace quickened.

They sifted through the last of the gathering crowd and emerged on the sidewalk. They glanced around to make sure no one was paying attention before they climbed over the fence and into the Acropolis gardens. A quick look back told them no one was paying them any mind, and so they hurried up the hill to the thicket where they'd left the shooter.

Tara suddenly wished she hadn't dumped the pistol in the trash, but it was too late to do anything about that now.

The two circled around behind the outcropping of greenery. Each picked up a stone that was slightly larger than their fists and held them up as they approached the opening in the rear of the thicket, as if two rocks could compete with a professional sniper. Then again, it had worked before—and they had the element of surprise.

As they neared the opening, it was their turn to be surprised. The sniper, his weapon, and his gear were gone.

12

ATHENS

"What was that?" Buri roared as he climbed aboard his private plane. The twin-turboprop aircraft wasn't as fancy as a Gulfstream or some of the other jets available to people of means, but it was perfect for getting to the capital and any of the two thousand islands that make up Greece.

It was the first time he'd spoken since they left the city. Until that moment, all he'd cared about was getting clear of Athens.

"I don't know, sir," Klaus said, following him to a seat in the back of the plane.

Four other men joined them and took seats in the opposite row. One man was missing.

"Where is Jan?" Buri fumed.

"He hasn't reported in, sir. I'm still waiting to hear back from him."

"Send him a text. Tell him we're leaving. He'll need to find his own way back to Crete."

"Yes, sir," Klaus said and began typing out a text message on his phone. The sniper had done a good job of eliminating the troublesome targets at the museum. Thanks to some inside information, Buri and his team had known exactly when the transport truck would be making its delivery.

What he hadn't been told was that there would be undercover cops running security around the museum. It wasn't luck that Buri had the sniper in position, it was a precaution, a failsafe in case something like this happened. Had they been betrayed? Still, with the precise delivery time and the ability to track the truck, it should have gone off without an issue.

Should have.

Buri had chosen the drop off as the perfect time to take the artifact, as it would make for an easier getaway than navigating the museum's many rooms and corridors.

He'd expected some resistance. It was, after all, a supposedly priceless artifact. But who else had known he would come for it, especially on such short notice? Buri thought he might know, but he needed to be certain. His contacts within the police department would be the first ones he questioned, and he had a man in the city who could handle that interrogation with callous efficiency.

"Milosh," Buri shouted at one of the four men in the middle of the plane.

A monster of a man stood up and turned around. He had a thick black beard and matching hair. His broad shoulders looked like they could knock over a tank, and his arms and legs were just as thickly muscled.

"Yes, sir?"

"Find out who set up that sting. I want to know who tried to catch us in a trap, and I want to know before we get back to Crete."

Then a thought occurred to him, and he turned back to Klaus while Milosh began looking through his phone contacts to begin his own investigation.

"Klaus, tell Jan to stay in Athens. Tell him to go to the safe house and await further instructions. I will be in touch with him shortly. Understand?"

"Of course, sir." Klaus knew better than to question the leader's orders, at least out loud. He kept his thoughts to himself, wondering why Buri would request their best sniper to stay in Athens.

Once the messages were sent, Klaus slipped his phone back into his pocket and looked across the aisle at Buri, studying the man for a moment. There was a fatigue wrapped around the leader's eyes, manifesting itself in thin crow's feet that stretched out from the corners of his eyes. There was still plenty of passion there, though, a desire that fueled the man's ambitions.

"You believe we were set up," Klaus said finally, breaking the thoughtful silence. It was a statement not a question.

The plane's engines whined outside, and the whir of the propellers steadied into a constant hum.

"Obviously, Klaus." Buri didn't hide his derision. "Someone knew we would try to hit the van today. I want to know who set that up. When Jan is secure, he will delve into this issue with the police. I pay far too much money to the cops for something like this to happen. This is an offense that I will not overlook. We will make an example of those who failed us."

Klaus knew that was coming. People didn't screw up and get away with in the new order of the Ahnenerbe. They would be punished in painful ways. In some instances, like the man Buri threw over his balcony, they would be confronted and executed without emotion or reservation.

"But we did secure the artifact," Klaus offered with a proud jaw set firmly in the hope that his employer's mood would lift.

Buri waved a dismissive hand. "It's obviously a fake," he said flatly.

This caused Klaus to tighten the muscles in his forehead. "What?"

"It's a fake. A phony. Whatever is in that box is not a real artifact."

Klaus still didn't understand.

"Open it up," Buri ordered. "Open the box and see what's inside. It's nothing more than an ordinary hunk of metal. Unless someone else has an expert opinion on ancient artifacts!" he shouted, and the other four men in the cabin turned around but said nothing.

Klaus still looked confused, his cold blue eyes still questioning through the narrow slit of his eyelids. He stood up and stepped over to the thick industrial-steel case they'd taken from the back of the van. Right away, he noted that there were no locks on it, which immediately raised his suspicions.

"Go ahead," Buri insisted, watching from the other side of the plane. "Open it."

Now Klaus was uncertain for a different reason. "What...what if it's a bomb, sir?"

Buri rolled his eyes. "The cops aren't in the terrorism business, Klaus. It isn't how they do things. I already checked the so-called artifact and removed the tracking device from inside the case. I disposed of it on the way here."

Klaus stared at the case for a long moment, deliberating on whether or not it was safe. "Why would you say it's a fake?"

Buri swore under his breath in frustration and stood up.

The plane turned as it taxied down the tarmac, preparing to take off.

Buri flipped up the clasps securing the lid to the metal case, pried the lid open, and pulled a piece of black foam off the top.

Inside was a misshapen hunk of dark metal.

"What is it?" Klaus asked, mesmerized.

Buri shook his head and returned to his seat. "You should sit down, Klaus. We're about to take off."

The man did as instructed but kept his eyes locked on the case as he strapped his seatbelt over his lap.

"It's just a hunk of metal," Buri continued. "Looks like iron, if I had to guess."

Klaus stared at the object. The plane accelerated, and his head rocked back slightly from the engines' thrust.

He turned to his employer, who was staring out the window, lost in thought.

"If this is a fake, a decoy, then we walked right into a trap."

"Astute observation, Klaus," Buri commented, his eyes still lingering on the terminal and runway zipping by in a blur. "We did indeed walk into a trap, which was our concern to begin with. Let that be a lesson to you. Always trust your instincts."

Klaus hung his head in shame and nodded. "Yes, sir."

Buri sensed the dejection and turned to face the man. "It's fine. From every negative experience, we can glean something useful. For example, we were completely surrounded, we were outnumbered, and yet we prevailed."

"That's true."

"More importantly, we know that there is someone after us. But that leaves questions. How did they know who we are to leak information to us?"

"You think they're onto our moles?"

"It's certainly possible," Buri said. "And with the evidence before us, I would say that's probable. But we shouldn't eliminate other possibilities."

"Such as?" Klaus raised an eyebrow.

"What if the British agent we killed had another contact? What if he told his supervisors—the higher-ups—about us? You'd have to believe he was relaying information at some point."

"That's true. But if he'd done that, why didn't they come after us already? Our headquarters should be swarming with Interpol, foreign agents, cops, the works."

"This is why I think he didn't have anything on us. Neil was with us for how long?"

"A few months, I think."

"That sounds correct," Buri said.

The nose of the plane tipped up and the aircraft lifted off the ground, aiming at a steep angle toward the clear blue sky above.

"What's your point?" Klaus dared to be direct, but he knew his boss appreciated that more than dancing around a subject.

Buri honestly didn't have one. He knew that the connection between Neil's arrival and the discovery of the stones was a coincidence. It had to be. There was no other logical explanation. Buri knew enough about cops and intelligence agencies to understand that when an undercover operative showed up they were standing behind hundreds of hours of research and investigation. That meant someone had been on his trail for a while now, probably for the better part of a year.

"Neil's arrival in our ranks was unfortunate timing...and all the more reason we need to be more careful."

"But he's dead now, so we should be clear going forward."

"Hardly. If Neil sent anything to MI6 or whoever he worked for, they might still be watching. That means we're going to have to change how we go about acquiring the final two stones. Smaller teams. More communication between everyone in our organization."

"Makes sense."

"Yes." Buri's mind wandered back to the subject of the stones, the strange artifacts that began appearing just a few months ago, all at the same time. In his mind, it wasn't a coincidence.

"What about our headquarters in Crete?"

Klaus' question was one Buri had already considered. He knew that they might be compromised and had already taken countermeasures.

"We are only stopping temporarily in Crete," Buri answered. "I can have a team sweep it for bugs, but that won't make much of a difference if MI6 knows about the place. We're flying to Boston."

"Boston?" Klaus looked genuinely curious.

"Our next target. We must move quickly."

Realization finally clicked in Klaus' eyes. "Ah. The university, then?"

"Yes. The university."

It was a long path they were taking. Buri knew the longer they were in the air, the higher the risk of capture.

Klaus understood his boss's decision. Boston would be a long flight. The plane would need to refuel on the island before departing, and it might need to make one additional stop, though he wasn't entirely familiar with the Gulfstream's fuel capacity. Instead of asking more questions, Klaus nodded and leaned his head back, resting against the seat.

Buri was glad the conversation had come to an end. He'd grown weary of the chatter and needed to think. He wanted to concentrate on the issue at hand: the fact that someone was after them. Intelligence agents had penetrated the veil he'd drawn over his operation, one he'd carefully woven to keep his activities cloaked in secrecy. Perhaps it was only a matter of time.

Not that it was of any consequence.

He had the only map, the only document in the world that could point to the exact location of the final two stones. Buri closed his eyes and tilted his head back, cursing himself silently for not thinking of it before.

Idiot.

He could have checked to see if one of the locations had been tapped recently. There'd been no news about such a discovery. He should have thought of that. He shrugged off the frustration. Today had been difficult, as he'd assumed it would be.

Buri never worked from the position of underestimating a situation. He always went in expecting things to not go according to plan. In a way, perhaps he'd known all along, deep down, that this was a setup, a trap intended to capture him and some of his men.

Cut the head off the snake, and the body dies. He knew that old adage wasn't always true. His new order of the Ahnenerbe was too strong for that. If he fell, someone else would step in and fill his place. He'd taken precautions for such an event, protocols that would delegate authority to the next in line.

He couldn't let it come to that. It was Buri's destiny to do this, to succeed where so many had failed. It was his birthright.

He turned his head to the right and glanced out the window, his eyes growing hazy despite it being the middle of the day.

His mind drifted back in time again, to his childhood and the day he found his grandfather's secret room.

Back then, his name wasn't Buri. It was Paul, named after the saint who'd become a leader of the fledgling Christian church.

He'd been playing in his grandfather's old office that day, kicking a soccer ball around since it was raining outside. His parents didn't like him playing with the ball indoors, but his father was at work and his mother was busy taking care of chores.

The office was mostly barren save for an old wooden desk in the corner, a matching chair, and an antique lamp that looked like it came from the 1940s. The old lamp had a cream-colored stained-glass shade and golden tassels hanging from the four points.

Paul was kicking the ball against the wall, working on his one-touch passes, when he lost his balance and fell toward the desk. He reached out his hands to brace himself and grabbed on to the edge of the desk in the nick of time. To his surprise, the desk didn't even budge. The wood wasn't lightweight, but it also should have shifted under his momentum. Curious, Paul stood up and nudged the desk again. It didn't move.

He frowned and tried again. Still nothing.

Then he hooked his fingers under the lip of the desk and lifted, wondering if it would go up since there were no signs of it being bolted to the floor.

What happened next changed his life.

The desk was much lighter than expected, and the legs nearest him came up with ease. There was a squeak from the left leg, and Paul looked down to see what caused it. To his surprise, there was a metal rod jutting out from within the hollow leg. That rod disappeared into the floor.

Paul raised the desk higher to get a better look and was startled by another noise, which caused him to drop the desk to the floor with a bang.

In front of him, to the left, one of the timber wall panels creaked and slid to the side, folding in behind the panel to its right. Paul stared into the cavity. A narrow wooden staircase ascended into an attic that the boy never knew existed. He had no idea what wonders awaited him.

He climbed the stairs with trepidation, seeing a dim light emanating from somewhere above. How was there a light on up there? Did the trick desk turn it on when the wall opened?

He ascended one step at a time, pausing on each to take a breath and steady his nerves. When he reached the top, Paul discovered a collection of items he never could have anticipated in a million years.

Pieces of Nazi regalia littered the area. A flag with a swastika hung from the sharply angled ceiling, illuminated by a single lightbulb that looked to be decades old. An SS uniform hung from a coat hanger off to his left in a corner. A long wooden table sat in the center of the dusty room. It was covered with papers, notes written in his grandfather's hand, and maps of various countries around the world with x's dotting certain areas.

On the far end of the table, something was covered by a sheet of glass. Paul walked around to the oddity and stared down at it.

It was the first time he saw the parchment, the map that would lead him to his destiny, his purpose in life. While he didn't know it yet, or even understand what he was seeing, Paul's world was about to change, and his path was about to veer into the footsteps of his grandfather.

13

ATHENS

"Sit." The chief of police stood behind his desk with his hands balled into fists that were firmly stuck to the top of his contemporary metal-and-glass desk. Like so many other furnishings found throughout the city, indeed the country, it came from IKEA.

The police chief, a hulking man named Atros, was five feet, ten inches tall, around the same height as Dimitris. He had a bald patch on the top of his head, surrounded by thinning black hair. The top two buttons of his white shirt were undone, revealing a thick crop of black hair on his chest. His belly bulged over his belt and was only partially concealed by the black blazer he wore. The man's nose was thick, matching his chin. He was the picture of a man who'd long ago given up on maintaining his physical appearance but still believed he was as sexy as a movie star.

Dimitris closed the door behind him, expecting the verbal onslaught that was about to be cast his way. He stepped toward the two chairs opposite the chief and chose the one on the right, sliding into it without hesitation. It was time to take responsibility for his actions.

"Four cops are dead," the chief started grimly. He lowered himself into the black leather chair and folded his hands in front of his chest. The gesture wasn't one of calm, but one of a man doing everything he could to hold back a tidal wave of emotions and resist strangling the cop across from him.

"I know," Dimitris said, genuine sadness and regret lacing his voice. He did know, all too well. It was his operation, and he was well aware of the consequences that awaited him.

News of the shootout in front of the Acropolis had spread throughout the world. The sudden outburst of violence would, no doubt, affect tourism for a short while. The city would have to take measures to put the rest of the world at ease, but it would be months before people felt safe enough to return to the ancient city to partake of its treasures.

And while the financial costs of the attack had yet to be calculated, what concerned the chief most was the lives that had been lost. The lives of his men.

"You know?" the chief roared like some unholy amalgamation of lion and bull. He slammed a meaty fist on the desk. A canister of pens rattled. The computer monitor wobbled back and forth, and for a moment, Dimitris wondered if it would topple over the edge. "I don't think you do, Frangos!"

"We had a chance to catch an international criminal, sir. Someone who I believe to be involved in something big."

"Something big?" Atros blurted. "Something big? What is this big...something? Huh? Four cops are dead because you circumvented protocol."

"I went through the proper channels," Dimitris defended.

The comment only served to send the chief into a spiraling vortex of rage. "Proper channels? You may have gone through a semblance of protocol, but those men were not assigned to that operation by me. I didn't approve any of that, and you know it."

"I thought I had the authority, Chief."

"You have no authority!" He slammed both fists on the table, striking it with the bridges of his hands. This time, the computer monitor wobbled more dramatically. Dimitris thought it would surely fall, but again it didn't.

"I am a detective, sir. I was trying to catch a killer and solve a case. On top of that, the killer happens to be a black-market artifacts dealer."

"Oh?" the chief said sarcastically. He widened his eyes and pursed his lips as if he might whistle. "Well, I had no idea. By all means, then, you're free to go, Detective. Thank you for your service. Now if you don't mind, please tell the families of the four dead cops your ghost story about an international killer who sells trinkets on the internet."

Dimitris' comment about the artifacts was a stab, a shot in the dark. He had no proof that the one called Buri was actually involved in that kind of business. He also didn't have proof Buri wasn't. What Dimitris heard on that recording was all he had to go on, and the dead MI6 agent, as well as the killer, had mentioned the artifact. What artifact? Was it one of those that had been stolen recently?

He forced himself to focus on the chief. Right now, catching the murderer or solving some strange mystery didn't matter. His job was on the line.

Dimitris had been a cop for twenty-five years. He'd seen it all and knew when something wasn't right. The death of the British agent was unquestionably a murder. But he couldn't give his boss the recording now. No way. If he was going to do that, it would have had to be the day Dimitris visited the crime scene. Now, it would just look like obstruction of justice, which would only make his situation worse—if that was possible.

"You have always been a loose cannon, Frangos," the chief said. "You've never been one who liked to play by the rules."

"All due respect, sir, but who does?"

"Shut your mouth." Atros jabbed a fleshy finger at the detective. "You are suspended indefinitely. An official investigation into this mess will be conducted, but right now, we are trying to clean up everything you've done. I have to personally visit four families and tell them about the deaths of their loved ones. Taxpayers are going to have to foot the bill for some of the damage done at the museum."

Dimitris wondered about that. More corruption, he figured, slipping money into pockets for "repairs." He didn't dare say anything to that effect.

"And all for what? Where is your mystery killer? Where is the gang that took out four of my cops, good cops, in this little operation of yours? Oh, right. You didn't catch the killer or any of the men. Every single one of them got away."

"The cameras probably—"

"The security cameras didn't catch anything useful. Neither did the street cameras. The men who hit that van in front of the museum were wearing sunglasses and hats. No one will be able to identify them. Not to mention we couldn't find any trace of their vehicles."

"And they didn't leave the country?"

The chief ran both hands through the remnants of his hair. "All airports in the region have increased their security and are on the lookout, but again, we don't know who we're looking for, do we?"

Dimitris knew better than to answer. He was already in up to his elbows. He also knew that there was no way to track the thieves since the device they'd placed in the case had been found on the side of the road. It was an easy assumption to figure the thieves had gone to the airport, but that was only if they were international, or perhaps based on one of the islands. That was certainly a possibility, but with about two thousand islands, it would be impossible to search them all.

The chief drew a deep breath and sighed, doing his best to suppress the rage he was almost involuntarily firing at the detective across from him. They'd worked together a long time, and Atros knew Dimitris was a good cop, though one that didn't always play by the rules. Maybe he'd navigated the proper channels for this operation, but he'd definitely danced in some gray areas. Now four cops were dead, and it was all on him. He knew Dimitris would do things differently if he could, would go back and come up with a better strategy, a plan that would have a better chance of working with fewer casualties.

But Dimitris wasn't a time traveler. He couldn't go back and change things, and that meant Atros had to take action.

"You're suspended indefinitely," he said bluntly. "With pay for four weeks. After that, we will evaluate your standing."

Dimitris had expected that. Actually, he'd expected far worse, but the chief's decision still hit him in the chest like a sack full of bricks. The air was sucked out of his lungs, and he felt his shoulders sag. His heart thumped harder. There was no defense, and he knew no amount of begging would change the chief's mind.

Atros had to do this, if for no other reason than to settle the public on the matter, to get the people who paid their salaries to see that something was being done to the person responsible.

Dimitris was a scapegoat.

"Yes, sir," he muttered, almost inaudibly.

Dimitris stood up, removed his pistol from the holster, and set it on the chief's desk. He took off his Hellenic Police badge from his belt and placed it next to the weapon.

"Thank you, sir," Dimitris said.

"For what?" Atros asked, confused. "I basically just told you you're fired."

"For giving me the opportunity."

He turned and started for the door, but Atros stopped him.

"Dimitris?"

The detective turned slightly and looked at the chief over his shoulder.

"I...I have always respected you. I don't want this, but you left me no choice."

"I know, sir," Dimitris said. "And when you failed to investigate the murder of the MI6 agent and were happy to declare it a suicide, you left me with no choice, either."

He faced the door again, opened it, and stepped out into the busy office.

A few eyes looked up at him as he passed by the rows of desks. Most of the cops working in the office kept their eyes averted. No one wanted to say anything to Dimitris for fear of being implicated by association.

He strode to the back of the huge shared office space, reminiscing about when his desk was in that area. He turned left and made his way to the corner where his office was situated and stopped short, looking at the two Americans who sat in the chairs in front of his desk, awaiting his return.

"Well, that could have gone worse," he said as he pushed the door all the way open and stepped inside. He closed it behind him, strode over to his desk, and eased into the seat.

"So, you didn't get fired?" Tara asked, hopeful.

"Oh, I'm fairly certain I'm going to be fired, but no, not at the moment. Suspended indefinitely, pending a thorough inquiry. Four weeks with pay. After that, who knows?" He threw up his hands. "Never mind the fact that we were correct about the thieves...and the fact that they're killers."

He slammed a fist down on his desk, startling the two visitors. "I'm sorry," he said, instantly regretting the outburst.

"Don't be," Alex said. "You're right to be angry. I mean, I understand that the chief has to do what he has to do to save face with the department and with the public, but you took a chance. It was a good plan."

"And now four cops are dead because of it. My plan killed them. They were good men." He stared down at the desk, regret blanketing his face.

Tara and Alex remained silent. A minute or two passed as they let the man swim in his thoughts, process the chief's decision, and probably some of his own in the last twenty-four hours.

"So, you are officially not a cop for the next four weeks?" Tara asked, breaking the silence when it felt right.

"Yes," Dimitris nodded. He only had himself to take care of at this point. His wife had left him more than a decade ago. His modest home was paid for, a small condo in the city. His car, too, was paid off, and his only bills each month were utilities and groceries. He'd lived a simple life, putting away as much money as he could in spite of his meager salary. "Something like that."

"You said they're paying you?"

"For the next four weeks, yes." It sounded like pitiful consolation.

"So, what you're saying is you have some free time on your hands." Tara looked at him with wild eyes. They were running with an idea, and Dimitris could see it.

"Seems that way. Why?" He slumped back in his chair and laced his fingers together, staring at the young woman.

Alex also stared at her, waiting to hear what she had in mind.

"Well, I know you won't have any authority or...jurisdiction... while you're suspended. Probably no resources. I'm guessing you turned in your gun and badge?"

He nodded.

"Thought so."

"I'm sorry, Ms. Watson, I don't know what you're thinking, but I have to figure out my next move. It would take a miracle to get me reinstated, and I'm short of those right now."

"Maybe you're not," she said, wryly curling her lips to one corner.

He cocked his head to the side and his eyebrows pinched together. "What do you mean?"

Tara looked over at her husband. It could have been mistaken for seeking approval, but that simply didn't happen between them. They were both their own people and did as they pleased. The glance was more of a courtesy since Alex was just as much a part of this as she.

"We still have a chance to catch these guys," she said. "And if we do that, maybe you get your miracle and we catch the men who killed the agent."

He drew a deep breath through his nostrils and steepled his fingers together, pondering the idea. Such a thing wasn't done, not by the good cops. What this American was suggesting went against everything he believed as a police officer. She was implying that they go vigilante, hunt down some criminals and bring them to justice. Except justice wouldn't look like the kind he stood for. Citizens, especially foreigners, couldn't simply arrest someone and haul them to jail. Vigilante justice would mean eliminating the bad guys.

"What you're suggesting is...illegal," he said finally.

"I know," she admitted. "Sometimes, though, breaking the rules is the only way to do the right thing." She leveled her gaze at him, her eyes piercing his with a furious energy that raged like burning emeralds. "This man Buri is going to keep stealing artifacts. It's what he does. Whether he needs the money or just does it for power or the rush of adrenaline, I don't know, but he is going to strike again. Somewhere. And what will happen then? More cops will die? Maybe some civilians this time? Security guards? We can't let that happen, Detective. We have a chance to stop this guy and his bunch...and bring them all to justice."

"Dimitris," the cop muttered after a long ten seconds of contemplative silence.

"What?" Tara asked.

"Don't call me detective. Just call me Dimitris."

She nodded, understanding.

"And I may still have a few resources I can call on, though most of them aren't with the department." He chuckled. "That's probably for the best."

His guests nodded.

He sighed as if he were Atlas setting down the weight of the world for the first time. "Count me in."

14

ATHENS

Dimitris pulled the car off to the side of the street and wedged it along the curb with little more than eight inches between two other cars. He stepped out and looked both ways before opening the door for Tara, who'd been sitting behind him.

Alex got out onto the sidewalk and looked around, a habit that might have been mistaken for sightseeing but was actually a form of precautionary reconnaissance—another trick he'd picked up from Sean.

Tara and Dimitris joined him on the sidewalk, and he led the way up three steps to the entrance of the apartment building.

The place looked pretty much like all the other buildings in the city. Sprawl had taken over Greece long ago, but diversity in architecture had resigned itself to the suburbs, government buildings, and of course, the ancient ruins that dotted the landscape. Only a few of the apartment and condo buildings were over four stories tall, and most of them looked the same, making it easy to believe the tales of tourists getting lost and turned around in Athens.

Dimitris unlocked the front door and held it open for his guests. As they walked in, he glanced out the entryway again, pausing on a shadow he thought wasn't there a moment before. The shadow didn't waver, and he shook it off, attributing the sight to paranoia. He closed the door behind him, stepped over to the elevator, and pressed the button. It dinged a second later, and the three crammed into the tiny lift.

At the top, they followed Dimitris to the end of the hall, where he stopped at a black door. He unlocked it and stepped inside, motioning for the other two to enter. Inside, the small apartment was clean and tidy. The entire space took up around four hundred square feet, with a bedroom to the right, a modest kitchen to the left, and the living room straight ahead with a breakfast nook merging with the kitchen space. It was impossible to ignore the touch of Swedish décor. IKEA, it seemed, was something many Greeks appreciated, probably because of the functionality and efficiency of the furnishings.

One thing that Tara immediately noted was the absence of pictures. The walls, tables, countertops, and the desk in the corner were all devoid of pictures of family or friends.

"So," Alex said after looking around, "this is really nice."

"Thank you," Dimitris said. He walked across the room and into the open bedroom. He reemerged a minute later with a subcompact 9mm pistol in one hand and a concealment holster in the other. He tucked the holster inside his belt and then shoved the weapon into it. Even without a jacket on, it was nearly impossible to tell the man was carrying.

"You got a permit for that?" Alex asked, half joking.

"I did," he said frankly. "It may not be good anymore, but I'm not going to stop and ask." He offered a dry grin with the answer.

Alex nodded his appreciation for the rule breaking.

"Do you live here alone?" Tara asked, probing the room with her eyes to see if there were any signs of another person, perhaps a roommate or girlfriend.

"Yes," Dimitris said, a distant sadness in his voice. "My wife left me a long time ago." He let the story fade, but Tara got the distinct impression there was more to it. She also got the feeling that whatever else was there, it was too emotional for him to talk about with two people he just met—or anyone for that matter.

"So," Tara broke into the awkward silence, "you two want to take a look at this paper again?"

"The notes from the dead man's apartment?" Alex asked.

"Yep."

"Sure," Dimitris said. "We have to start somewhere."

The three sidled up to the table, which just so happened to have three chairs—probably because one side of it was wedged against the wall. Still, in Alex's mind, it begged the question as to where the fourth chair had gone. He let the trivial thought go and refocused.

Tara flattened the note on the table, doing so with the greatest of care. This was, after all, their only lead left, and if they damaged it—well, that would be problematic, to say the least.

"Okay, so we agree that we're looking at the symbol of the Ahnenerbe," Tara said, pointing to the familiar emblem drawn on the paper.

"Yes," Alex said.

Dimitris nodded.

"Which means the agent saw this somewhere, leading us to the conclusion—albeit a tenuous one—that we might be dealing with a new iteration of the Ahnenerbe. I doubt it was done as a doodle during a boring staff meeting with an underworld artifact thieves' guild."

Alex snorted a laugh. "Good one."

"Thanks." She went on. "These runes"—she pointed at the symbols drawn haphazardly on the paper—"are Scandinavian in origin, but we need our computers to know what they say."

"Actually," Alex corrected, "we could use our portable scanner with one of the laptops at the apartment. That would tell us exactly what these runes mean in just a few minutes."

"Portable scanner?" Dimitris asked, somewhat confused. "Your computers can read ancient Scandinavian languages?"

The two Americans cast a knowing glance at each other and nodded to him.

"The ones back in our lab can do way more than that," Tara answered. "These laptops aren't as powerful. We haven't been able to get the tech from our main units into the smaller cases yet, but we're working on it. Now, the thing that I don't really get is all these letters on the right side of the page." She ran an index finger along the rows, fourteen in total. Again, she noted that some of the groupings contained two letters, others three or four. There appeared to be no consistent pattern. There were lines through eleven of the groups of letters. And another line through one of three others that seemed to be separated by extra space.

"I was wondering about that," Alex admitted. "It looks like some kind of checklist based on the lines through most of the acronyms, if that's what they are."

"That's true," Dimitris agreed, tilting his head slightly to get a better view of the paper. "But it still doesn't tell us what they are or why they are on this paper."

Alex chewed his bottom lip as he considered the problem.

Tara rubbed her jaw with a thumb and forefinger.

For nearly two full minutes, no one said a thing, pondering the issue of the odd letters.

Alex finally broke the silence. "Okay, so maybe we're thinking about this wrong."

"How do you know what I'm thinking?" Tara asked wryly. She added a wink for effect.

"Funny. Seriously, though, I know I'm trying to connect the letters in some way, but it's clearly not a word puzzle where all the letters tell you the answer if you combine them correctly."

"True."

"So, what if we do this backward?"

"Backward?" Dimitris asked.

Alex could feel his heart rate pick up as the solution clarified in his mind. "These guys, the Ahnenerbe, are thieves. The heist at the Acropolis Museum was just one."

"Museums," Tara said with a frustrated sigh as she realized the answer was right in front of them. "Of course. Emily told us that several artifacts had been stolen recently from museums all around the world, especially in Europe. One was from a dig site."

"And you remember how many had been taken, don't you?" Alex asked.

"Twelve," Tara said plainly, her keen memory snatching the information in an instant.

"Exactly. Twelve. And there are twelve of these letter combinations marked off the list." His eyes danced from his wife to Dimitris. "Every one of these letter groups represents the name of the place where an artifact was taken. They're the initials of the museums, and the dig site for the one other location.

"How can you be so sure?" Dimitris asked. The scowl on his face depicted his skepticism.

"Look up one of the locations," Alex said to his wife. "The file Emily gave us lists all twelve."

Tara nodded and pulled the folder out of her bag. She set it on the table away from the sheet so as not to disturb it. She opened the file and pointed to the list of targets where artifacts had been stolen.

"Museo Nazionale Romano," she said, pointing at the listing.

Alex used his finger to hover over the letters *MNR*. "Got it. Another one," he said.

She looked back into the file and called out the next. "Archaeological Museum of Andros."

Alex pointed to the AMA on the list. "You seeing a pattern yet, Dimitris?" He looked up at the man, his vision barely clearing the bottom of his eyebrows.

Dimitris looked baffled, but also accepting. "Yes. I see it. There are still two locations left, assuming you are correct with your analysis."

"It's a safe assumption," Tara said. "Of course, I can keep going down the list if you like."

He waved a dismissive hand.

"So," she went on, "we need to figure out the next two targets. Based on the order of these acronyms, it's easy to see they are going down the list when I compare it to the locations that have already been hit."

"Which means the next one on the hit list is HMNH."

The three exchanged a bewildered glance.

"No one knows what that one is?" Alex asked, hopeful.

Dimitris shrugged and shook his head. The flesh on his neck jiggled a little from the movement.

"On it," Tara said. She pulled her laptop out of the IAA bag and set it on the table, flipped it open, and waited for a moment before the screen blinked to life. Then she began typing in her search query. She hit the enter key and waited for a second. Then the screen populated for the search "Museums with the Letters HMNH."

The first one at the top of the page gave them the answer they wanted.

"That was...easy," Tara said.

"Yeah, I guess it was," Alex agreed.

"What?" Dimitris asked, twisting around to see what they were looking at on the screen.

At the top of the page was the link to the website of the Harvard Museum of Natural History.

15

ATHENS

"But that's a natural history museum," Alex protested, though he didn't fully believe his argument against Harvard as the solution to their question. "Do they even have artifacts relating to archaeology?"

"The Peabody does," Tara answered with a smug grin.

"The Peabody?" Dimitris asked. He stood and walked over to the kitchen sink, produced a glass from an overhanging cabinet next to the refrigerator, and then filled the glass with water before returning to the table. He took a long sip and then waited for the others to continue. He was clearly lost in this part of the discussion, unfamiliar with the names the other two were throwing around.

"The Peabody Museum of Archaeology and Ethnology," Tara explained. "It's located in the Harvard Museum of Natural History in Boston."

"That's right," Alex realized. "I forgot about that. I've never actually been there before."

"Well, their exhibit isn't huge. All of the smaller artifacts are real, but when I was there, it was disappointing to see that most of the larger items were replicas, copies made from plaster. It was still cool to see the scope and size of what those ancient societies could do, but I don't go to museums to see copies."

"So, you believe that this artifact, like the other...twelve, is something that is going to be kept at this museum in Harvard?"

"It matches the pattern," Alex said. "And it also makes me wonder what that last one is."

He looked at the letters *BM* at the bottom of the page.

"Bill Murray?" he offered with a chuckle. "Doesn't he have that on the gates to his mansion or something?"

Tara rolled her eyes, shaking her head in disapproval. "Such a dork. I'd guess it means the British Museum. But that isn't where these guys are heading next. Their pattern has been to follow this list. The MI6 agent must have figured that out before he died. I'd bet their next stop is Harvard."

Dimitris was on his phone now, flipping through his own search results to double-check the information Tara was flinging his way.

"She's right," he said, finally. "Those museums were recently hit, though only one artifact was taken from each. The reports on those artifacts are...scarce, though."

"Can't imagine why that would be the case," Alex joked. "Based on what we know about these things, they have unusual scientific properties, affecting everything around them, especially electrical devices." He almost slipped and mentioned the piece of Quantium they had back in the lab in Atlanta, but he bit his tongue and stopped before he divulged anything.

"Then we need to let everyone in Boston know what's going on."

"On it," Alex said as he retrieved his cell phone from his pants pocket.

Dimitris' head spun. "Who are you calling?"

"Our boss in Atlanta. He can get in touch with the right people in Boston to put everything on lockdown. They'll secure the artifact and make sure those villains can't get to it."

"Good thinking. What about the other one?"

Tara held her phone in her hand for the detective to see. "We have a contact at the British Museum. They should be able to verify who I am. Once they do that, I'll run the same drill with them: secure the artifact, wait for the bad guys. Simple."

"Well," Dimitris said, putting his hands up in the air, "glad I could help."

Tara grinned at him as she found the number for the British Museum.

Alex saw the status on his device change to *Calling*, and he held the phone up to his ear.

Then the moment seemed to stand still. Each sensed it as it happened.

The window behind them shattered, and a canister struck the floor.

Alex reacted instantly, with nothing but the instincts that had been forged through the last several years of training with Sean. He kicked the canister with his toe, driving the object back toward the window.

He was shocked to see the can fly through the broken window. Alex initially believed it was a tear gas canister, but that theory was incinerated the second the device exploded.

The concussion from the blast blew through the wall, sending debris flying into the small apartment. Dimitris was thrown from his chair.

Tara flew backward and struck the base of the kitchen counter with the middle of her back, then her skull struck the surface. Stars filled her vision, which until that point she'd believed was just something artists drew in cartoons to demonstrate confusion or dizziness. Now she understood the reality. She blinked rapidly to dispel the hallucination, but it wasn't so quick to leave.

Alex felt himself leave the floor for a split second, then his shoulders slammed into the interior wall near the door. Somehow, he managed to keep his head from striking the surface, which would have sent him reeling the same as his wife. He dropped to the floor, smacking it hard with his knees and crumpling down onto his face.

What was happening?

His ears rang painfully. Another sensation of pain throbbed from both shoulder blades. He felt woozy, but he was okay. He could control his arms and legs, fingers and toes.

Alex braced himself on the floor with his palms and pushed himself up. A cloud of black smoke rolled into the sky just outside a gaping hole in the wall. It was a wonder nothing was burning, though the smell of fire was still prominent in his nostrils.

Momentarily disoriented, Alex forced himself to think: Sean. What would Sean Wyatt do now? Nothing his friend had taught him could prepare him for this. Or could it?

What was it Sean always said? Alex had to shake the cobwebs from his mind, which didn't take long once he took in the sight of his wife lying on her side next to the kitchen counter and the detective close by, unmoving and lying prostrate.

Assess, he thought. Sean always told them both that if they were ever in a desperate situation, quickly assess it, then take action.

Alex checked Tara again. His wife was dazed, probably experiencing the effects of a concussion, though he couldn't be sure since he'd not seen what happened to her after the explosion.

Dimitris was on the floor near Tara. The detective had regained his faculties enough to prop himself up on his hands and knees, but it was evident the man was still woozy. Alex also noted the file and the piece of paper they'd been studying. He felt his heart sink at the sight.

The sheet of paper had fallen to the floor, and the glass of water Dimitris had been drinking lay shattered around it. The paper was soaked. The folder containing the mission details was still intact, but their lone clue to this entire mystery was in jeopardy.

Alex grabbed the sheet and the file then glanced back toward the new opening in the wall. Dust and smoke still blocked the view to the street beyond, but that wouldn't last long. Whoever sent that explosive into the apartment would surely be waiting outside, watching. Alex knew he could sit tight and wait. An attack like this would draw first responders to the scene within minutes. Cops would seal off the area. Fire trucks would rush to the sidewalk. Medical personnel would tend to the wounded in triage tents all along the street.

Would the person who tried to kill them stick around and risk capture?

Not likely. There was another option that concerned Alex, and it was the one he believed would prove to be the most probable.

Whoever did this would check the apartment. That meant Alex and the others had to leave immediately.

He rushed to Tara and lifted her head with a gentle thumb on her chin. He looked into her eyes, and she looked back, finally clearing the cobwebs and stars from her vision.

"What...happened?" The way she asked the question sent a combination of fury and pity through Alex's mind.

"Can you walk?" Alex asked.

She nodded. The feeble gesture was barely noticeable, but it was enough. With his help, Tara stood and regained her balance. She shook her head again to clear the remaining effects of the explosion and the impact to her skull. She immediately wished she hadn't done it; the movement sent a sudden throbbing through her head again. She winced and grabbed the back of her skull.

"You okay?" Alex asked.

"Yeah," she half lied. "I'm good. Just a headache. Check on Dimitris."

"I'm fine," he groused, clambering to his feet. He reached for his weapon, eyes darting around with a crazed, ravenous fire in them. "What was that?" He added a Greek word that sounded like an expletive.

"Someone wants us dead. My guess is we have less than a minute before the would-be killer is in this room."

Dimitris nodded. He shot a glance over to the doorway and spied the three metal hooks on the key ring next to a coatrack. "Come with me," he said.

The other two watched the detective march over to the door, grab a set of two silver keys off one of the rings, and open the door.

He looked back at them. "Now!"

They startled out of their haze and followed.

Dimitris closed the door softly behind him and looked toward the stairwell, then at the elevator.

Tara and Alex wondered if he was trying to decide which exit they should take.

Then they heard the footsteps down below. They weren't hurried, clumsy steps but careful and calculated ones, the way an assassin would move. They were so quiet, it was a minor miracle anyone heard them.

Dimitris motioned to the door at the opposite end of the hall. It was only twenty feet away, but with the hit man ascending the steps, time wasn't exactly on their side.

The detective reached the door first and silently thumbed one of the keys. He inserted it into the doorknob that was oddly located in the center of the door. He twisted the key, but nothing happened. Another Greek expletive escaped the cop's lips, and he withdrew the key. No sounds came from the stairwell, which was more disconcerting than if they'd heard ten pairs of boots tramping up the steps.

Alex and Tara waited anxiously behind Dimitris as he inserted the second key and twisted it with the greatest of care. Alex glanced back over his shoulder, expecting to see a man with a gun, or multiple guns, emerge from around the corner.

The door's lock didn't even click as Dimitris twisted the knob and pushed the door open. Luckily, the hinges didn't make a sound as the detective stepped through and moved aside to let his American companions slip inside. Once they were in, he eased the door shut, holding the doorknob on the inside to make sure it didn't click when the bolt returned to the receiver in the frame. Once shut, he gradually let the bolt slide into the frame until it stopped.

Dimitris gripped his pistol close to his jaw and peered through the peephole. Two seconds later, a man appeared at the top of the steps. He wore a dark green T-shirt with a tan jacket and matching pants and boots. He carried a pistol in black-gloved hands. Another was at his side, and he wore a belt that carried three spare magazines.

Alex and Tara knew better than to ask if Dimitris saw anything. They didn't need to. The way their host was holding his weapon, intently staring out through the peephole, told them everything they needed to know.

The killer was mere feet away.

16

ATHENS

Jan swept his pistol to his right as he stepped onto the top floor landing, then immediately to the left, to ensure the corridor was clear.

The sunglasses on his face concealed his eyes, and a mask covered his nose and mouth. While he was on the street, he'd kept the mask off and his weapons hidden under a jacket. A gunman walking the streets of Athens would lead people to think he was the one who had caused the explosion.

Although that was true, he didn't need to advertise.

Something had gone wrong. He had to find out what, and then finish the job.

He'd fired the projectile with an air-compressed launcher he developed and fabricated. The device was small and easily portable, unlike most rocket launchers, and it was extremely quiet. He would have preferred to eliminate his target with a sniper rifle, but he'd been forced to abandon that idea when he ditched his prized weapon after the failed heist attempt.

He didn't call it a failure, but his boss did. Jan knew it had been a trap, and he was determined that wouldn't happen again.

He stepped around the corner and padded over to the door. He reached out and twisted the knob, careful not to make a sound. He pushed his shoulder against the door and nudged it inward, holding his weapon up near his face. The second the door was clear of the frame, he swung it open quickly, sending a swoosh of air through the apartment that roused a plume of dust from the floor.

He whipped the pistol around to his left, checking the kitchen first then the living room. He then aimed into the open bedroom door and strode toward it, pinning his back against the wall for a moment before stepping into the darkened chamber. The room was clean, though a few items had been knocked to the floor from the explosion. Jan quickly maneuvered to the bathroom attached to the bedroom. It was empty. He looked under the bed, checked the closet, and then returned to the main room. An acrid smell lingered in the air from the explosive. Sirens screamed from somewhere in the city, and Jan knew he didn't have long.

There were no bodies, which was a problem.

The targets had all been in the apartment. Of that, he was certain. He'd watched them enter the building. Through the blinds in the window, he could see their silhouettes and noted when one of the lights flicked on, all signals that his prey were right where he wanted them to be.

Using the improvised launcher allowed him to fire one time and eliminate all targets. The explosion would also cause mass chaos and hysteria, allowing him to escape with greater ease amid the panic.

All had gone according to plan—except the explosion itself.

He stepped closer to the open crater in the living room and stared at it for a moment. The damage was mostly on the outside of the building. While the living room and kitchen were badly damaged, it should have been completely obliterated. He knew the canister struck the window and flew into the apartment, and the charge would have taken mere seconds to detonate. So, why did it not destroy the apartment from the inside?

There was only one conclusion Jan could reach. Somehow, the targets had managed to redirect the explosive back out of the window. Whether they threw it or used some other means, he didn't know, and it didn't matter. Perhaps these targets were more skilled than he was initially led to believe.

Buri had relayed the message that Detective Frangos wouldn't be a difficult kill. The man had been suspended from his job and would likely return home to wallow in pity and self-loathing, so it was a surprise to see he had company.

Jan didn't recognize the two younger people, but that changed nothing. They were collateral damage—in the wrong place at the wrong time.

Jan clenched his jaw as he tried to figure out what had happened, how his plan had gone wrong.

The sirens drew closer; he was out of time. He strode toward the door and took one last look into the apartment before exiting, letting the door close behind him. Rounding the corner, he was about to descend the stairs when he thought he heard something farther down the hall. Jan narrowed his eyes and stared intently at the other apartment door, twenty feet away.

He furrowed his brow, studying the portal, waiting for the sound to reveal its origin once more. He craned his neck to the side and looked hard at the narrow gap at the bottom of the door. There were no shadows, and no other sounds indicating anyone was home.

Jan shrugged it off, attributing the sound to a pipe or water heater—some random noise in the otherwise silent corridors of an apartment building.

He turned and made his way back down the stairs. When he reached the tiny lobby at the bottom, he walked over to the coatrack where he'd left his jacket and slipped it on. Wearing outerwear might make people pause and wonder on a warm day like this, but having his guns exposed would be far worse, especially with the army of cops on their way to the apartment.

He zipped up the jacket and stepped out into the open air, skirted down the steps and turned to the right, walking away quickly as the sound of sirens swelled around him.

Jan deftly avoided some of the debris from the side of the building and looked up at it with fresh wonder. He feigned both curiosity and fear as he blended into the crowd of people trying to escape the area. Occasionally, he looked back over his shoulder as many of the other panicking people did. With each glance, he used the opportunity to look around for signs of his quarry, but they were nowhere to be seen.

He knew Buri would not be happy about such a failure, but Jan consoled himself with the fact that he'd been forced into rushing this job. He'd been given a tight timeline in which to work. When things were hurried, mistakes were made. Buri would understand that, though it would hardly make him happy.

Then Jan had a thought: There was no way Buri would know he'd failed. Who was to say that he couldn't still get a win out of this?

Jan cut to his left, dissecting himself from the main throng of people. He walked across the street toward a news crew setting up for a report on the damaged apartment building.

He recognized one of the reporters, a young woman with thick black hair. The order had used her before, scouting her when she was just an up-and-comer. Now, she'd become one of the foremost news reporters in Athens—the help of the Ahnenerbe attributed with most of her success.

Jan made eye contact with the woman as she brushed her hair over her shoulders in final preparation to stand before the camera. She swallowed uncomfortably then nodded to the cameraman.

"Hey, can you get me another lapel mic?" she asked. "I think this one has a bad battery."

She fumbled with the device and dropped it on the sidewalk. The case split open, and one of the batteries rolled out.

The cameraman shook his head at the clumsy move but made his way to the rear of their minivan to retrieve a replacement.

The young woman looked both ways and then hurried across the street to where Jan stood in the shadows.

"What are you doing here?" she asked, irritated.

"It's lovely to see you, too, Mari."

She hated that he knew her name, but that wasn't new. It was the reality she lived with every day.

"What do you want?"

"Me? I don't want anything." He looked innocent and hurt. "I just want you to report the news."

She glanced around to make sure no one saw her talking to the stranger; not that they would know who he was. "Oh?"

He nodded. "Yep. Turns out three people were killed in that explosion. You won't see any bodies coming out of there, but they were in there. And one of them might have been a cop. You won't have to dig much to find out who."

Mari clenched her jaw. She wanted to ask if he'd been the cause of it, but she felt she knew the answer. And she knew better than to challenge the order. Jan wasn't her usual contact, but she'd met him before. The mysterious head of the order made certain all of his puppets were at least a little familiar with the others.

"Anything else?" she asked, doing her best to sound tough.

"Nope. Remember, three dead."

She nodded. "Got it."

"Good."

Mari turned to walk back to the sidewalk where the camera was set up. Her cameraman was returning from the back of the van, a new lapel mic dangling from his fingers.

She turned and looked over her shoulder, but the man from the shadows was already gone. She pinched her lips together and tried to avoid the chill that shot through her spine and caused her skin to pebble.

With a new mic pinned on her lapel, she stared at the camera lens and prepared to deliver the news.

17

ATHENS

Dimitris watched until the mysterious man disappeared down the stairwell. He felt a bead of sweat roll down the side of his face, but didn't dare rip his eye away from the peephole.

His American friends hadn't made a sound since they stepped into the neighbor's apartment, but something out in the hall had, causing the killer to pause at the top of the steps. If the man had tried to get into the apartment where they were hiding, Dimitris was confident he had the upper hand and could use the element of surprise to take down the intruder.

That calmed his nerves, but there was still the matter that someone had tried to kill him. Maybe whoever sent the explosive through the window was trying to kill Alex and Tara, but he doubted it. Very few people knew they were even in Athens, much less that they were working with him on a case.

No, Dimitris had been the target. He was sure of it. The only question was, who wanted him dead?

His mind flashed through the names and faces of the cops he worked with. Through the years, he'd pissed off his fair share of people—a crooked cop now and then—but he doubted it was them.

They were long gone, moved to other countries or were serving time for more serious crimes.

This was something different; he could feel it. Dimitris wondered if the murder investigation had something to do with it. He snorted. Of course it did. What else could it be?

It would seem he'd stumbled onto something much bigger than an ordinary murder case. Whatever this was had some serious players, and he didn't know what game they were playing yet.

Dimitris waited two full minutes before he pulled himself away from the peephole at the door. He turned to the others and nodded. "I think he's gone now."

Everyone breathed a collective sigh of relief.

"Who was that?" Alex asked, still more coherent than Tara.

"I don't know," Dimitris said. "If I had to guess, it was the man who tried to kill us." He looked down at Alex's feet and then back up into his eyes. "That was a good kick. It saved our lives."

"I just reacted," Alex confessed. "I was lucky."

"Perhaps," Dimitris said as he sized up the American. "But that was an extremely fast reaction. I wouldn't have thought of that."

"Honestly—I thought it was tear gas."

"That would have been bad, too, though preferable to incineration."

Tara looked to the door and then into the living room behind her. "Where are we?" she asked.

Alex turned to her, gazing at her with regret-filled eyes. "I'm so sorry, honey. You must have hit your head pretty hard back there. We're in Athens, Greece."

She rolled her eyes. "I know where we are, smart guy. I'm asking who owns this apartment."

His cheeks reddened, and he lowered his head in embarrassment.

"My neighbor," Dimitris said. "She goes out of town now and then and asks me to check on her cats."

On cue, one of the furry felines rubbed up against the gruff man's shin. It was a gray cat with short hair and a rotund belly.

"Looks like you haven't forgotten to feed it," Alex quipped.

"This animal eats better than most people."

The newcomers took in their surroundings. The walls were dotted with a hodgepodge of images ranging from cats lounging on the couch to pictures of the homeowner traveling abroad. There was a picture of her at the Great Wall of China, one in Paris at the Eiffel Tower, one at the pyramids in Giza, and another in England at Big Ben, just to name a few.

The lady appeared to be about Dimitris' age, with dark curly hair that featured streaks of gray. She was attractive and didn't appear to use much makeup to highlight her dark lashes and strong cheekbones. Tara and Alex wondered if there was anything going on with their host and this woman, but they didn't bother asking. They had more pressing matters than gossip to worry about.

"So, they know where you live," Tara said, bringing the topic of conversation back on point.

"It would seem so. Which means they probably have someone working for the police department. That's not so surprising. What *is* surprising is the way they tried to bomb my apartment in broad daylight."

"They don't fear anything. Just like the Ahnenerbe during World War II. They operated with almost total autonomy, and impunity, reporting only to the highest members of the Reich." Tara met the gaze of the two men before continuing. "This organization is ruthless. They play by their own rules, and they will stop at nothing to achieve their goal."

"Which is what, exactly?" Dimitris asked.

"They have already tried to create the super race, and we know how that turned out."

Alex looked down at the sheet of paper in his right hand. He held the file in his left. The paper was still soaked, but the ink seemed to be staying in place for the most part. His forehead crinkled as he noticed something that hadn't been there before. Two lines had appeared at the top of the sheet, on the reverse side of the page.

"Guys?" Alex said absently.

The other two looked at him and then down at the paper he held in his hand. Alex's eyes were locked on the message. He handed the file to Tara and then walked over to a small table next to a window where he gently laid the sheet down.

Tara followed him with Dimitris in tow. "What is it?" she asked, stopping so close to her husband that their shoulders brushed.

"I think it's a piece of the puzzle we were missing before."

Dimitris looked over his shoulder at the note but didn't understand it. "What does it mean?"

Alex read the lines out loud.

"The eleven with three are none without one. Scattered are they that open the gate. The power of the gods awaits he who walks through."

"Eleven with three?" Dimitris said, confused. "What does that mean?"

Alex lifted the page carefully and turned it over. The ink was still holding on the other side, though he knew if he was careless, it might smudge or run.

"This must have been written with invisible ink."

"Invisible ink?" Dimitris looked up at him questioningly.

Alex nodded. "Through history, people have used invisible ink to conceal notes or secret messages. Some are revealed with heat. This one must be water activated."

Tara watched as Alex turned the sheet over. She immediately counted the number of sites that had been hit by the thieves, and the dots were easy for her to connect.

"Fourteen artifacts," she said. "They've nearly completed their mission." There was a distant fear in her voice that wasn't lost on the two men. "It sounds like they're collecting these artifacts so they can open some kind of portal, something that would grant some form of power. The power of the gods."

Alex nodded. "But what gate are they talking about? I've never heard of anything like that before."

She shook her head. "I don't know." She turned to Dimitris.

He simply shook his head dejectedly. The man was out of his element now, and he knew it.

"Well," Alex said with a sigh, "we do know where they're heading next. At least we think we do."

Tara agreed with a nod. "Harvard. We need to get to Boston."

"I'll give Emily a call and let her know what's going on," Alex said. Then he cocked his head and stared at the sheet of paper. His eyes widened with a combination of wonder and fear.

"What?" Tara asked. "What is it?"

He licked his lips and then pursed them for a moment, pressing them together tightly. "The BM," he said.

"Uh, what?"

Alex pointed at the two letters on the sheet. "I know we thought that this one meant the British Museum, but it also gives me an idea."

"Call ahead and make sure they have all their security in place?"

"Well, yes. We definitely need to do that. But do you remember something, or someone else, with those initials?"

Her brow tightened for a second as she considered the riddle. "Other than Bill Murray?"

He snorted a laugh. "Yes."

Then her eyes widened as if window blinds opened to reveal the sunlight. "Oh," she exclaimed. "Boston!"

Dimitris frowned. "Yes, we're going to Boston. We just said that a minute ago."

She rapidly shook her head. "No. No. I mean, yes. We are going to Boston. But it's not just a city."

Dimitris' scowl deepened. "What do you mean?"

"Boston is also a person."

"A boy, actually," Alex added.

"A boy?" Dimitris looked more lost than ever.

"Yes," Tara went on. "His name is Boston McClaren. He's something of an expert in ancient history. The kid has a penchant for rare artifacts. Studies stuff that most people think is pseudohistory."

"If anyone knows anything about these fourteen artifacts and a gate to the power of the gods, it would be that kid."

"You don't think the people behind all this are going to target him, do you?" She looked genuinely concerned.

The question brought a new set of concerns.

"It's possible, I suppose." Alex didn't sound certain.

"Wait a second," Dimitris protested. "Why would these men, these killers and thieves, target a young boy? Surely he doesn't have what they're looking for?"

Alex and Tara shared a worried glance, then both turned to face the detective at the same time.

"Boston," Tara said, "is no ordinary boy."

"In the archaeological community, he's known as the Collector. Cliché, I know, but you can't fault the kid for that. And it's what he does. He collects ancient artifacts, especially ones that have been deemed fake or aren't understood by the historical community. The kid is only ten years old, and he's read more history books than me. He's a savant of sorts, I suppose. I haven't spoken to him in nearly a year, but we've talked before when I had questions that were a little too out there for our usual network of professors and researchers."

"A boy," Dimitris said. "A ten-year-old boy." He made no effort to hide his skepticism.

"He made his money playing video games," Alex explained. "Millions, actually. He had a knack for one of those online multiplayer games. So he created some streaming accounts, started streaming his gameplay, and before he knew it the kid had millions of followers. He uses his money to collect things like artifacts and relics. From what I've heard, it started because he thought some items looked cool. Now, though, I think he has a more curious approach and tries to find things that are misunderstood or not understood at all."

"Things like these artifacts that keep disappearing," Tara said.

"How does a boy, a ten-year-old boy, find ancient artifacts?"

Tara smirked, her eyes narrowing with the grin. "The antiquities black market, of course."

The detective arched a suspicious eyebrow.

"We don't know everything about him," she admitted. "How he found the black market and all that? But we know he has a courier, a guy who used to be in the military and then started his own private security company. From what I know, he was a tough character. Did several stints in the Middle East, both with the military and with his company. He wanted to settle down a bit, so when Boston made him an offer, he took it. Still runs his company but now does it from the States while he works for the kid."

"A man. Works for a child."

"Like we said, he's no ordinary boy."

Alex's face twisted with concern. "I just got a bad feeling."

"What?" Tara asked, her face mirroring his anxiety.

"What if...what if the BM on this page really is for the kid? What if he has one of the artifacts these guys are after?"

Sirens blared on the streets outside the window. Dimitris shifted over to the glass and drew back the curtain. He peered outside for a few seconds and then looked to the others. "As you Americans say, the cavalry is here."

Alex scooped up the wet page and strode over to the kitchen. He pulled out a drawer, then another and another, until he'd checked them all. Then he opened a cabinet.

"What are you doing?" Dimitris asked.

Alex opened another cabinet door and found what he wanted. He pulled out a box of large plastic zip bags and removed one from the box. "Looking for this."

He carefully shoved the paper into the bag and zipped it closed.

"How do we get out of here?" Alex asked, satisfied the page was temporarily salvaged.

"Out the front door. Like anyone else."

Dimitris grabbed some napkins from a stack on the counter and handed one to Tara and one to Alex. "Follow me."

They hurried down the steps, unsure if the elevator had been damaged in the blast. It wasn't worth the risk either way. They covered their mouths and noses with the napkins as they reached the bottom floor, mere seconds before they rounded a corner and almost bumped into four firemen who'd entered the building.

The three kept the napkins against their faces and did their best to look afraid as one of the firemen escorted them to the door, while the others started up the stairs.

Once outside, the fireman shouted at another who was standing on the sidewalk issuing orders. The second man motioned for the three to make their way over to where people were gathering. Most of them were crying or looking around in confusion, trying to make sense of what happened.

Dimitris obeyed, leading Tara and Alex to the designated area.

The fireman in charge of the triage area motioned for them to join the others. Paramedics were helping some, and one was speaking to a cop. Dimitris avoided eye contact as they moved through the collection of victims and continued down the street.

The first responders didn't notice the trio leave as they were busy taking care of the shocked or wounded. Dimitris didn't risk looking back over his shoulder for fear of being recognized, although it wouldn't be long before the investigators realized it was his apartment that was targeted in the explosion. He hadn't done anything wrong, but if he wanted to get out of the country and help the two Americans—who, in turn, he hoped would help solve his investigation—then it was better if he went unrecognized for the time being.

He cut to the right at the next intersection and headed toward the nearest train station.

Once they were around the corner and out of sight from the growing crowd, he tossed his napkin into a trash bin and looked at the others. "We'll take the train to the station nearest to your apartment. We can get your things and head to the airport. Your plane, can it be ready to fly soon?"

"It will be by the time we get there," Tara said. She took out her phone and sent a text message to the pilot.

"To Boston, Mass?" Alex asked.

"No," she said. "We can call and make sure Harvard is on alert. Same with the British Museum—if we happen to be wrong about our young friend. But I think we should head to Tennessee."

"Tennessee?" Dimitris asked.

"It's where McClaren lives," she said. "We can take all the precautions we want with the museums. They can handle themselves. Our friend, Boston, though, I'm not so sure."

"You said he has that...courier working for him, the one who collects things from the black market."

"Even so," Tara acknowledged, "he could be in danger. His whole family could be. If the last of those fourteen artifacts is with him, then it's where we'll have to make our stand. And maybe he can help us with this strange riddle our deceased MI6 agent left in invisible ink."

18

ATHENS

"It's done?" Buri asked.

"I trust you saw the news," Jan's voice echoed through the earpiece.

"I did." Buri had seen the reports on his phone from the comfort of his private jet.

"Then why did you ask?"

Buri hid his irritation at the question. Jan had always been loyal, respectful. It was out of character for him to respond in such a way.

"I simply wanted to clarify. You know how the media is. They obey the will of others."

Jan knew that was true. After all, he was the one who had engineered the lie about the three bodies found in Detective Frangos' apartment. It would be hours, maybe days, before the media corrected the erroneous report, if they even bothered to retract anything.

"Of course, sir," Jan said, tweaking his tone to a more subservient one. "I'm aware."

"So, the detective is dead."

"Along with two others."

"Friends? Family?"

"He has no family. And I don't know that the man kept anyone close. I believe it might be someone who helped set up the ambush. I'll get more information when it's available."

"Good. I'm curious to know who might have been helping him."

"That makes two of us," Jan said as he looked around the area. He was standing on the sidewalk a block up from where the explosion had rocked the apartment building. People were everywhere. Cops, paramedics, and firemen kept a tight perimeter at the intersections of each block.

He spotted the female reporter and was happy to hear she'd done as he ordered. There hadn't been much doubt in his mind, but people had a tendency to go rogue now and then. That was something he couldn't abide right now. His quarry had managed to elude him, but he gambled that they couldn't have gone far. He wondered if they'd managed to get to another floor in the building. If that was the case, they would have to leave at some point. They'd have to. Cops and firemen were in the midst of a full evacuation of the area in case there were more explosives nearby.

The incident was being called a terrorist attack, which wasn't surprising. Anything like that was tagged as such, even if it wasn't true. This was anything but a random hit on innocent people.

"Let me know if you hear anything," Buri said. "If our late friend the detective had outside help, it's possible someone else knows about our...endeavor."

"Yes, sir."

Buri ended the call.

Jan looked down at his device and then slipped it into his pocket. When he lifted his gaze, he noticed three people exiting the apartment building, each pressing what looked like paper towels or napkins to their faces. There was a young woman with dark auburn hair and pale skin, a man who looked approximately her age, and a second man who was a few decades older.

Jan recognized him immediately.

"Detective Frangos," he muttered. "Where do you think you're going?"

Jan stepped out of the shade of the awning overhead and strolled casually down the sidewalk. He matched the pace of his prey as they disappeared behind a cluster of emergency vehicles. When he reached the end of the sidewalk, he looked to his right and saw the three making their way toward the subway station.

Jan slipped a pair of sunglasses onto his nose and trotted across the street, closing the gap by half. He walked by a table where an elderly woman was selling cheap hats and necklaces. The woman was staring at the chaos down the street and didn't see him scoop one of the baseball caps and fit it onto his head.

It wasn't much of a disguise, but it would have to do. If Frangos had seen him in the apartment, or at any point, the cop would recognize him. The sunglasses and ball cap would only buy him a few extra seconds when the time came, but it would have to be enough.

Jan would make sure it was.

He stuffed his hands into his pockets and looked across the street, as he would if he were a tourist taking in the sights. Not that there was much to see on that particular street, or even in that part of town.

Where was Frangos going, and who were the people with him? A throbbing in the back of his skull caused him to think back to the ambush at the museum. Could one of them have knocked him out while he was in his sniper nest? It was certainly possible, though he knew there was no way to prove it. Not that it mattered. They were guilty by association. The fact they were with Frangos meant they had to die, same as him.

Jan paused to look in the window of a small bakery and then to his left at his targets as they reached the top of the subway steps.

Frangos glanced around, presumably to make sure he wasn't being followed. So predictable. Jan knew the man would do that, which was why he'd stopped by the bakery to feign interest in a pastry.

When Frangos was satisfied that he wasn't being followed, he and his two companions continued into the station, disappearing from view.

Jan grinned. He loved the chase, the hunt. It wasn't often he got to do something so exhilarating. Sure, he was tasked with killing people now and then, but it was typically from a sniper position where he picked them off like cattle. This was a rare and delicious opportunity; one that he would relish.

It was unfortunate he wouldn't be able to tell anyone, especially the leader of the order. Buri would be furious that the kill hadn't gone according to plan. That meant Jan would simply avoid the truth altogether. Sure, he'd have to rid himself of the bodies, but he could handle that. It wouldn't be the first time.

He took off at a brisk pace to recover the ground he'd lost between him and Frangos, and covered the distance to the station in time to see the feet of his targets disappear under the ceiling below.

He reached into his pocket as he descended the stairs, finding a metro pass he'd used earlier in the day. Jan found it convenient to keep a loaded metro card handy, just in case he needed to use the train.

At the bottom of the stairs, he turned toward the row of computer touch screens where a couple of travelers were purchasing their metro credits. To the left, he noted the three targets moving toward one of the stairwells leading to the platforms below. They were heading to the one that would take them to the Acropolis station. Why were they going there?

Jan ignored the alarms going off in his head, warnings about returning to the scene of a crime. The area around the Acropolis and its museum was already clear, the investigation into the heist buried in paperwork. No one would recognize him there. He'd been hidden, after all.

Jan hurried after Frangos and turned right at the bottom of the landing. Frangos and his two associates were straight ahead, standing at the edge of the platform waiting for the next train.

Jan slipped in between a sparse line of people who were likewise waiting for a ride. He stood next to a woman in a leather jacket and ripped acid-washed jeans. She was tall and attractive, with bright blonde hair and a jawline that would make any supermodel jealous.

That wasn't why Jan chose her as his visual shield. She was tall, and that would conceal his presence.

The sounds of wheels on rails screeched from within the tunnel, and soon the train's headlights appeared in the darkness. Jan took one last look down the line of travelers to make sure Frangos was still there. Once confirmed, Jan faced straight ahead and waited. When the train came to a stop, he stepped on board, taking another glance toward his quarry. They entered a few cars down just before the doors closed.

Now, he would simply wait and watch.

19

ATHENS

The phone only rang twice in Tara's ear before someone answered on the other end.

"Well, well, well. Look who came crawling back." The young boy's voice brimmed with mischief.

"Hello, Boston," Tara responded dryly.

She stood in the small kitchen of a luxurious apartment across the street from the Acropolis gardens. As Dimitris predicted, the chaos from the shootout during the attempted heist had been replaced by the usual traffic that occupied the street. Tourists were once more standing on the sidewalk, taking pictures of the ancient ruins. It was almost as if the entire incident never happened.

Alex worked in the bedroom to make sure everything was packed and they could leave as soon as possible. He also checked their weapons were still stowed in their backpacks in the top pouch where they were easily accessible. That was a tip he'd picked up from a friend—a hiker who had walked several sections of the Appalachian Trail.

Dimitris wandered over to the large window that all but covered the entire street-facing wall and looked out through the long vertical blinds. He peeled one back and spied the street, the sidewalk beyond, and clusters of olive trees and bushes that occupied the foot of the hillside beneath the Acropolis. He let the blind fall back in place and looked back at Tara as she continued her conversation.

"So, what can I do for you today?" Boston asked. "I hope you have something juicy for me."

"Be careful what you ask for," she warned.

He chuckled. "What's that supposed to mean?"

"Alex and I are tracking down some artifact thieves here in Europe. We're concerned that they're going to hit the Harvard Museum of Natural History next." She hedged her information for the time being, not wanting to cause the young man on the line any undue concern.

"Oh, the Peabody?"

"Precisely."

"Hmm. What do they have on display that someone would travel across the world to steal?"

"That's just it. We're not sure."

"And that's why you called me," he said with a degree of certainty that far surpassed his years. It was borderline cocky, but it suited the kid.

"You're one of the best," she said.

"One of?"

It was Tara's turn to laugh. "Fine. *The* best. Happy?"

"Happier," he emphasized the *er* on the end. "Someone's stealing artifacts, huh? What kind of stuff are we talking about?"

"The kind that you're interested in," she offered.

There was a pause on the line, and Tara knew she'd played the right card.

"Mysterious? Rare? Unusual?"

"All of the above. And more."

"Well, color me interested."

She could hear his fingers tapping on a keyboard and knew he was already getting ready to look for something.

"I am texting you the names of the museums that were hit. There was a dig site that was robbed as well, but I don't think you need that. The museum names should be enough for you to go on."

"Okay, hit me with it."

She lowered the device and began typing.

His phone dinged, and she could tell from the silence on the line that he was reading though the list of museums. "That's interesting," Boston said. He spoke loud enough that she heard the comment even while holding the phone near her waist.

She raised it back to her ear. "I only sent you three museums."

"I don't need any more. Remember who you're dealing with? I keep my finger on the pulse of stuff like this. You're talking about the stones that were taken. Right?"

"You tell me."

She looked across the room at Dimitris but said nothing.

The detective looked nervous, and she knew that the concern on his face was because they'd already lingered too long in the apartment. If the person who'd tried to kill them at Dimitris' place was still out there, it was possible he'd followed them here.

"Well, from what I can tell, the three museums I'm seeing did have some thefts, though what was taken wasn't reported. They left that little detail out; instead claiming it was some old pottery shards in two cases, and a vase in another."

"But it wasn't those items, was it?"

"No way. I've seen this kind of thing before. My courier has, too. Museums can't get insurance for the kind of stuff I'm interested in, so they're forced to list it in their inventory as more conventional commodities. That doesn't stop some of us from finding out what's really there."

"Which is what?"

"I'll get to that. How did you get pulled into this? Handling these kinds of cases isn't really your thing, Tara. Did Mr. Schultz put you up to this?"

She sighed. "We're heading up a new division—a project, if you will, called the Paranormal Archaeology Division."

"Well, that sounds like it's right up my alley."

"I know." She rolled her eyes. Sometimes, talking to a ten-year-old was like...well, talking to a ten-year-old. Exasperating. It was the only flaw in dealing with Boston. He hadn't quite learned social cues yet, but she knew that would come with time. Or she hoped it would.

"You don't have to get snippy," he groused. "Is there anything else I need to know about before we continue this conversation? Any details you're leaving out? That might help me confirm what I already suspect?"

She'd held back on the MI6 agent's death, and still wasn't sure how that would help the boy help them, but maybe throwing a little danger in the mix might hurry things along. After all, she could see Dimitris was ready to go, and Alex was standing in the doorway of the bedroom holding both backpacks.

"We found a note from someone. They're dead now. We think they were murdered for what they discovered."

"A murder mystery? That's definitely not my normal kind of thing, or yours for that matter."

"No, it isn't. But this note contained a bunch of weird initials. That's how we determined the names of the museums. The dead man who created it must have figured out the targets these thieves were going to hit and hoped to relay the message to someone."

"Sounds plausible."

"Yeah," she agreed and spun around to face her husband, holding up one finger to signal she was hurrying as fast as she could. "Anyway, the note had a hidden message that said, 'The eleven with three are none without one. Scattered are they that open the gate. The power of the gods awaits he who walks through.'"

Another pause filled the phone line for several seconds. There was no typing from Boston's end, and no heavy breathing or ticking sounds that some people liked to use when they were trying to work out a problem in their heads.

Then the boy spoke abruptly and with a newfound concern in his tone. "Yeah, so you're talking about the lost Sun Stones."

"The what?"

Alex looked at her with genuine curiosity. His shoulders rose slightly to beg the question as to what the boy was saying.

"The lost Sun Stones. They were scattered—as your riddle suggests—centuries ago, to protect the Sun Gate of Tiwanaku."

"Sun Gate? There was something about a gate on the note."

"Well, it's in Bolivia. Pretty famous archaeological site, actually. I'm surprised you haven't heard of it."

"It doesn't ring a bell."

"Oh. Well, I'll spare you most of the details. It was built by a pre-Columbian people. When explorers discovered it, the gate and many of the pillars and other surrounding stones had been knocked over. The ruins were in...umm, ruin." He laughed at his accidental play on words. "Anyway, the gate was cracked and lying on its side. Restoration efforts returned the entire site to more like how it appeared hundreds of years ago. The feature attraction is what's called the Sun Gate. There are eleven pillars that stand opposite the gate. These pillars track the movement of the sun just like a calendar, which is pretty amazing. It's like a South American Stonehenge."

Tara took a second to process everything. It never ceased to astound her how much the young boy knew about history. She'd happily wager that he knew more about certain aspects of history than some of the most renowned historians in the world.

"So, what does all this have to do with the guys who are stealing these stones? What's the connection?"

"Ah," Boston said. "That's the big one. I know for a fact that those three museums in your text were keeping stones from the Sun Gate. Over the years, nearly every single one of the stones has been recovered and placed under tight security in museums all over the planet. Most of them seem to be in Europe. It would seem another one was discovered and then taken from the dig site by the thieves...if what you're telling me is correct."

"It is," she confirmed.

Tara looked over at Dimitris. He grew more on edge with every passing second, and she could tell he wanted to get out of there. She didn't know what spooked him, but it was enough for the man to twirl a finger in the air, signaling for her to hurry up.

"Yeah, someone is gathering the Sun Stones, and that's not good."

"Why isn't that good?"

Boston chuckled. "I don't know if you've seen one of those things, but I know you guys found a sample of Quantium in North Carolina. Before you confirm or deny, you should know that I already know. Don't worry. Your secret is safe with me."

That might have been true, but it reinforced that there was a leak somewhere, and that was something Tara and Alex needed to get to the root of, sooner or later.

"Go on," she said.

"Whoever is stealing these stones obviously thinks that reuniting them will allow them to open the portal, the Sun Gate, and that it will bestow them with great power."

Tara rubbed her forehead with her free hand, massaging the center with her thumb and index finger. "How in the world do you know so much about this stuff?" she asked.

"First of all," he replied, "like I said, this is my kind of thing. Secondly, I have one of the real stones."

20

ATHENS

"You have one of the stones?" Tara asked. "And what do you mean real?"

"Of course I have one. I collect that kind of weird stuff. And by real, I mean there is one out there—probably several—that look like the real thing but are fakes."

"How in the world...? No. You know what? I don't want to know." She wasn't sure how to say it, so she just pushed ahead. "Boston, you and your family could be in danger."

"Danger?" Boston laughed. "Why would I be in danger?"

"Because the last two letters on the list of targets are the letters *BM*. We thought it meant—"

"Bill Murray? I love that guy, even though he was way before my time."

"I was going to say the British Museum, but we did have a laugh about the Murray thing."

"Ah, the British Museum. No, they don't have any of these. Not that I know of. And if they do, it's likely a forgery. If someone tries to take mine, though, they have another thing coming."

She didn't doubt the kid's resources. He had considerable assets now, including a full-time security detail to keep him safe from both fans and jealous enemies. A ten-year-old with enemies was a strange thing to consider, but the world could be a dangerous place sometimes. Tara knew that all too well.

"Either way, we're coming to you. We need to make sure that stone is secure and that you're safe."

"In that order?" Boston joked. "I'm kidding," he added, sensing her embarrassment. "Seriously, though, we're okay. You know my courier is former Special Forces, right?"

"Still..." Tara insisted. It was easy enough to tell that Boston wasn't taking the threat seriously. "We need to have a look at that stone. And I want to make absolutely certain these guys don't get to you. In fact, you should probably leave town. Is there somewhere safe you and your family can go?"

"My parents are out of town," he confessed. "They went to Italy for a concert or something. And before you say anything about being home alone, I'm not."

Tara clenched her teeth. She knew he wouldn't be left at home alone. Maybe he was there with his grandparents. Or perhaps his courier was the one who was on babysitting duty. Maybe it was a combination. At the moment, it didn't matter as long as the boy was safe. From the sound of it, he wasn't going anywhere, which meant Tara and company had to get to Tennessee as soon as possible.

She decided to take a different path with her conversation. "If we were to come to your place, would we be able to see this stone of yours, maybe ask some more questions?"

"Sure. Come on over. Y'all still in Atlanta?"

"Um, not exactly."

"What's that supposed to mean?"

"We're...abroad at the moment, but we're about to head to the airport. We will come by first thing tomorrow morning if that's okay with you."

"Sure. Sounds good. I'll have Dak make you guys pancakes. He makes the best pancakes. Don't tell my mom, though. She might get jealous."

There he was again, reminding Tara that he was still just a young boy—a young boy who was beyond gifted when it came to history.

"Pancakes would be great, Boston. I'll see you then."

She ended the call and looked at the two men standing by the door. Alex had a look of utter confusion on his face, while Dimitris' expression was irritated.

"Pancakes?" Alex asked.

"I'll explain later."

"Yes, on the way to the airport. Come. We've already been here too long." Dimitris spun and twisted the doorknob.

As the detective pulled the door inward, Tara's eyes widened as she caught sight of the slender shadow on the threshold. She couldn't react fast enough.

The man kicked the door and it burst open, knocking Dimitris back three steps. He only managed to keep his balance by grabbing on to the counter to his right. Tara and Alex started to go for their weapons, but they were already staring down the barrel of a gun.

The intruder eased the door shut behind him and stared at Alex and Tara first, then turned his gaze to Dimitris.

His steel-blue eyes pierced theirs, flashing an unspoken warning.

"Give me your bags," the man said, his accent a thick German.

Alex and Tara cast wayward glances at each other, and then Alex set their bags down on the floor. For a second, his gaze lingered on the top pouch of his bag where he knew his gun was packed. There was no way he could get to it, not before he caught several bullets from the gunman, but he couldn't help the fanciful thought.

"Where is it?" the man demanded.

"Where is what?" Alex asked, sincerely confused.

The man brandished the weapon, pointing the lengthened barrel of the suppressor straight at Alex's chest. "You know what."

Alex looked at his wife with questioning eyes. She shook her head. "He really doesn't know what you're talking about. I don't know what you're talking about."

"I heard you talking from outside the apartment. You said something about a note with the list of targets. The museums? Who were you talking to just now?"

Dimitris watched the intruder with a calculating stare.

"Your mom," Tara said dryly.

The joke went over the man's head for a moment, and when it clicked he simply narrowed his eyes and pointed the weapon directly at Tara's face. "Who was on the phone?" he asked again.

Alex shifted in front of her, putting himself between the gun and his wife. "Don't point that at her."

"You are not in a position to negotiate," the intruder said. "Where is the note you were talking about? And tell me who you were talking to."

"And you'll what? Let us go? We both know that's not going to happen." Alex spoke with courage, though he could feel his heart pounding in his chest. His fingers quivered slightly, and he hoped the gunman wouldn't notice.

"True. I'm going to kill you all, but I can do it quickly or slowly. That is up to you." He lowered his weapon but kept it trained on Alex. He maintained a peripheral eye on Dimitris to his left, but the detective was unarmed and several feet away. "The note. Please." He held out his free hand expectantly.

Alex clenched his jaw, grinding his teeth behind his lips. "You don't know what you're dealing with," he warned. The truth was he didn't know what they were dealing with, either, but somehow this man had found them.

Was he sent by Buri, the man who was behind the heists? Or was he working alone? The latter was doubtful. Most likely, he was one of Buri's operatives. Then it clicked. Alex recognized the man from the hillside overlooking the Acropolis Museum. He was the sniper who'd been picking off cops before Alex and Tara flanked him.

Out of the corner of his eye, Alex saw Dimitris inching his hand toward his weapon. The gun could level the playing field, though Alex and Tara would still be danger and in the line of fire, at point-blank range.

"Okay," Alex said, raising his hands innocently over his head in surrender. "Take it easy. I'll get you the note."

"And who were you talking to on the phone?" The gunman directed the question at Tara.

"Just a friend," she said. It wasn't a lie, and her body language confirmed that.

"Yes, but you told this friend what you were up to. That means your friend is now a loose end. We can't have those, as I'm sure you can understand. I will need their name. Don't worry about any other details. I can find them with nothing more than a name. It's unfortunate you just signed your friend's death warrant. They didn't have to die. I would have just killed you three, but one more shouldn't be a problem."

Tara glared at him but offered no answer to his question.

Alex could tell she was stalling and used the chance to make his move.

"The note is in my bag," he said. "I'll get it for you."

"Do it slowly," the gunman directed. "I know you Americans can't bring guns into the country, but I don't want any foolishness."

He was wrong about the gun, but Alex knew the second he went for the pistol, he'd get a bullet through his earhole. He noted Dimitris' movement again, now more pronounced since the gunman was focusing much of his attention on Alex.

Alex bent down, moving gradually and deliberately so as not to spook the intruder. He unzipped the front pouch of his bag and fumbled for a folded piece of paper inside.

"Here it is," he said and pulled the page out of the bag. The second the gunman saw the paper, he took a step toward Alex, involuntarily lowering his weapon in the process. Alex noticed the gunman flinch slightly, perhaps noticing the movement of Detective Frangos behind him. "How's your head?" Alex asked, coming up with the first thing he could think of to keep the man's focus on him.

The gunman cocked his head slightly in question.

"Your head," Alex said, motioning with a nod. "I imagine you have a pretty bad bump from yesterday. The rock to the skull?"

Realization struck, but he didn't offer up a reaction. It didn't matter. The barb had done its job. Now the killer was focused entirely on Alex.

Sensing his window, Dimitris moved like lightning. He drew the pistol he'd kept hidden and whipped it around in a flash. His finger twitched and the weapon popped with a deafening sound. Three pairs of ears instantly started ringing with a high-pitched tone. The fourth pair heard nothing as the intruder slumped to his knees and collapsed onto his face.

Dimitris' shot was perfectly placed. The entry wound was just below the back of the gunman's left ear. The exit wound was directly on his right temple. He'd died instantly.

The smell of smoke lingered in the air, with a thin haze escaping the muzzle of the weapon.

Dimitris lowered his gun, stepped over to the body, and kicked the weapon away from the limp hand. He looked up at the other two and nodded. "Now we go," he said.

Tara and Alex stared at the cop for several seconds. The sounds of everyday traffic filled the apartment as cars honked their horns in frustration. It was surreal to hear those noises over the pall of death that now hung in the room.

The Americans nodded. They needed to get to Tennessee. Whether he believed it or not, their young friend was in trouble.

21

BOSTON

Buri watched from a picnic table just outside the gate leading into the quad at Harvard University. His elbows rested on an old wooden surface. A breeze blew off the river beyond the buildings to his back, tickling the hair on his head as it washed over.

He was hiding in plain sight. Dressed in a gray Boston Red Sox hoodie and a pair of blue jeans, he looked like a local. His sunglasses shielded his eyes from the bright sun of the cloudless day, and kept anyone from coming remotely close to recognizing him.

He wasn't worried much about that. As far as he knew, no one in the States would know who he was or what he was up to.

He hadn't heard from Jan since arriving in the US. That wasn't uncommon. Jan often went deep on certain missions and wasn't always able to report in a timely manner.

Buri twisted his wrist and absently checked his watch. It was almost time.

Thanks to inside information, he knew that security in and around the museum had been heightened. That fact caused him to wonder if Jan had failed in some capacity, or even completely.

It was too soon to judge, but Buri had connections in all the right places. He'd learned of the security upgrade through one of those connections, a mole in the Boston Police Department, though the information was hardly surprising.

Buri always operated with caution. He expected the unexpected, and that had served him well, helping him to establish a new, more powerful order than any of his predecessors had ever imagined. They, of course, had possessed the luxury of being able to operate openly in World War II Germany. Now, such methods of doing things would be impossible to pull off. A more clandestine approach was required, something he was more than adequately equipped to handle.

He looked at his watch again, giving no outward sign of emotion or concern. Thirty seconds.

He folded his hands on the tabletop and stared ahead at the Harvard Museum of Natural History.

Freshmen were running around in matching T-shirts, going through their orientation. Bass thumped in the distance from a concert that was going on in the middle of campus. Buri had walked by earlier in the day when they were setting up the stage and running sound checks.

He'd made the rounds of the entire campus, taking in every square foot before giving the go-ahead for the plan.

The students would have no idea what was going on. Their confusion would only serve to elevate the panic around the area, panic that would allow him invisibility.

A twist of his hand and Buri saw the timer was at ten seconds. He counted down in his head as he watched the numbers fall. "Three," he muttered. "Two. One."

A boom sounded from eight blocks away. A second later, the ground shook. The table under Buri's elbows vibrated. Pedestrians nearby froze and spun around to find the source of the sudden noise.

Then they started pointing toward the waterfront where a plume of black smoke roiled into the sky like a beacon of destruction.

Instinctively, many of them started shouting. Others began retreating in the opposite direction. Somewhere nearby, a woman screamed.

Within twenty seconds, the street descended into anarchy. More screams filled the air. Students who had been laughing and joking with classmates now sprinted through the quad and down the streets to get away from what they could only perceive to be a terrorist attack.

That was a natural reaction in Boston, especially after the events surrounding the tragic attack on the Boston Marathon years before, not to mention the 9/11 attacks that began at Logan International Airport.

As the world fell apart all around him, Buri remained poised. He stood casually, as if he hadn't a care in the world, then strolled toward the museum. When he reached the base of the steps, he paused and looked around. He'd already witnessed several people running out of the building to either see what happened or find safety elsewhere on campus, but no one had bothered to lock it up.

The diversion had worked perfectly.

Buri didn't consider himself a monster. He could have ordered that the explosion take place in a heavily populated area. Any target with lots of people would have been fine, but it would have also been a waste. Instead, he'd purchased a small commercial fishing boat and parked it just offshore in an area that was far enough away but close enough to the city that it would suck in every single cop, fireman, and EMT within two dozen blocks.

Media reports would initially carry information regarding a terrorist attack on a boat in Boston. The misinformation wouldn't be corrected until later, when it was discovered to be a ruptured fuel tank on an empty fishing vessel. It would be days, maybe weeks, before the actual cause was revealed—that the boat had been destroyed deliberately. By then, the entire world would have moved on to the next story, the next trending item of interest. That was, after all, the state of the social media-enamored world.

A young Asian woman with black glasses and a burgundy Harvard University hoodie burst through the door of the museum and hurried down the stairs. She blew by Buri with a whoosh of air and sprinted down the sidewalk, disappearing around the corner as she headed for the middle of campus.

Buri reached the entrance and pulled open the door. He donned a concerned face as he saw more students and museum staff rushing toward the exit. "Come on!" he shouted, waving a hand to direct them in the same direction as the other woman. "Get to the quad! Rally point is in the quad!"

He'd heard those terms used before with emergency evacuation procedures. Some people called them rally points. Others called them safe zones. He figured as long as he sounded like an authority figure, the panicked people wouldn't think much of it. They just wanted to get somewhere safe.

When the last of the staff were out of the building, Buri stepped inside and let the door close behind him. Inside, an ancient and reverent silence permeated the air.

He gripped the railing on the stairs to the right and began his ascent, moving quickly until he reached the top level. The gift shop was divided in two, one part to the left and one to the right. The cash register was unmanned, as was most of the building.

Buri stepped through a doorway to the right and made his way through the huge room. The area stretched from one side of the building to the other and was filled with crystals, gems, rocks, and even a few pieces of a meteorite. It was an impressive geological display and represented thousands of hours of work by hundreds of people. Buri didn't care about the geology exhibit. He walked through the room, quickening his pace as he passed through the next exhibit featuring information on global climate change.

He worked his way to the left in the corridor and found himself standing at the entrance to the Peabody Museum. On both sides, artifacts from Mesoamerican history lined the walls in huge display cases. Shards of pottery, stone and wooden tools, pieces of fabric, and jewelry filled the cases.

Buri drew in a long breath, letting the smell of antiquity fill his nostrils.

His pace quickened, and he worked his way through the replicas of ancient pillars from the Aztec empire, cases that displayed more artifacts from centuries long lost, and statues of warriors in animal skins.

He floated up the stairs at the end of the room and reached the top, where another exhibition displayed more items from South American cultures. Buri continued on to the right, reaching another set of stairs that went to the top floor, a floor that wasn't accessible to the public.

Warnings lined the walls of the stairwell going up to the next floor, advising visitors that the area above was off limits to anyone but authorized personnel. Buri glanced to the right and left and then hurried upward.

He reached a door on his right, again with similarly plastered warnings. He reached out and twisted the doorknob, expecting it to be locked. He'd gone to the trouble of bringing his lock-picking kit and felt the light weight of it in his back pocket. The doorknob, however, turned easily, and he let out a delighted snort.

"Too easy," he said.

Buri walked through and found himself in a different kind of room. This was where all the real work happened. Computers, tubes, glass cases, wires, pipes, and all sorts of research and diagnostic equipment littered tables in the middle of the room and the counters that lined the walls.

Again, he focused all of his attention on the one thing he was there for, and it stood right in the center of the lab.

The glass case was large enough to hold a football or basketball and stood about five feet high. Inside, however, there was no sports equipment. It was a rock with a strange figure carved into the side. The stone was about the size of Buri's head, and he already knew how much it would weigh. He was more than capable of handling the item, though some of his men had insisted that they be permitted to retrieve it.

Buri declined their offers. Too many things had gone awry in recent days, and he knew that if you wanted something done right....

He weaved around the tables and chairs in the lab and stopped at the case with the stone. Buri cocked his head to the right and smiled.

Then he looked to his left at a table where a series of tools were laid out in an orderly fashion on a mat. He grabbed a wooden-handled carpentry hammer from the collection and turned to the display case. He swung the hammer hard at the side of the glass. It shattered easily under the sudden force, and glass rained down on the floor around his feet and onto a nearby worktable.

Buri took the hammer back to the mat and placed it just as he'd found it. Then he returned to the stone and eyed it warily for a moment. The sound of klaxons filled the air now, not that anyone would notice. Every first responder within two miles was on their way to the site of the explosion—another brilliant piece of planning and why he was so willing to take the risk himself to get the job done.

He slid the hoodie off his torso and over his head, revealing a white New England Patriots T-shirt underneath. He brushed a few shards of broken glass off the top of the stone and then wrapped the artifact in the hoodie before lifting it off its pedestal.

Buri waited for a second, just in case his assessment of the security system had been incorrect. No metal doors dropped out of the ceiling to seal him in. No audio warnings echoed from hidden speakers. He smirked with satisfaction, then tucked the heavy stone under his armpit, concealed by the hoodie, and walked out of the museum's front door.

One stone to go, and thankfully, it was only a few hours' flight to Chattanooga, Tennessee.

22

CHATTANOOGA

Alex pulled the car up to the security gate at the bottom of White Oak Mountain. The guardhouse was never occupied, that he knew of. The few times he'd been to the McClaren house, there was no one keeping watch, though that was only partly true. There were security cameras on the sandstone guardhouse, and there were others positioned in strategic places around the perimeter and on the house. It was a far cry from where the boy and his family lived before, in a small apartment a few miles away.

Alex rolled down the window and pressed the call button. The sound of a phone ringing came through the speaker. On the fourth ring, Boston's voice interrupted.

"Well, look what the cat dragged in. How are you, Alex?"

"Tired," Alex answered honestly. They'd been halfway across the world twice in the last seventy-two hours, and jet lag was beginning to catch up to both him and Tara. Dimitris, sitting in the back of the sedan, didn't seem to be affected yet. That would change come bedtime, or five hours before it.

"I'm sure you are," Boston said, "but I'm going to need you to pass a test before I let you through the gate."

"Test?" Alex looked at Tara, who shrugged.

"You know how he is," she whispered.

"Test?" Dimitris echoed from the back. "What do you mean, test? I thought you knew this child."

"Who was that?" Boston asked though the speaker. "I can't see in the back seat. Are those windows at legal tinting levels?"

"No," Alex admitted. "That's Dimitris. He's a cop from Athens, Greece. He's helping with this investigation."

"Investigation?"

"Boston, can you please just let us through the gate?"

"Not until you answer my question correctly."

"Or I could just drive on the grass and around the gate." Alex's eyes drifted to the right where the gate was attached to a column covered in sandstone tiles. Just beyond that, four thick Azalea bushes wrapped around the column, and that's where the barricade ended. It didn't continue along the property line. Instead, it offered any trespasser willing to get a little dirty a grassy patch of land that was wide enough for a truck to cross. From there, an intruder could simply merge back onto the driveway and head up to the manor.

"You wouldn't," Boston hedged.

"I will if you don't hurry up and ask me the question you so badly want answered."

Boston grunted and then sighed. "Fine. What was the score the last time you and I played FIFA Online?"

Silence enveloped the interior of the sedan as Alex turned away from the keypad and speaker, facing toward the winding driveway that led up the foot of the mountain.

"What is the problem?" Dimitris asked. "Don't you know this?"

"Oh, he knows it," Boston said, answering the question from the detective before Alex could. "He just doesn't want to say it."

"Alex?" Tara urged. "We may not have a lot of time here. We need to get moving."

"That's right. You do need to get moving. Wait. Why do you need to get moving? I thought y'all might hang out for a while."

"We'll explain when we get up to the house. If you'd kindly move the gate, I would appreciate it." Alex sounded like he was begging. Desperately begging.

"I will as soon as you say it, Alex." The taunting in Boston's voice was overwhelming.

Tara could tell that her husband was irritated and probably a little embarrassed, which told her the answer was humiliating.

"Fine," Alex relented. "Seven-nil."

"And who had the seven?" Boston prodded.

"You did. Okay? Happy?"

"Yep." The gate immediately started retracting inward, and Alex inched the sedan forward, impatiently trying to get through in case the boy in the mansion decided to change his mind and make him answer some other ridiculous question that would make him feel inadequate.

Dimitris frowned for a moment, then burst out laughing. "You couldn't score a single goal on him? He's a boy!" The exclamation was followed by thirty seconds of laughter while Alex steered the car up the gently sloping hill toward the four-story brick mansion.

To the right, across a broad field of grass and sporadically planted hemlocks, spruce, red maple, and sweetgum trees, a wrought-iron fence wrapped around a pool and pool house. The walls surrounding the pool matched those of the pool house and of the mansion perched at the top of the hill. The driveway split off in two directions, one leading to the garages and lower parking area, the other circling around the central yard in front of the house where two massive ancient oak trees stood defiantly against time and weather.

"First of all," Alex began his defense, "everyone knows that kids are better at video games than adults. We have responsibilities, things we have to do, jobs, bills to pay. What does he have? An hour's worth of homework, and then six hours of video games every day."

"That's not fair," Tara said. "He spends most of his time studying history and geographical anomalies."

Alex rolled his eyes. "Fine. Whatever."

Dimitris laughed again as Alex pulled the car around to the front of the house and stopped in front of a set of beige brick steps that led up to a door set into the right wall. The main entrance located in the center of the house was rarely used, except for when Boston's family entertained guests for parties or holidays.

Alex killed the engine and flung open the door, ready to get out of the car as quickly as possible. He looked up the steps to the porch and realized he was probably jumping out of the frying pan and into the fire.

A young boy with curly blond hair and dark-rimmed glasses stood defiantly at the top of the steps with his arms crossed and wearing a smug grin. A Pittsburgh Penguins jersey was draped over his shoulders and hung down past the beltline of his faded blue jeans.

"Hello, Boston," Alex said, a reluctant tone to his greeting.

The boy remained stoic for several seconds, taking on a look that almost came across as angry. Then his façade cracked, and he offered a broad smile to his guests.

Tara stepped around the car and passed Alex, rushing to give Boston a big hug, a gesture that the boy happily returned.

He let go and stepped over to Alex to give him a handshake. Alex paused for a moment, then stuck out his hand and firmly gripped the boy's.

"No one likes a sore winner," Alex remarked.

"No one likes a sore loser, either," Boston countered.

"Fair enough. But I want a rematch."

"You should pick a better team next time."

"Maybe."

Boston turned to Dimitris and offered his hand, which the detective shook. "So, you really beat him seven to nil?"

Boston nodded proudly. "Do you play FIFA?"

Dimitris laughed. "No, I don't, but I know the game. It's very popular in most of Europe, though admittedly we prefer basketball in Greece."

"I've heard that about the Greeks," the boy said.

The comment brought another round of laughter from the detective. "I like this kid," Dimitris said.

"Give it time," Alex quipped.

Boston ignored the barb. "Come on in, guys. Dak is making some pancakes."

The group followed the boy into the house. The mansion was elegantly appointed but without the over-the-top opulence that so many other nouveau riche people put on display.

An elevator that featured a forest scene, painted on the doors by a local artist, was a prominent feature in the foyer. The floors were covered with the same kind of sandstone that had been used on the guardhouse and the gate columns at the bottom of the hill.

Looping around the corner and beyond the elevator, a dining area opened up with a twelve-foot-high ceiling. A brick fireplace sat silently across from the table and chairs. Beyond that and to the left, a circular dining room for more formal occasions featured a huge round table with ten place settings, perpetually waiting for a dinner party. It held a massive floral centerpiece with broad leaves and vibrant flowers of yellow, white, and orange gracing the arrangement.

The kitchen countertops were made from granite that swirled with shades of cream, tan, and chocolate brown, all accenting the surrounding colors of the cabinetry and floors.

"You guys didn't have to come all this way just to see me," Boston said as he led the group into the sitting area. He motioned to a collection of leather chairs near the smaller table by the fireplace.

"You know why we came," Tara said. "You're not safe."

"Oh, that again."

"Yes, that again."

The boy shrugged into his seat and crossed one leg over a knee. "Yeah, you're probably right."

Tara instantly became suspicious.

"What?"

"Right. You guys have been traveling all day and all night. I guess you didn't hear what happened in Boston a few hours ago."

"What happened in Boston?" Alex asked, leaning forward in his deep chair.

"There was an attack. Well, so far they're calling it an attack. You know how the media is. They're saying it was a terrorist group. One cell was even claiming responsibility for it on social media."

Alex and Tara shared a worried look. Dimitris simply looked on, waiting for more information.

"Turns out you were right," Boston continued. "Whoever these thieves are, they hit the Harvard Museum of Natural History. Specifically; the Peabody."

"And they got the artifact?" Alex asked.

"No one from the university is confirming anything. They're oddly silent about the entire incident, but it's pretty clear what happened."

"Which was what?" Dimitris spoke up.

Boston turned to him. "Whoever you guys pinned for these heists are smart. They knew security would be tight. I'm assuming you called ahead to warn them?"

Tara and Alex both nodded.

"Well, they either didn't take it seriously, or the diversion worked perfectly. I'd guess it was the diversion that did it."

"Diversion?" Dimitris asked.

"Distraction," Boston clarified. "The attack they're claiming was terrorists...it wasn't. If I had to bet all my money on something, I'd wager it wasn't any extremist group. It was those thieves. The cops found a boat on the river engulfed in flames. Thing was mostly destroyed by the time they got there. Hardly anything but the shell of a hull left and a bunch of melted and burned fiberglass."

"No one was in it?" Tara asked.

"Nope. No bodies found. But you know how things are up in the Northeast right now. Ever since 9/11, they've been on full alert for stuff like this. The Boston Marathon bombing didn't help. Anytime something like this happens, the media takes it and plays on the fears of the people."

The boy was far beyond his years in understanding the nation's political climate. For only ten years of age, he had a firm grasp on things that many adults still did not.

"So, the thieves blew up a boat, knowing that the first responders would go there right away," Alex said, working through the event.

"Not just first responders. Whoever did this knew that the city would converge on that particular area. Streets were closed. Every cop within ten blocks was sent there to help."

"Which left no one to watch the museum," Tara realized.

"Alarms went off in several buildings, including the museum. People evacuated. Again, no one was hurt, but with the museum empty, the thief just walked in and out the front door."

"Thief?" Dimitris asked. "You said thief. As in only one."

Boston nodded. "Camera footage shows one guy going in and one guy going out. When he went in the building, he had a Red Sox hoodie on, which I like by the way."

"I thought you were a Braves fan," Alex digressed.

"I am. But Sox in the American League. Anyway, when he came out of the building, he had the hoodie tucked under his arm. It was pretty clear he was carrying something."

"The artifact," Tara muttered.

"Yep. The museum won't release what it was. They know if they do that, the black-market value could skyrocket and motivate the thieves further. Of course, they could come out and say it's worthless, but then they run the risk of having it dumped somewhere. It's a lose-lose situation."

Alex arched an eyebrow and ran both hands through his thick brown hair. "I guess you have a pretty good handle on things."

"I try to keep up," Boston said with a shrug. His face turned grave. "I was actually a little worried when I heard what happened up in Beantown. If those guys are capable of pulling off a heist like that so easily, maybe I'm not as safe as I thought." His expression changed to one of gratitude, and when he spoke again, humility melted over his words. "I'm glad you're here. I feel a lot safer now than I did a few minutes ago. So, thanks for coming. I know I said not to worry about it and that I would be fine, but I'm sure Dak will appreciate a little extra help, too."

"I'll appreciate what now?" A husky voice echoed from a corridor around the other side of the fireplace. Footsteps followed it. A man appeared in the archway to the pantry. His dark hair was cut short and brushed over to one side, tangled and messy. It was shorter above the ear, all the way around. His sideburns were trimmed even closer to match the deliberate five o'clock shadow accentuating his strong jaw and sharp chin. A few strands of gray salted the man's head and beard, but the lack of lines stretching from his eyes told the visitors that he was probably still in his late thirties or early forties. The army-green Pearl Jam T-shirt he wore featured a Cyclops skull on the front, and his jeans were torn slightly at the knees, along with one ripped hole near the left pocket.

"Speak of the devil," Boston said happily. "Dak, these are my friends Tara, Alex, and a new friend named Dimitris. He's a cop in Athens."

The three guests stood to take turns shaking Dak's hand. All of them looked up into his emerald-green eyes. They were eyes that reflected distant pain, perhaps regret, but also confidence and determination.

He was holding an apple and lifted it to his mouth to take a bite. The move displayed his rippled forearm, thick with veins. Dak was in peak physical condition, a tribute to the habits he'd formed as an army ranger. He still worked out six days a week and spent an hour each day training in various forms of martial arts.

"Better the devil you know," Dak quipped as he chewed the apple.

"Indeed," Boston agreed. "Dak saved my life. Did I ever tell you guys that story?"

"Yes, Boston," Tara said, her words drawn to emphasize they'd heard the tale more than once.

"Oh. Well, anyway, Dak's the best." The boy's face reddened.

"You're all right, too, kid," Dak said. He tousled the boy's curly hair, making a mess of it.

Dak turned to the others, his face turning serious. "Boston tells me the museum at Harvard was hit. Said some thieves have been taking artifacts from museums around the world. He also said you three figured out the pattern."

"That's true," Alex said. "Although it didn't help much, I guess."

"Well, it helped us. We've moved our artifact to a secure location."

Dak's lips curled at the right corner of his mouth. "Not that we didn't have it in a secure location here. Our systems are the best money can buy. The vault that houses the most valuable stuff is modeled after some of the security systems at the National Archives in Washington. Not as expensive or elaborate but similar in design."

"That's impressive," Alex acknowledged. "Why'd you move the artifact, then?"

"I'd prefer the McClaren home not be a target for these guys, whoever they are. It's in a safe deposit box in a bank downtown, in the most secure vault in the city. There's only one way in or out of that place. I checked it out myself. If these thieves want to get to it, they're going to have to spend a lot of time working on a plan."

"So, you bought us some time," Tara realized.

"Exactly. Maybe those guys find out where the relic is. Maybe they don't. The only people who know are in this room and the president of the bank. I have the sole passcode to gain access to the safe deposit box."

The fact that the kid gave his head of security the only access to the vault with the relic spoke volumes to how much Boston trusted Dak. The kid's parents, too, must have trusted the man implicitly.

Alex and Tara knew why. Dak had thrown himself into harm's way to save Boston's life. Immediately after that, Boston's parents had brought Dak into the fold, hiring him as head of security. The job, however, came with a twist. Dak didn't just maintain security around the house. He accompanied Boston to big video game tournaments on occasions when his parents couldn't. When his parents were around, Dak was often sent on other...errands.

Alex and Tara only knew a little about Dak's missions for the young boy. Boston called him a courier, but the truth was, Dak did much more than that. Rumors filled in most of the details about the man's exploits in the dangerous world of black-market antiquities dealing. Some of it was the stuff of legend, whispers in the shadows of a relic runner who could get anything, though no one could ever pinpoint who the mysterious relic hunter was or who he worked for.

"So, the artifact is safe?" Dimitris asked, jumping into the conversation.

"Yes. As safe as it can be," Dak confirmed. "My plan is to leave it there at the Millennium Bank for a month, then move it to another location. I'll keep my ears open, and if I hear anything about a heist here in town, I'll have the item moved sooner."

"Why would you move it?" Tara asked.

"A moving target is harder to hit. Not just that; if they put together a plan to rob that bank, that will take time. By moving it, they're forced to come up with another plan. And they won't know the day it's being shifted, so there's no concern about them taking down an armored car or something like that. Only I and the bank president will know."

"Sounds like a good plan," Alex said.

"I try." Dak offered a wink.

"There is one problem with that plan," Tara said. She'd been contemplating it as she listened. While it was a sound strategy and one that should keep the thieves perpetually a step behind, it had one flaw.

The guys in the room turned to face her.

"The thieves could still come here," she said. "They could come after you and Boston and force you to get it out of the bank for them."

"True," Dak agreed. "That's why we've taken measures to keep us safe."

"Measures?"

"Well, we could leave and go on the road for a while, but sooner or later you have to come home. I mean, Boston has school to attend, after all. So, we've increased security around the perimeter of the property as well as hired some additional men to watch the place at night."

"Well," Tara said, "that's reassuring." She pointed her attention at Boston. "What else can you tell us about these stones?"

The boy was about to answer when he saw something move out of the corner of his eye. Dimitris had stood up a moment before and was leaning against the stone hearth with his arms folded across his chest.

Boston's eyes widened at the strange sight of the red dot slowly climbing up the left side of Dimitris' torso.

"What is that?" the boy asked, pointing at the Greek detective.

Dak turned his head and followed the boy's finger. His brain flipped a switch, and instantly Dak was on full alert. "Everyone get down!"

23

CHATTANOOGA

Glass popped from one of the windows to the right. Everyone's reaction was quick, everyone except Dimitris. He took a fraction of a second too long to dive to the floor. He dropped down as the bullet punctured the glass and tore through his left shoulder, narrowly missing his heart and neck.

Dimitris barked a quick shout of pain as he rolled over, grasping at the stinging wound with his free hand. The pain shifted quickly, adding a sharp burning feeling to his nerves.

He stayed down, though, knowing that if he tried to rise and make an escape, the gunman would take him down instantly.

"Are you okay?" Dak shouted at the injured man.

Dimitris grunted and then nodded. "I'll live." He didn't sound convinced. A puddle of blood collected beneath him, and the sight of it sent a queasy feeling through his body.

Dak kept Boston pinned to the ground, using his own body as a shield. He held a black pistol in his right hand. The others hadn't even seen him draw the weapon, so quick and instinctive were Dak's movements.

Tara and Alex also drew their .40-caliber Springfields as they pressed their chests to the floor. They could see Dak was already assessing the situation.

"Got a way out of here?" Alex hissed.

Dak gave a nod. "Back through that hall, stairs to your right go down under this floor. The garage is down there. If we can get to the vehicles, we might be able to get out."

Another salvo of gunfire blasted through the windows. This time it came from automatic weapons. The glass crashed and shattered on the tile floors all around. There were no loud reports from outside, which could only mean the attackers were using suppressors.

Everyone's attention went to the boy under Dak's hulking frame. He was curled up in a fetal position with his hands over his head, as if the protective position had been practiced before.

Dak's eyes, however, remained fixed on the injured detective. "Dimitris?"

The cop's eyelids hung low, providing only narrow slits to see through. He perked up slightly at the sound of his name.

"Can you move?" Dak asked.

Dimitris nodded his head weakly. "Go. I'll hold them off as long as I can. Get the boy...to safety." He labored to breathe, and speaking didn't seem to be helping.

"We're not leaving you here," Tara said. "You're coming with us. One way or the other."

Dimitris offered a feeble smile and shook his head again. "Leave me." He drew his own pistol and clutched it with frail fingers. "Go," he ordered. "I'll be fine."

Dak knew there was no time to argue with the stubborn man. "We have to move. He's made his decision, Tara. Follow me."

Dak eyed the trajectory of the rounds that were flying in through the windows. Bullets thumped into the walls, the stone hearth, and a portrait of a blonde woman in a flowery dress and black horn-rimmed glasses.

He noted that the brunt of the attack appeared to be coming from the front of the house, though he was certain if they moved toward a window in the back they would be met with a similar barrage. That didn't matter. They weren't going out the back.

"Come on," Dak said. He rose to a crouch and fired three shots through two of the destroyed windows. Then he scooped up Boston, tucked him under his armpit with one arm, and darted down the hall, careful to keep out of sight.

Dak and Boston disappeared around a corner halfway down the corridor.

Tara watched them and then turned her attention back to Dimitris. His eyes were closed. His shallow breaths lifted and lowered his chest in a steady rhythm.

"Dimitris?" Tara belly-crawled over to the man, careful to keep her head low. She shook him by the arm, but he didn't respond.

Alex joined her. He stared at Dimitris with a forlorn gaze. He and Tara both felt helpless, utterly incapable of helping their new friend. And now he was going to die because they'd dragged him halfway across the world. The realization hit them both in the gut with the force of a cannon.

"He's unconscious," Alex said. His voice bore regret with every syllable.

"I know," Tara said. "We can't leave him here."

"We don't have a choice. He told us to go. I don't want to leave him, either, but we can't carry him, and if we try, we'll be caught or killed. We have to finish this for Dimitris. I don't like it any more than you, but it's our only choice."

Tara knew he was right, but that didn't keep the tears from pooling in her eyes.

Alex fought hard to keep his own tears at bay, and seeing hers didn't help. "Come on," Alex insisted, reaching out his hand.

Tara looked at it for a moment, almost as though it were an alien object. Then she took it and reluctantly followed Alex down the hall on hands and knees until they were clear of the windows and around the corner to the basement stairs.

At the bottom, they landed on a black-and-white checkerboard tile floor and looked to the left and right. The left side opened into what looked like a den with a large leather couch facing a flatscreen television on the opposite wall. Beyond that, the walls were painted with elaborate scenes of animals. Lions, tigers, tropical birds, giraffes, deer, snakes, lizards, elephants, and a slew of other creatures adorned the wall space, all playing together. Toys littered the floor in that section of the long basement. Bins lined the walls with more playthings.

To the right, the couple could see through the open door and into the garage, where Dak had already loaded Boston in the front seat of the strangest-looking truck Tara and Alex had ever seen. The hood slanted back at a shallow angle. Where it met the windshield, the angle only increased slightly. It featured a flat roof made of glass. The sides were boxy and angular as well, the frame riding atop wide off-road tires with black rims. The garage door shone brightly against a row of headlights that stretched across the grill in a thin seam.

Dak was already in the driver's seat and holding his finger over the button that would open the garage.

"You coming?" he shouted.

Tara and Alex didn't need to be asked twice. They rushed to the angular vehicle and climbed into the back seat, Alex allowing Tara to get in first and slide over to the driver's side.

The second the door slammed shut, Dak hit the button over the dashboard, and the garage door climbed.

"Better strap in," Dak suggested. "This thing has some pep."

"Is this...the new Tesla truck?" Alex asked, both curious and already certain of his guess.

"Yes. One of the first they produced," Boston said. To the kid's credit, he didn't sound scared at all.

"The shell and windows are almost impenetrable," Dak added. "This thing is almost a tank."

"An electric tank."

"It's not bulletproof, but it's the next best thing."

The truck didn't make a sound even though all of the dashboard instruments were on. But once the garage door was clear overhead and Dak stepped on the throttle, the thing exploded out of the garage like a silent rocket, the only sound coming from the tires screeching on the smooth concrete surface.

They shot out of the building in a flash. Dak wheeled the vehicle left toward the driveway. To his surprise, the assailants had failed to block off this part of the asphalt, instead choosing to position their three SUVs around Tara and Alex's vehicle.

Two men were standing in the front yard holding automatic rifles with long black cylinders attached to the barrels. Another was perched on top of an SUV to get a better, higher angle. To the right, two men were on the hillside in the back of the house. Their guns were—at first—hanging at their waists. The second they saw the pickup burst out of the garage, though, they raised their weapons and opened fire, peppering the ground around the vehicle with bullets. Several rounds pinged off the tailgate and the bumper of the truck, but it was too fast. The electric vehicle barely let out a whine as Dak hammered down on the pedal and shot the truck over a slight bump.

The sound of bullets striking the 30x cold-rolled steel tailgate subsided as Dak whipped the vehicle around the first curve going down the hill. He cut it back to the left and reached up to press a second button over the dashboard.

Up ahead, the wrought-iron gate was closed and approaching rapidly.

Dak hit the button again. Nothing happened. They were less than a hundred yards from it now, and it still wasn't moving.

"Um, Dak?" Boston said, worry building in his voice.

"I see it."

The driver pressed the button repeatedly, but the gate remained closed. Fifty yards away from the gate, Dak realized that either the attackers had disabled the motor to the gate, or they had to be closer to it to get the thing to open. One way or the other, it was going to slow them down, and they needed every second they could spare.

Dak made his decision and cut the wheel hard to the left, driving the left side of the truck up onto the embankment leading into the field. Just ahead, a wide circle of landscaping surrounded a thick oak tree with azaleas, rhododendron, and hydrangea bushes.

Ahead, the stone column of the gate loomed dangerously near and was approaching uncomfortably fast.

"Dak?"

"Come on, kid. You gotta trust me."

The truck passed the oak tree, and a split second after, Dak cranked the wheel another notch to the left, deftly steering up the hillside and then back to the right, narrowly avoiding several boxwood shrubs and, more importantly, the sandstone column. The right-side mirror almost clipped the pillar, missing it by scant inches.

Dak corrected the wheel again and expertly steered the truck back onto the lower end of the driveway and out to the street beyond.

Boston looked back over his shoulder and noted the gate was now slowly opening.

"Gate's working now," he said with chagrin.

"Of course it is," Dak complained. He hit the button again. Tara and Alex looked back, along with Boston, to see the gate closing again just as an SUV tried to get though. The vehicle was moving too fast to stop, and the gate's sensors wouldn't allow the barricade to open quickly enough.

The driver of the SUV tried to slip through an opening that was way too narrow and slammed into the gate and the column with a loud bang.

"That should slow them down," Dak said.

No one said anything as he guided the pickup to the main road. A pall hung in the cabin of the truck. They'd managed to escape with their lives. It was a minor victory but one that came at a terrible cost. Dimitris was still in the house, unconscious at best. At worst....

Dak glanced in both directions. After a moving van passed, he stepped on the accelerator again and launched the truck out onto the road.

"I'm going to take the back roads," Dak informed.

"Where are we going?" Tara managed through the swamp of guilt filling her throat.

"Safe house. We have a place over on Belvoir near the Brainerd area. No one else knows about it. We'll get some supplies and then head north."

"North?"

"To the mountains. We have a cabin in Tellico Plains, up on the border of the Cherokee National Forest. We can lie low for a while and figure out our next move."

"What is our next move?" Alex asked.

"Not sure yet," Dak confessed. "That's what we have to figure out. The good news is they can't get to that artifact. Thanks to you two, it's safe. You got me curious, though. What do those guys want with that stone? It's just a rock."

"Not necessarily," Boston interrupted. The boy had been silent since they left the house. By rights, a boy of his age should have been shaken, maybe in tears. Being shot at was a harrowing experience, one that haunted people's lives forever. Someone had tried to kill them, yet he seemed relatively unaffected. Alex wondered if it was due to training with Dak or if Boston simply possessed that inner steel naturally.

When he saw he had everyone's attention, Boston went on. "The calendar at Tiwanaku is said to have the power to open the Gate to the Sun, a portal into another plane of existence."

"Like another dimension," Alex said.

"Right. We know the Nazis were experimenting with stuff like that during the war. There was a group who was dedicated to learning about such off-the-wall science, but I can't remember the name right off the top of my head."

Alex and Tara shared a knowing glance.

"The Ahnenerbe," they said together.

"That's it," Boston confirmed, raising a finger. "They've been gone a long time, but it's possible that someone stumbled on to their work. Perhaps some of the records or research they did during the war wasn't lost or destroyed. Or maybe it was, and these guys found it."

Tara eyed her husband and then drew a deep breath. "Yeah, so... we're pretty sure that the guys who just attacked us are the new version of the very group you're talking about."

"The Ahnenerbe?" Dak asked.

"Looks that way. We learned that the guy who's behind it calls himself Buri."

"Buri?" Boston thought for a moment. "That's an odd name."

"It was the name of one of the Norse gods, although he was more like a demigod. According to the legend, he was the first human."

The cabin of the truck fell silent again. Dak steered through a roundabout, then continued down the country road, passing between farms and neighborhoods where farms had been just a decade before. The area was changing, just like everything else in the universe. Nothing was ever still, permanent.

Tara considered that as she watched the pastures turn into subdivisions and long-term retirement villages. Her mind drifted back to Dimitris again, hoping his final minutes had been relatively painless. She felt another tidal wave of guilt wash over her, driven by a maelstrom of regret.

It was all she could do to refocus on the task at hand. "This new Ahnenerbe is more dangerous than the last. Before, they operated with a government's direction and endorsement. Now, they work from the shadows, but it would appear they can infiltrate any nation. Look how fast they got here to the United States."

"They must have been planning this for some time," Alex added. "I wonder if the discovery at the dig site was what jump-started everything."

"Probably," she agreed. "We need to look at the timelines again. Even though they didn't steal the artifact from the dig site first, it could have been announced that the archaeology teams there had made an important discovery. If we can find that information, it could be another piece to the puzzle."

"Not that it matters," Boston said. "We have the last piece to that puzzle."

"That's right," Dak said. "And without it, they have nothing to bargain with."

24

CHATTANOOGA

Buri pushed the door open with a hand wrapped in a black leather glove. He craned his neck to look inside and took a step. Glass crunched under his feet from some of the shards that exploded outward during the gunfire.

He'd watched his quarry enter the house, having arrived just minutes before he and his team. His FLIR thermal scanner, short for Forward-Looking Infrared, had displayed all the targets inside the home and in one place. Initially, he couldn't believe how lucky he was. He'd cursed when he saw the troublesome couple and their new Greek friend show up at the gatehouse, but Buri learned long ago that he needed to always have a contingency in place. Fortune favored the prepared mind. He'd heard that somewhere along the way but couldn't recall where or who had said it.

Either way, Buri rapidly implemented his backup plan.

The team spread out quickly, covering the perimeter of the property and then closing in toward the house like a constrictor, squeezing until they were certain none of their prey had managed to sneak out. Then, when he was within range, Buri used his thermal scanner to search the house. It took seconds to find the group of people inside, all huddled near the kitchen in what appeared to be a sitting area.

What he hadn't expected was the sudden escape.

As he and his team closed in on the home, showering it with a volley of bullets that obliterated windows and tore through drapes, shattering fragments of brick along the way, he saw the targets drop to the floor, though one had fallen slower than the others.

Buri's feet crunched again on the interior side of the threshold. He turned and examined the area to his right. A huge stainless-steel refrigerator and freezer stood against the wall between two cracked and broken windows. The sheer white veils hanging from the tops were nothing more than tattered strips of loose fabric drifting in the breeze.

He spun around the corner on the tips of his toes and continued past the ornately decorated elevator, only pausing briefly to either admire the painted scene or wonder why someone would do that.

The men around him swarmed the house. They reached the upper and lower floors in groups of two, scouring it for the artifact he knew had to be here, the object that would enable him to finally complete the mission his grandfather had started so many years before.

His quarry had managed to escape...temporarily. He was confident his men who took off in pursuit would be able to catch them, and the loud bang he'd heard from the foot of the hill likely signaled the end of an extremely short chase. The driver of the bizarre pickup truck must have tried to push his luck and driven into the gate or lost control of the vehicle and plowed into one of the stone columns.

Buri worked his way around the shattered glass that seemed to litter the entire area and found a man lying on the floor, his back leaning against the wall next to the fireplace. Blood soaked his shirt, despite someone having attempted to stem the leak with a few paper towels from the kitchen. The man was unconscious but alive; his chest barely rose and fell. A quick look at the wound told Buri the man could live if he received medical attention. It didn't appear that anything vital was injured by the bullet, though it must be painful—the round being near the collarbone.

For a moment, Buri stood with a pistol dangling at his side. "So, Detective Frangos," he said with unbridled disdain, "looks like your investigation has reached its end."

Dimitris said nothing. His only response was the slow, rhythmic fall of his chest as his lungs pulled in air and expelled it through his nose.

"Unfortunate it had to end this way," Buri said. He raised the pistol and pointed at the detective's head. His finger rubbed on the trigger. He started to squeeze, but was interrupted by the sounds of hurried footfalls ascending the steps.

Someone was in a hurry.

Just then, one of his men spun around the corner and into the room, kicking loose bits of broken glass along the tiled floor with a light clattering sound that mimicked that of sleet hitting the pavement on a cold winter's day.

"Sir?" The young man was blond, hair cut short in a military style. He had a tattoo of an eagle on his neck just below the right ear. Like many of the men in Buri's order, the man had blue eyes.

"What is it, Marcus?" Buri asked, irritated that his kill had been interrupted. His finger relaxed ever-so-slightly on the trigger.

"They got away, sir," Marcus informed him. He knew the boss wouldn't be happy about that and did his best to sound apologetic. He also knew the consequences of failing Buri. He'd seen what the man could do to those who betrayed him or who came up short in their tasks.

"They got away?" Buri asked, seeking clarification. "How?"

"The gate," Marcus said, still panting. "They got around the gate. We tried to go through it, but it closed and we wrecked our SUV. I think Mueller might be dead. He hit the windshield pretty hard. I think I heard a pop. He wasn't moving. I was lucky. I hit the back of the driver's seat with my shoulder."

Buri was tempted to ask about the SUV's driver, but he focused on the more important information. "It won't matter as long as the artifact is still here. I doubt they were able to get it out of here in time."

"Yes, sir," Marcus said. "We don't believe they had the relic in their possession when they made their escape."

Buri wondered how the man could possibly know that, but for the moment he was willing to give Marcus the benefit of the doubt.

Another member of his team hurried to his side from another room beyond the hearth.

"Sir?" This man's thick black hair shook as he slowed to a stop. Dark stubble framed his thin face.

"Did you find it?" Buri asked, letting his hopes get the better of his intonation.

"No, sir. The artifact isn't here."

Buri's lips tightened in anger. "What?"

"The artifact is gone, sir. We found the vault wide open. The kid has quite the collection, but one of the display cases was empty."

"Scanners?"

The man shook his head. "Sorry, sir. Scanners didn't show anything close to the signatures we've seen from the other stones."

Buri gritted his teeth. The muscles in his jaw tightened and throbbed. A big part of him wanted to shoot the messenger, both messengers in this case. The artifact was gone? How could they have missed it?

"Based on the security setup of the vault, sir, I'd guess they removed the artifact before we got here." The black-haired man's information sparked a new possibility in Buri's mind.

"How so?" he pried.

"The entire room is password protected with a keypad and retinal scanner. There is also an additional key required to open the display cases, along with individual keypads for each one."

"We had eyes on the targets the entire time we were here. We saw them come in," Buri added.

"Correct. They didn't have time to extract the artifact and make their escape."

"Which means they must have anticipated our visit." He looked down at the unconscious cop, slumped on the floor. "How is that possible?"

"We're not sure, sir. But the heightened security in Boston; now this?" The man leveled his gaze at the leader. "Sounds like they figured out our plan."

"But who would have been privy to that?" The answer hit Buri the second the words slipped through his lips. "Neil." He muttered the name so quietly that the other two men in the room didn't hear him clearly.

"What was that, sir?" Marcus asked.

"Our mole, Neil. It appears he was taking note of our targets and plan of attack. It's the only explanation. He must have conveyed our operations to someone, somehow. Not that it matters now. We've nearly accomplished our goal." He felt the Quantium necklace pressing against his chest, just below the neckline. Wearing it pushed him, kept him focused on what he had to do.

"The only challenge we have to face," he continued, "is figuring out where our little collector placed the artifact." He turned to the dark-haired man. "Search the rest of the house, and let me know if you find anything. I want the place turned upside down. If you have to break down walls, do it."

The henchmen nodded obediently and wheeled on their heels, ready to carry out their leader's orders.

Buri looked down at the bleeding man still heaped against the wall by the fireplace. His chest still went up and down in the same deliberate rhythm.

"Stop," Buri commanded. He held up his left hand to reinforce the order. Then he inched closer to the detective and lowered his pistol. He stared at Detective Frangos as though he were a juicy steak, ready to be devoured. "I have a better idea."

25

CHATTANOOGA

Tara and Alex sat on a deep, black leather couch. They'd been silent for nearly twenty minutes. Regret throbbed at their minds, chased by a lump in their throats that couldn't be washed down with any amount of drink.

Dimitris Frangos was dead. And it was their fault.

The lone consolation the young couple could muster was that the man lived alone, didn't appear to have any family, and if he had friends they were few. Some of the people he worked with in the police department would miss him, though it was unlikely his bosses would, especially after the suspension. Then again, his passing might give them a moment's pause to consider whether their actions had led to his untimely demise.

Boston sat on a leather club chair that was positioned at an angle to the right of the couch. Cartoons played on the 65-inch flatscreen television, though the boy kept the sound low. Truthfully, he wasn't watching the show anyway. His brain wouldn't let go of what had just happened. While he'd taken the harrowing events at his home like a seasoned pro, he was now showing signs of shock. It was inevitable, Tara thought. Even though he was smart beyond his years, Boston was still a boy, still innocent in many ways and inexperienced with violence and death.

Dak returned from the kitchen with three bottles of water. He handed them out and then plopped down on the other club chair opposite Boston.

Silence permeated the room as the cartoons flashed brightly on the high-definition screen.

A ringing phone ruptured the silence. The device sang and vibrated from inside Alex's pocket, startling him and everyone else in the room.

With a frown, he reached into his pocket and withdrew the phone. His face drained, turning an ashen color as he looked at the number on the screen.

"What is it?" Dak asked.

"Who is it?" Tara added.

Alex looked up from his phone. The device was still ringing.

"It's Dimitris."

He tapped the green button and put the phone to his ear as the others stared with blank expressions, bewildered by the strange call.

"Dimitris?" Alex asked.

At first, the only answer was the sound of rhythmic breathing. It was silent, unlabored, and sounded deliberate, as if the caller was trying to intimidate Alex. Perhaps it was a butt dial, and Dimitris' body had been moved, accidentally calling the last number he'd dialed.

"He's alive," a strange voice answered. "For now."

Alex's face blanched further. His eyes flashed to Tara.

She knew that look. He was afraid, but of what?

"Detective Frangos is alive?" Alex asked so the others could hear.

Tara was washed with relief, but she could tell all was not well.

"And if you'd like to see him remain that way, you and I are going to work out a little deal." The smooth voice spoke with the confidence of someone who was accustomed to getting their way, an authoritative tone that leaders often used.

"Buri," Alex groused.

"Very good. You know who I am. It isn't often I find myself in a position where I am the one who is known and my counterpart is not. We usually have impeccable intel. In this instance, however, it seems someone infiltrated my organization."

"You mean the MI6 agent you killed?"

"An unfortunate incident, but necessary. Before you start prattling on about innocent people's deaths, you should know that no one is innocent. Not even you."

"You don't know me."

Buri snickered. "Not yet, but I will."

"You won't find us. We'll be a step ahead of you."

"Of that, I have no doubt. Fortunately for me, I have another card in play."

It took all of two seconds for Alex to connect the dots. Dimitris was his ace in the hole. Had the detective been dead, Buri would have had no play, or at least fewer options. But with Dimitris alive, he had a hostage.

"What do you want, Buri?" Alex sneered.

"You know exactly what I want."

"And if I don't give it to you?"

Buri let out a chuckle. "Do you really have to ask? I have the resources to sustain your Greek friend's life for a long time. During that time, I'll make certain that I keep him alive merely so he can be tortured. Every day of his life will be harrowing, painful, pure agony. Every morning he wakes, he will beg for death. Every night, he will desperately try to sleep, but it will not come. Your detective will not know peace or rest. And every single day, the cycle will begin again."

Alex clenched his jaw as he listened to the man on the phone. He wanted to jump through the device and pummel Buri until his face looked like a bloody fruit that had been through a blender. Dimitris was a good person. He didn't deserve any of this.

"Where?"

"I can see you're a man of reason," Buri commented. "I'm glad you're done pretending. You already know where you need to meet me. And since you were just in Greece, I know your passports are in order."

Alex was quiet for a moment. His wife and Dak stared at him expectantly. Boston was trying to listen in, but could only hear a fuzzy voice.

"How do I know where?"

"Come now. You've managed to get this far. You're telling me you don't know what those stones are for?"

The answer hit Alex in the gut. "Tiwanaku?" He whispered the word, and everyone's ears pricked.

"Very good. See? I knew you were smart. Bring the stone to Tiwanaku. Be there tomorrow at noon, or I begin your friend's...treatment."

"If you so much as touch him—"

"Please," Buri interrupted. "There's no cause for bravado here. We both know there's nothing you can do about it other than bring me what I asked for. The stone. Noon. Bolivia. Or the pain begins for your friend, and it won't end until you arrive. Understood?"

Alex swallowed hard, wincing as he did so. He didn't notice his breathing had quickened, though he could feel his heart pounding much harder than normal. "Fine," he relented. "We'll be there."

"That's a good boy," Buri said. "I'll see you then."

The call ended before Alex could say anything else. Not that it mattered. They were mere words, forming in his head to make him feel better—nothing more than impotent sounds.

Everyone in the room stared at him, waiting for Alex to tell them what was going on.

"You said Tiwanaku," Tara noted.

"Yes," Alex confirmed with a nod. "That was Buri. He has Dimitris."

"He's alive?"

"For now. But Buri has plans for him. I won't tell you what they are, but it's bad. We're to take the stone to him at Tiwanaku, and he'll give us Dimitris." Alex realized, as he spoke, that Buri had never agreed to such a deal. The villain merely said to bring the stone. He never promised to give Dimitris over to them. He also didn't promise no one else would be hurt. Alex decided not to share that little detail with the rest of the group.

"Tiwanaku?" Boston asked. "So, he's going to try to do it." The kid's voice drifted like clouds on a saltwater breeze.

"What do you mean?" Alex asked.

Boston sat up straighter. "The portal. The Gate to the Sun. He's going to try to go through it, just like Edmund Kiss did all those years ago. Except now, if he has all the stones, he might actually pull it off."

"So?" Dak asked. "Good riddance. You said that Kiss character never came back. Problem solved."

"No," Boston corrected. "His assistant from the village never returned. Kiss disappeared, but not through the gate."

"Where did he go?"

"Kiss? He returned to Germany for a while, fell into poverty and depression, then disappeared. No one really knows much about his life after the war. He died in the 1960s, I believe. Other than that, though, the guy fell off the radar."

"So?" Dak pressed. "If this Buri goes through the gate, he'll be gone. All's well that ends well."

"Kiss didn't have all of the stones. If we give Buri my stone, he'll have the entire collection. With that, he may be able to open the portal from both sides. The legend suggests that there is tremendous power waiting on the other side. What that means I don't know, but it can't be good, especially in the hands of someone like Buri."

"Which means we're going to Bolivia to stop him," Tara said.

"You'll need some extra firepower," Dak said. "I'm coming, too."

"Me, too," Boston ventured, even though he already knew the answer.

Dak leveled a gaze at the boy that he'd seen many times before.

"I know. I know," Boston relented. "I have to stay here for school and stuff."

"And your parents wouldn't let you go on this trip anyway. It's too dangerous, kid."

"But when I'm eighteen, you can't stop me."

Dak grinned. "I'll see you in eight years, buddy."

Alex turned to the boy. "Thank you for all your help. But Dak is right. We can't risk you getting hurt." He could see the boy understood but was still dejected that he'd be stuck at home. "But we may need someone here to find information quickly while we're gone. Can you be available for us?"

The boy's demeanor instantly switched back to excitement. "You bet. I'll run point from here."

"Perfect."

"His parents will be back later," Dak said. "Then I can accompany you to the bank to retrieve the stone. We'll be cutting it close to get to Bolivia by noon tomorrow."

"Not to worry," Tara said. "We have a fast ride."

26

LA PAZ, BOLIVIA

The minibus rumbled to a stop in a drop off area just outside the ruins of Tiwanaku. Alex, Tara, and Dak sat in their seats until everyone else had left the vehicle.

The crisp mountain air smacked them in the face when they stepped out. It was dry and smelled of dust and stone. On cue, Alex took a quick drink from his water bottle.

La Paz stands on top of the world as the highest administrative capital on the planet. Wedged between high mountains in a natural basin, the city offers sweeping views of vast plains, a volcano with snowy peaks, valleys, clusters of green trees and shrubs, and high rocky cliffs. These combine to make La Paz one of the most unique cities in the world.

The only downside was the elevation sickness that hit many visitors, and Alex found himself struggling to fight the symptoms.

Fortunately, they'd taken precautions with a dose of Diamox. Tara hated to think of how Alex would feel had he not utilized the medication.

Dak seemed unaffected, though the man was hardened and didn't show much emotion or weakness. At least none she could detect.

Tara looked at her watch. They still had plenty of time—nearly an hour—before their rendezvous with Buri. Of course, *plenty of time* was relative. They had an hour to kill, but if there had been any more delays, they would have missed their appointment, and subsequently, Dimitris would have suffered the consequences.

"I'm going to have a look around," Dak said, motioning to a hillside several hundred yards away. "I'd like to make sure I know what we're getting into."

Tourists meandered around the ruins, snapping pictures with their phones or with high-end cameras. All told, only a few dozen such visitors took up real estate around the ruins, which made it easier to spot trouble. This caused Dak a growing sense of concern because, at the moment, he didn't see anyone suspicious.

The other two also surveyed the immediate area but sensed nothing amiss.

"See anyone who looks like they might be a member of a defunct Nazi secret society?" Alex asked.

"No," Dak said, ignoring the humor. "And that's what bothers me."

He didn't show up expecting a red carpet pointing them to the rendezvous spot, but everyone in his field of view looked like ordinary people. None of the tourists appeared to be a threat, not even to the most paranoid parts of Dak's imagination. Still, he wasn't about to be caught with his pants down.

"You two wander around a bit, have a look at some of the ruins. Try to look natural." He squinted against the sun even with the protection of his Ray-Bans. He zipped up his windbreaker and tightened the daypack on his back until it was snug.

"What are you going to do?" Tara asked.

"Like I said, I'm going to have a look around. Out there," he added after he could see they were still uncertain.

They followed his gaze to the hills surrounding the ruins. Rolling prairies gave way to high mountain peaks in the distance. It reminded Dak of Texas—the prairies, anyway. He'd grown up in Waco, a town of more contrasts than a box of crayons.

He remembered going to one of the football games in the old stadium when he was younger, a trip he'd taken with his friends. He recalled the game fondly, still appreciating his friends' parents who took him in and treated him like one of their own.

Texas could have filled Dak's mind with a host of unpleasant memories, but although those still loitered in the background, he chose to recall the good times he had with the people who drove him to be better, to be more.

"I'll head over to that knoll and take a look around," he said, motioning nonchalantly to a small rise to the east. "Might be good to have me out there in case something happens."

"Like what?" Alex asked.

Dak merely gave him a glance that conveyed the dire possibility.

"Oh," Alex said. "Right."

"Don't worry about it, kid," Dak said with a wink. "I'll be watching your every move. Just don't do anything stupid, and we get out of this alive."

Alex wanted to believe him but felt there were still elements at play that were out of their control.

"Keep calm. Do everything like we rehearsed it. Okay?"

Tara and Alex nodded.

"And if things go haywire—" Dak paused for a second, thinking. "Eh, just improvise."

He turned and trudged toward the hillock to the east. He carried a sand-colored tactical backpack over one shoulder, stocked with a few weapons.

Tara tightened her jacket against a cool breeze. She rechecked her own rucksack for the third time since climbing onto the minibus and then motioned at one of the walls of stacked stone a hundred yards away.

"What do you say we go take a look at the ruins for a bit, get the layout of the area?" Her auburn hair fluttered in the breeze, brushing across a small patch of exposed creamy skin on her neck.

"Sounds good to me," Alex said. He continued to look around, eyeing the location warily. Something wasn't right, but he didn't want to make his wife jumpy—that is, any jumpier than she already was.

He secured the bag against his shoulders and ran his fingers against the front pouch where he'd stowed Boston's artifact. Alex had no idea how this was going to play out, but a sentimental part of his mind hoped he could return the object to the boy.

Alex and Tara hiked over to a wall to the west and stopped. They inspected the seams between the enormous blocks. The original inhabitants had cut the stones so exactly that—much like the ruins in Cusco, Peru—they required no mortar to remain securely in place. Some of the stones appeared to be cut with something far more precise than the ancient tools supposedly afforded humans long ago.

The imminent confrontation with Buri made staying focused on Tiwanaku's sights nearly impossible. Every passing second brought them closer to the unknown, the clock hammering away in their minds, filling them with both wonder and dread.

"How does this guy think he's going to get rid of all these tourists?" Tara asked, looking around at the people wandering the property.

"Yeah," Alex said, eyes darting from place to place. "I see what you mean."

They were spread out, a few here, four or five there. If the visitors were in larger groups, perhaps taking an organized tour, it might have been easier to rid themselves of so many witnesses, but as it was, Buri was going to have his work cut out for him.

Then another thought hit Tara, one that shook her to the core. "I hope he doesn't plan on hurting these people."

"Yeah. I was thinking the same thing."

"Is there a way we can get them out of here?"

Tara looked around, searching for something they could do, a way to get all the bystanders away from the ruins. She realized it was too late when she saw the caravan of SUVs arrive at the parking area just outside the ruins.

"Looks like we're too late to take care of the tourists." She inclined her head, indicating the six SUVs.

Alex let out a long sigh and twisted his jaw back and forth. "Well, let's just hope that bullets don't start flying."

The sounds of engines groaning shook them from their conversation. They looked toward the last bend in the road. Within seconds, they saw the source of the sound. Three school buses rumbled up the road and around the curve. The buses featured a cornucopia of colors swirled and splashed over them in a chaotic display of art.

"Why are those buses empty?" Tara asked.

"That's a good question. And here's another one: Why haven't Buri and his men gotten out of their SUVs yet?"

"Maybe it's not them."

He fired a *not-a-chance* smirk at her and kept his eyes on the peculiar convoy of buses as they turned around in the drop off area and then grumbled to a stop. The doors folded open, but the drivers remained in their seats with hands on the wheels, waiting.

The doors of the SUVs abruptly swung open, and men in black sunglasses and sand-colored tactical gear emerged. They carried matching weapons, short-barreled AR-15s from the looks of them. Those guns would, no doubt, be equipped with a modification to make them fully automatic.

"What are they doing?" Alex asked.

His answer didn't come from Tara. The men in the tactical uniforms began ordering the visitors to evacuate the premises and board the buses. They would be taken back to the city and could return after a quick security check.

Buri's men worked efficiently, rounding up the tourists within ten minutes. Alex and Tara could only watch as the henchmen finished their job and sent the buses down the road. Few had put up much of an argument, assuming these men were the local cops.

Tara stole a discreet glance around the ruins. Dak was nowhere in sight, which was partly relieving and partly cause for concern. She didn't see him with Buri's men, so he hadn't been captured, which meant he was still in position for whatever he had planned.

Then a back door on one of the SUVs opened, and Buri stepped out. He was dressed the same as his men but only carried a sidearm on his right hip. His head twisted around and locked on to the young American couple standing by the ancient stone wall. A cryptic smile seeped across his face.

Buri strode toward Tara and Alex with four armed guards, two on either side staggered slightly behind their leader. The rest of the men fanned out and continued searching the ruins to make sure they hadn't missed a straggler. Alex hated to think about what these men might do to someone who'd deliberately or accidentally skipped the free bus ride.

"Five bucks he says something cliché like 'I'm so glad you made it,'" Tara hissed.

"No bet."

The villain stopped five yards short of the couple. He paused for a moment, assessing both of them.

"Well, I'm impressed," Buri seethed. "I'm so glad you could make it."

"Close enough," Alex whispered with a bridled snort.

Tara passed him an *I-told-you-so* smirk.

"I have to be honest," Buri went on, "I wasn't sure if you could. That's a lot of travel on such short notice."

"No one was using the company jet."

"Ah. How fortunate." He put out his hand and pointed to the ground at their feet. "Put the stone on the ground and step away."

Alex shook his head. "Wait a second. How about a little foreplay first? Or is that how you get down, straight to it?"

"I'm sorry if you thought we were going to sit down for coffee and cake, Mr. Watson. As much as I'd enjoy that, especially with your lovely wife, I prefer not to beat around the bush. Direct always works best. So, if this is your attempt to stall, please, spare me."

Alex didn't like the way he looked at Tara when he mentioned her, though it was difficult to see the man's eyes though his sunglasses.

"So, that's it? You want us to give you the stone and walk away? Where is Detective Frangos?"

Buri motioned to one of his men nearest the parked vehicles. The guard trotted over to the one on the far left and swung the door open. Dimitris was inside, hands and feet bound with zip ties. His face was pale, the color of death, though it appeared he was stable for the moment. He turned his head weakly to the side and looked out with vacant eyes wincing against the bright sunlight. He said nothing, but he didn't have to. His eyes told the story. He was dying. It was a miracle he was still breathing, but there was no telling how long he could survive without medical attention.

"Your friend is alive for now. And to your other question, I didn't say anything about you walking away," Buri said. "After all, I'm going to need a test subject, maybe two, before I enter the portal. And since the two of you have done me the courtesy of coming together, you'll be the perfect specimens." He waved a hand and the guard slammed the SUV's door shut.

There was something creepy about how he called them specimens. The word hearkened back to the era of the original Nazis conducting experiments on their prisoners. The thought turned Tara's stomach, and she could see out of the corner of her eye that it had a similar effect on Alex.

"What are you talking about?" she asked. "We're not going to be anyone's guinea pigs. And what are they doing with those?" She motioned with a nod toward two guards who carefully placed a stone on either side of the gate, just in front of the supporting columns.

"Oh, but you will be my guinea pigs," he said and took a dramatic step forward. Buri folded his hands in front of his belt. "You see, I need two of you. One will go through the portal while the other remains here, on this side of the other dimension. As to the stones, I'm surprised you haven't learned how this mechanism works. I thought you were smarter than that, but allow me to explain. The stones act together to produce a containment field. Without them, the portal will collapse or at best, be unstable. That is why any who tried to pass through it before failed. And why I will succeed."

"What will that prove?" Tara demanded. "You want to send one of us through to die? That won't accomplish anything."

"It will, my dear, because you'll be holding hands. Of course, if you two don't want to do it, I could always call the driver of one of those buses and have them bring back a truckload of test subjects." He reached into his pocket and took out his phone, then held it threateningly in front of the two Americans. "Is that how you'd like to play this? With innocent lives?"

Neither Tara nor Alex could say yes to that, even though it meant one of them was going into the portal. Unless....

"You won't get away with this," Alex barked.

"How cliché." Buri's condescending response sent Alex into an inferno of rage, but he could do nothing. The villain's guards stood with their weapons pointed at him and Tara. "Perhaps you're referring to your friend who was watching over our meeting."

Concern smashed Tara and Alex in their faces.

"I assure you he won't be a problem."

Two more armed men rounded the corner behind them. They dragged Dak with a hand under each armpit, the captive's head bleeding from a gash over the right eye. He looked dazed and wasn't putting up much of a fight except for the occasional leg kick or a twitch of an arm.

They must have gotten the drop on him, which had to be a feat considering Dak was a former special ops guy.

"You didn't have to work him over like that," Alex said, anger boiling in his throat.

"I don't like loose ends," Buri answered. "We can't have those, can we? So, as I requested before, put the stone on the ground, and we will begin. Who knows? Maybe you'll get lucky and survive the initial test. I must admit, that's what I'm hoping for. You see, if you come back alive, that means my analysis of the gate was correct, and I will be able to return, as well."

"And with all the power of the heavens," Tara muttered.

Buri's face twitched, confused. "Heaven? Oh, no. I intend to return with the power of hell itself."

27

LA PAZ

The sun neared its zenith in the clear blue sky, not a wisp of cloud in sight. Tara and Alex stared straight ahead at the Sun Gate and wondered what awaited on the other side. At the moment, the only thing on the other side was the view of the hill through the stone columns that supported a header overtop.

They watched as Buri's men placed the eleven artifacts, one atop each of the eleven calendar stones that surrounded the gate. The same guards who had escorted Buri upon his arrival still stood next to him, carefully watching the three prisoners.

Dak remained on the ground, conscious and complaining about a pain in his head. He still seemed in a daze and a touch confused. A guard had been assigned specifically to Dak and was ordered to shoot him in the head if he tried anything. He didn't, instead staying in a slumped heap on the ground.

Once the stones were in place, Buri's men circled the prisoners to make sure there was nowhere to run. The only place Buri didn't position his men was directly ahead, through the gate itself. That made sense if his assumptions proved correct, but it was hardly an escape avenue. Even if there was no interdimensional portal within the gate, any attempt to escape straight through it would end with the rattle of gunfire and a quick death.

Buri stepped to Tara and Alex, stopping short by a few feet. He held his hands behind his back, a gesture that appeared to be an attempt to look dignified. All they could see was a monster, a neo-Nazi without all the pieces of flare and regalia the originals had donned.

"Have you decided which one of you will go through?"

"I will," Alex said quickly before his wife could speak.

"No," she protested. "I can't let you do that."

"One of us has to," he said.

They faced each other with tears building like tidal waves against a cracked dam.

"Let me do it," she insisted.

"I can't go on without you." Alex gazed into her green eyes, losing himself in them for what he assumed would be the last time. "I have to do this."

"You think I can go on without you? I love you. We're like—"

"Don't say peas and carrots," he interrupted.

She snorted a resentful laugh. "See?"

"I don't mean to be rude," Buri said, cutting her off, "but we really must be going. The sun will be at its peak soon, and I don't want to waste the moment. According to the legend, the portal will only be open for a few minutes."

The two Americans scathed him with furious glares.

Tara sighed and turned back to her husband. When she spoke again, it was in a whisper only Alex could hear. "If you go and don't return, I don't want to think about what these men would do to me."

His face flushed red-hot. He wished he could pull out a machine gun and mow them all down in one Rambo-esque attack. But this wasn't the movies. There would be no miracle to save them from their fate. Their only hope was that whoever went through the portal would return safely. That was still a possibility, however small.

"Hey," Dak slurred, propping himself upright on the ground.

Tara and Alex looked over at him, as did Buri and his men.

"Just remember, Beantown will always have your back. All you gotta do is throw caution to the wind."

"He's delirious," Buri snapped. "Shut him up."

One of the guards delivered a blow to the back of his head and he slumped forward again, though he didn't pass out. Dak's head rolled around as his torso tipped one way then another. He made eye contact with both of his companions and gave a drunken wink. Then his lips cracked into a mischievous grin and he toppled over onto his face, his body limp.

If Alex and Tara thought their new friend was going to miraculously save them with some kind of superhuman abilities, they were wrong.

Buri took one more step forward he nodded to a guard who stood directly in behind the gate, holding the last stone in front of his waist. The guard returned the unspoken order with a bob of his head, then set the final stone down on a smooth tile and retreated twenty paces back.

Buri stuffed his right hand into a pocket and then withdrew it again. He extended his hand toward the couple and opened his fingers. A small blue crystal rested in the center of his palm. The object was only an inch long and half as wide. It was difficult to tell in the sunlight, but the gem appeared to glow.

"Where did you—" Alex started to ask.

"Please. You can stop with the games, Mr. Simms. We both know what this is. Whoever is going through the gate will carry this. Only Quantium can activate the portal."

Tara focused intently on the crystal.

"But if we go through the gate with that," Alex said, pointing at the precious stone, "you won't have a way to get through."

"You're assuming you'll make it back alive."

Alex swallowed a chunk of uncertainty.

"And you're also assuming that is the only piece of Quantium I possess."

Disbelief splashed onto the Americans' faces.

"That's impossible," Tara seethed. "It's one of the rarest elements on Earth."

"Improbable. Not impossible. If one knows where to look."

The insinuation haunted Tara and Alex. Was he suggesting he had access to a lode of Quantium? The idea was as terrifying as it was preposterous. Yet here Buri was, giving them a sliver of the element as if passing them a quarter for a tollbooth.

Tara took the opportunity to snatch the crystal from Buri's hand while Alex was lost in thought. He reacted a moment too slow, and Tara wrapped her fingers around the object and jerked it away from the man.

"Hey," Alex demanded, reaching for her hands.

"No," she stopped him with a word and a blazing glare. "You know you have to let me do this. And you know why."

He did know. The last thing she'd said still tortured him. If she stayed and he didn't return, these guards and their leader could do what they wanted with her. Considering their roots, that could take any number of directions, and none of them were pleasant.

The tears broke through his fortress and spilled over the walls of his face. His lips trembled, and the aftershock reached his fingertips. He grasped her hands with his, desperate not to ever let go.

"Touching," Buri said sardonically. "The woman takes the lead."

The barb didn't touch Alex. His heart was already rent into a million pieces.

"It's okay," Tara said, offering a weak smile. Her lips drowned in tears as she spoke.

Alex pulled her close and wrapped his arms around her, squeezing her with every muscle he could summon. Deep down, he hoped she would survive. Maybe nothing would happen. Even then, the best-case scenario would be execution at gunpoint.

"I love you," he said.

"I love you, too," she replied.

"Okay, wonderful," Buri blathered callously. "Escort them to the gate." He motioned to the couple, and two of the guards lowered their weapons, stepped forward, and grabbed Tara and Alex by the arms.

The men ushered the two captives forward until they were only ten yards from the opening between the behemoth stones. Hope kept banging on the door to Alex's heart.

"Say goodbye," Buri ordered. "Of course, I'm hoping you see her again in a minute. And remember to hold on to her hand. If you let go..." He let the answer hang in the dry air and flutter away on a cool breeze.

Alex tried to ignore him, but the fear and sadness storming through his mind cluttered his focus.

"Hey," Tara said. She grabbed his face with both hands and peered into his eyes. "It's going to be okay." Then she embraced him again and brushed her lips against his right earlobe. "Hold my hand tight," she breathed. "And when I tug on it, you jump."

His expression tightened in confusion. He wanted to protest, but she pulled away before he could say anything. He certainly didn't dare speak it out loud. Tara was up to something, and Alex had to trust she knew what she was doing.

She turned and pulled on his hand, leading him toward the gate while holding the sliver of Quantium in the other.

When they were five yards from the opening, a distant hum filled their ears. The crystal in Tara's hand pulsed slowly, like the rhythm of a heartbeat. To her surprise, it only gave off a small amount of heat, barely noticeable if she hadn't been paying attention.

The two stopped four yards from the gate. Tara hesitated, holding on to Alex's hand, gripping it tighter with every passing second. He wondered if she was doing that because of what she'd said or because she was afraid. He still didn't understand what was happening. She'd told him to jump, but where were they jumping? Through the gate together? So it was a double suicide? That wasn't a great plan. But at least they'd be with each other. Her eyes hadn't insinuated such a scheme, though, and he had to refocus.

Then his mind flashed back to what Dak said and the funny wink that followed. He'd said Beantown, something about Beantown having his back. *What does Boston have to do with any of—*

Then the epiphany struck. Boston was still connected somehow.

Buri's troops must have checked Dak for weapons and any kind of communications device, but the villain hadn't checked Alex or Tara.

She glanced over at him with a flirty eye, and he caught a glimpse something inside her jacket's inner pocket. A red light flashed intermittently against the interior fabric.

Her radio.

He nodded to her, finally understanding. Then he faced the gate and searched it carefully. It took less than three seconds for him to spot what Buri and his men missed. A pile of dirt ran up to the base of the stone pillar on the right. The clump was small, packed tight, and if he hadn't been looking, Alex would have missed it.

A bomb.

They were going to blow the Sun Gate to pieces. That plan carried with it an inherent danger, especially to Tara and Alex. Too close, and they would be taken out with the column.

The couple took another step forward, this time with more reservation. When they drew another shortened step closer, a tiny blue orb appeared in the center of the opening, under the header and between the pillars. It hung in midair, as if from an invisible string. As Alex and Tara inched closer, the light swelled, growing in size threefold. It swirled from the center out in a mesmerizing and terrifying vortex.

Buri stared at the wonder with his eyes wide open.

"I knew it," he whispered. "I knew he was close." He spoke just loud enough for Tara and Alex to hear, but no one else.

Tara risked a discreet look around. The men—hardened and battle-forged—stared blankly at the incredible sight. Some of them let their guns slump in their hands. It was only slight, but she noticed. Every one of the gunmen stood in rapt awe. Their reactions would be slower, though not by much.

She squeezed Alex's hand, signaling she was about to make her move. He twisted his head toward her and gave a subtle nod.

Tara pinched the glowing shard and took another step forward. They stood mere feet away from the swirling vortex. Alex tried to see into it, to catch a glimpse of what may be on the other side, but it looked like he was staring into the ethereal abyss of a blue nebula, something both real and imagined. He wasn't sure, but he thought he heard voices.

Tara heard them, too, amid the constant humming that filled the air. She gazed into the swirling blue light. Part of her wanted to step through. Or did she? Was it her own desire or the desire of the portal calling out to her, drawing her into the abyss beyond? *What was on the other side?* She wanted to know. She felt herself pulling Alex toward the opening.

What was Tara doing?

He pulled on her hand, but she didn't budge. He tried again, but to no avail. She squeezed his hand harder, almost painfully so. He clenched his jaw, teeth grinding in his mouth as he struggled against his wife's grip.

Her feet moved unconsciously now, dragging them both closer to the portal.

Alex knew Buri and his men could see him trying to hold back his wife. He didn't care. Tara was only one step away from going through the gate. The hills and prairies on the other side were gone, blocked by the ethereal, swirling blue portal.

"Tara," Alex barked.

Though her eyes stayed fixed on the gate, her mind tore away from the sounds that begged her to step through. Something evil lurked there, beckoning her to enter. It felt cold, dark, sinister. She couldn't put her finger on what it was, but there was a presence on the other side of that gate that she never wanted to see or hear again.

She took a step toward the opening as if to walk through, but at the last second snapped her wrist to the left, flinging the Quantium sliver into the earth at the base of the pillar on the right.

Then Tara pulled hard on Alex's hand and shouted, "Now, Boston!"

Back in La Paz, a ten-year-old boy had been watching and listening to the entire drama play out. His video feed had gone down when Dak was taken, but he could still hear, and understood what his friend had suggested when he said Beantown had their backs.

The boy wouldn't be convinced to stay at home with his parents, so Dak made up a story about them going to Bolivia to check out some fascinating ruins. That wasn't a lie, not entirely. The kid was still at the hotel with a bodyguard Dak trusted. Now, Boston was the hinge for the whole operation.

Dak had given the young man the backup plan and warned him that it would only be used if things went south. Desperate times, he'd said.

"Do it, kid," Dak confirmed.

Boston didn't hesitate.

The base of the right column shuddered under a loud thump. Dust and smoke erupted in an instant. Rock fragments sprayed across the courtyard. Some of the debris struck the gunmen. Most of it did little harm to the armed men, though a few were caught in the face, neck, or head. At least three dropped to the ground, incapacitated.

The rest hit the dirt the second the explosive blew. Visibility was nearly zero for several seconds and it took them a moment to recover and get their bearings.

In the confusion, Tara and Alex made the most of the opportunity. They dove to the side of the left column, using it as a shield from the blast. The gate header collapsed under the blown pillar and fell to the ground with a heavy thud, effectively closing the portal forever.

Thankfully, the left one stood firm. It trembled and even teetered a couple of inches, but its foundation didn't yield to the explosion.

Alex looked to his wife through the airborne debris. "Now," he said.

The two of them scrambled to their feet and rushed headlong toward two of the gunmen who were down on the ground. One writhed awkwardly, clutching at his face. Blood seeped through his fingers. The other lay prostrate, motionless on the ground.

Tara and Alex scooped up the gunmen's weapons and turned them on the closest members of Buri's team.

"Light 'em up," Tara said. She leveled the gun and squeezed the trigger.

28

LA PAZ

Sirens whined from somewhere down the mountain, drawing closer with every passing second. Buri picked himself up off the ground without bothering to dust himself off. He felt a sting coursing through his right cheek and touched his face with a finger. A smear of red streaked the flesh. Buri looked at it with more anger than concern. The wound wasn't mortal, but it sent a surge of rage through his body. He searched the area, desperate to figure out what had happened.

Had he done something wrong? Were one of the calendar stones misplaced? Perhaps one was a fake? There'd been an explosion, and the only explanation he could conjure was that he'd forgotten a step in the process. No, that couldn't be it. He'd been meticulous about everything.

As the dust and smoke caught the breeze, the thin air cleared to reveal the destruction. The man's face lengthened into an unbelieving scowl. The right column to the gate was gone, a pile of rubble with huge chunks of broken stone littering the ground.

The swirling blue light was gone; the hum that accompanied it now silent. Somehow, the gate was utterly destroyed.

The sirens drawing near handed him another piece to the puzzle.

Someone had called the police, and from the sound of it, they were in a hurry. Who could have done that? All of the prisoners were under his control. Could someone on one of the buses have called it in? *Impossible*, he thought. They believed the cops were the ones who ushered them to safety, away from the ruins. Someone else had called it in.

Buri peered through a haze, panning left to right until he noticed movement beyond the rubble. He winced in the bright sunlight and realized his eyelids scraped against his eyeballs like a cheese grater. Some of the debris had hit him in the eyes, and he was just now feeling it.

Ringing filled his ears with a high-pitched tone. He rubbed his eyes and blinked rapidly to clear out the debris.

Then he heard the gunshots.

The weapons belonged to his men. Something was wrong.

Buri stepped forward, drawing his pistol. Orientation returned, and his vision settled, though the ringing still lingered in his ears.

He brandished the pistol and stalked slowly through the swirling haze like a panther hunting its prey. More gunshots echoed from nearby, less than thirty feet away. He narrowed his eyes against the bright sunlight and made out two figures firing on his men. His vision cleared at the moment a breeze lifted the remaining dust from the air.

The Americans had subdued two of his men and taken their weapons. Three more lay on the ground, unmoving, while the others tried to return fire. Had they caused the explosion? If so, how?

That didn't matter now. The gate was destroyed, and if he had to guess, they had something to do with it.

He raised his pistol, taking aim at the girl first. Buri would make Alex watch her die first. He lined up the girl's neck with the pistol sights. His finger tensed on the trigger. Buri shook the remaining cobwebs from his mind and focused on the target. He applied more pressure to the trigger.

A heavy object suddenly struck him in the lower back. The gun discharged and the bullet sped into the blue sky as Buri's arms involuntarily flailed on impact. He hit the ground face-first, only narrowly managing to twist his head at the last second. His cheek paid the price instead of his nose. It was painful, but not as bad as it could have been.

The gun. Where is my gun? Fear gripped him. Buri's fingers scratched blindly at the dirt, searching for his weapon.

Another heavy blow to the ribs knocked him onto his side. He realized the gun would have to wait. He had a fight on his hands, and if he didn't retaliate, it wouldn't last long.

He rolled to his feet and took a few staggered steps back as he regained his bearings. Then he saw his attacker. Dak approached like a wolf being tossed a porterhouse, hungry and fearsome. His eyes burned as green flames, accented by the dark five o'clock shadow wrapping around his jaw. Behind him, two more of Buri's men lay in a heap, unmoving.

"Sorry about your little science experiment, Professor," Dak said as he neared.

"You?" Buri sneered, taking cautious steps backward.

"Oh, you thought it was an accident?" His head snapped back and forth. "I planted the explosive before you arrived. I would have blown it myself, but your goons worked me over pretty good. Still, I wasn't as bad off as I let them think. Their mistake."

Dak stopped a few yards away from his enemy and kept his hands lowered to his waist. "Now, we can do this the easy way, or we can do this the hard way."

"What?" Buri hissed.

"Well, you see, the easy way is where you get down on your knees, and I bind you, then leave you for the Bolivians to handle." He glanced over at the damage to the ancient gate. "I have a feeling they won't take too kindly to having a national landmark destroyed. Lot of money goes into this area just to see that thing." He motioned vaguely toward the portal—what was left of it. "Then, of course, there's the hard way. That involves a considerable amount of pain on your part, and comes with a complementary beating within an inch of your life."

"Do you think me afraid of you? You're nothing. I am descended from the gods!" He drew a long hunting knife from his belt and brandished it with his right hand, dancing back and forth on his tiptoes.

"Fine with me," Dak said. "Hard way it is."

Across the mesa, Tara and Alex split up as they pursued Buri's gunmen. More than half of the enemy was dead or wounded, but those who'd been less affected by the explosion had been able to regroup and retreat to cover behind several sections of stone walls, columns, and rocks. Most of them had been on the other side when the bomb went off. Stunned by the blast, confusion set in. Well trained or not, the combination of the explosion and then gunfire soon after caused the men to believe they were under attack from an external foe, not their prisoners.

Tara and Alex had initially pushed back the gunmen with their sudden and brutal attack, but the enemy quickly dispelled their shock and regrouped. Five of their unit remained, and now that they had reorganized, it wouldn't be long before they produced a counterattack.

"We're outnumbered," Tara said, rising from behind a huge stone to fire another shot.

"Yeah, I don't like it, either!" Alex shouted back as another volley of bullets rained down on their position. He crouched behind a huge chunk of wall sticking out of the ground. He heard the sound of sirens, barely audible over the repetitive, intermittent popping of enemy guns. "Cavalry is on its way. We just have to hold them off until the cops arrive."

One of the men behind a barrier shifted to his left—to Alex and Tara's right. They were fanning out to encircle the two. The man on the far left moved to his right, confirming the enemy's strategy.

They would create a perimeter, surrounding the two Americans in a kill box. Then they could squeeze in around the targets, exposing them on both sides where they had no cover.

Tara looked over her shoulder. She saw Dak squaring off with Buri. The latter held a long knife in his hand, while Dak remained unarmed. Based on the man's résumé, Dak was hardly an underdog in the fight even though he held no weapon. Still, it was a disadvantage, and without knowing much about Dak's opponent, the scales might be tipped in favor of the villain.

"Maybe we can kill two birds with one stone," Tara said. One of the men to the left moved to his right, taking the position where the previous gunman had crouched. It would be less than a minute before they were completely surrounded, and exposed on both sides.

"Gotta move fast whatever your plan is," Alex replied.

"We head to the gate, what's left of it. That will keep these guys at a safe distance."

"Okay, but that only solves the problem until they move again. They'll be able to flank us from all sides, not just two."

"Right," Tara agreed, "but not if we cut the head off the serpent."

Alex looked toward Buri, who stood with a blade extended toward Dak. Then Alex realized what his wife was suggesting. "I like it. You go first. I'll cover you. Head to the backside of the gate. Use the header as cover. When you get there, fire on their positions, and I'll join you."

She eyed him dubiously, but there was no time to argue. "Okay. Be careful," she said. Then she leaned over and kissed him hard on the lips. "I love you."

"I love you, too," he said with a smirk. "This will work. Don't worry."

"Who's worried?"

Tara turned toward the ruined gate and readied herself to take off.

Alex pressed his shoulder against the big stone and waited until the reports from the enemy guns slowed. Then he poked his weapon around the corner and fired. He aimed at the right side first and planted a bullet right at the base of a section of wall where the farthest guy to the right had taken refuge. The round nearly caught the man on an exposed foot, which he quickly withdrew. Alex continued down the line, firing single shots at each one of the men in quick succession.

Tara took off the second Alex opened fire. It felt like she had bags of sand tied to her legs. She pumped her muscles harder, fighting the lethargy that had settled in after being crouched on the ground. Adrenaline kicked in, and her muscles loosed slightly. The gate was only another twenty feet away. She heard Alex's weapon fire two more rapid shots before the enemy weapons answered.

She glanced back and saw the dirt and sand kicking up around Alex as he knelt behind the giant stone. For his part, he didn't look scared. A fierce determination and grit covered his face, to the point he looked downright angry at the fact they were shooting at him.

Then one of the men noticed Tara escaping across the plateau and turned his weapon on her. He opened fire with a series of quick pops. His weapon wasn't built for long-range targets. The shorter barrels of the pistol-framed AR-15s meant the weapons would be effective in an urban setting, particularly in an interior assault, but out here in the open, their accuracy was compromised.

Clouds of dust and debris exploded around her as if from a field of miniature land mines. She lowered her head and dove to the collapsed header that now rested at an angle, propped on rubble like a one-ton seesaw.

Bullets smashed into the stone as she pulled her feet in close under her. Her weapon would be less effective from this range, but she didn't have to hit anyone, she only had to buy Alex time to reach her.

She glanced around the right edge of the angled header and met his gaze. He nodded.

The men were repositioning themselves to tighten the noose around Alex's position. For the moment, it seemed they were content to let Tara go as they focused on Alex.

Tara slid to the other side of the stone and took aim on the nearest target, a man who was slipping around to Alex's left flank. She raised the sights slightly, accounting for distance, then squeezed the trigger. The round missed to the right of the man's left shoulder. He ducked instinctively, and she fired again. This one missed just inches away from the gunman's left hip. She took a breath and held it, then fired again.

The third round sailed through the air, across the twenty-five yards to the target. Luck was on her side. In the man's haste to get to a boulder lying just ten feet away from him, he ran straight into Tara's bullet. The round tore through flesh and crashed into his pelvis. He screamed in pain and dropped to the ground in a heap, rolling to a stop. Within seconds, he clutched at the wound to stem the bleeding.

He was no longer a concern, but the other four men were, and it was unlikely she'd be able to pull off such a crack shot a second time—much less four more. She had two spare magazines she'd taken off the men they'd incapacitated, but even with that many rounds there was no way she'd be able to pick off all the enemy gunmen. She turned her weapon to the next man in line and fired. He'd seen his comrade go down and retreated cautiously to cover once more. Then she peppered the others with slow, deliberate rounds.

Alex stood from his position and started to run, but a series of gunshots from the killers echoed across the ruins. Dirt exploded around him and he was forced to dive back to cover again.

They were in a stalemate. Tara knew she held the advantage. If she could keep the men at bay long enough, the cops would arrive. That plan quickly evaporated. The gunman on her right realized she and Alex were trying to retreat to the gate to regroup and buy time. So, in a desperate but calculated move, he sprinted hard toward one of the calendar pillars and dove behind it. She emptied her magazine trying to take him out, but he was too fast and too far away.

Now the gunman was close to Alex's right flank. From there, he could take out Tara's husband without much effort. Then they would surround her and Dak.

Another idea emerged from the soup of problems simmering in Tara's head. She looked back toward Dak and Buri who were forty feet away, then made up her mind.

29

LA PAZ

Buri held his knife at arm's length, waving it around cautiously as if he were trying to hypnotize a venomous snake.

Dak didn't flinch, keeping his stance wide and his positioning narrow to limit the target area for his opponent. The back of his skull pulsed with a dull pain, a result of the multiple blows he'd received from Buri's men. Dak pushed the pain away and locked on to the man with the weapon.

Buri stepped forward and thrust the knife at Dak's side.

Dak deftly dropped back a step and easily avoided the jab, but it was a mere test. Buri was feeling him out, as any good fighter would.

He switched his stance slightly and made a quicker move, feigning to the left with a snap kick, then driving hard with his right hand that held the blade.

Dak swatted the kick aside with his left hand, twisted 180 degrees, then deflected the stab and grabbed the assailant's wrist. He started to jerk Buri toward him, a move that would have brought the enemy within range to make one swift strike at the man's throat.

Buri sensed the move, and as Dak's fingers wrapped around his wrist, he turned his hand palm up and yanked back. The sharp edge of the blade sliced through flesh, and Dak snatched his hand away before the knife could do permanent damage.

He looked down at his fingers as the thin slits opened and bled. Three of the cuts were deep, but they hadn't hit nerves or bone. Dak was lucky he'd reacted so quickly. He'd sensed the man's intention at the last second and received nothing more than severe paper cuts to his fingers.

Still, he'd have to be more careful. He ignored the stinging pain in his fingers and retreated with a twist and a drop step to separate himself from the enemy.

Buri wore a satisfied, smug grin. "You seem to be bleeding."

"Lucky move," Dak countered.

"You're lucky I didn't take all your fingers at once. Not to worry. I will make quick work of you."

"You gonna just stand there and keep running your yap, or are you going to fight me?" Dak risked a peek out of the corner of his eye and saw Tara crouched by the toppled header. He also made out Alex, who was pinned down in a dangerous position out in the open. He had cover from a direct assault, but Buri's men were flanking him. It wouldn't be long before they had the upper hand.

Dak sighed, resigned himself, and stood with his feet shoulder width apart, facing his opponent head-on.

"Shall we? Or do you want to keep up with the foreplay?" Dak groused. He flicked his bloody fingers toward the man, beckoning him to make a move.

"Very well," Buri said with gravel in his voice.

He lunged toward Dak and sliced at his midsection.

The move was sudden, but Dak was ready. He'd presented an easy target for his opponent, a ruse to get the man to attack first. One thing Dak had learned when dealing with an enemy with a knife was to let them make the first move. Putting them on the offensive made their moves more predictable as opposed to taking the initiative and letting the chips fall where they may.

Buri corrected his momentum with a pivot and whipped the blade around again, narrowly missing Dak's right wrist.

Dak dropped to an elbow and kicked out his right leg.

Buri saw the move and jumped in time to miss the blow, but he was thrown off balance and had to dive to his side to maintain body control. He rolled to his feet just as Dak leaped at him. Buri extended the blade tip toward his opponent, stabbing hard like a cornered badger.

The sharp point dug into Dak's side, ripping a line through his shirt and skin that stretched from his armpit to his lowest rib. He tucked into a ball and dove clear of further damage, then took several steps back as he assessed the wound. Again, he was lucky. The knife had only scratched surface. It stung like an army of yellow jackets had struck his torso. He winced but fought off showing pain, unwilling to give in to the enemy.

He wouldn't be so lucky again.

The man with the knife circled around him like a shark in a swimming pool of chum. He tossed the knife back and forth from one hand to the other in a cocky display of ability.

Dak had to hand it to the guy. He'd underestimated Buri's skills with the blade, or in combat in general. The man was older, but fit, and clearly knew what he was doing in a fight.

Dak needed to get the knife away from the guy, but that would only be half the battle.

The world spun a little, and his head throbbed. The injury from his capture was clouding his vision and judgment ever so slightly. Dak realized the exertion of combat was the probable culprit of the symptoms returning, the effects enough to give his enemy a much-needed edge.

Buri sensed his opponent's struggle. Moments before, the man had been nearly unconscious. He'd been beaten badly and was in a weakened state. All Buri had to do was finish him off.

He relaxed visibly and took a predator's step toward Dak. He bared his teeth, moving in for the kill.

Dak wavered, but he stayed on his feet. The throbbing in the back of his skull caused him to grimace. His eyes tightened against the bright sunlight. Dak called on every ounce of focus he could and concentrated on the enemy.

Buri held the knife down at his side, twisting it back and forth so the sun's rays glinted and flashed across the dirt. "What's the matter? Not feeling so good?"

He feigned a charge at his opponent, and Dak flinched, raising both hands to block the attack that never came. Buri let out a laugh, then faked a jab.

Again, Dak raised his fists to block, but the blow didn't come.

Instead, Buri raised a boot and kicked Dak in the midsection.

Dak felt the air explode out of his lungs, and he instantly hunched over, gasping for air that his lungs wouldn't accept. Then something smacked him on the back of the head. Fingers dug into his neck and jerked upward. He fought against the hand pulling on his head, but his muscles wouldn't obey. His lungs still ached for air, and he felt himself desperate to collapse into a fetal position until his airways cleared.

Buri wouldn't allow that. He wrapped an arm around the former Delta Force operator and squeezed his forearm against Dak's neck just under the chin, forcing the man's head up and exposing his throat.

"Well," Buri said, "this was fun. Unfortunately for you, it's time to die." He brandished the blade and brought the razor-sharp edge to Dak's throat.

Dak mustered every ounce of courage and focus he could. He made out a figure across the mesa next to the destroyed gate. He narrowed his eyes and realized what he saw.

"I'm surprised you didn't ask me something stupid, like, any last words." Dak spat at his attacker.

Buri relaxed for a moment but not enough to allow his victim to escape. "No. I don't care what you have to say." He pressed the knife's edge to Dak's throat and was about to draw the blade across the carotid artery and jugular vein when a pop sounded from the center of the ruins.

Dak felt his captor's muscles tighten for a second, and then the hand holding the knife fell away, the rest of the man's body following seconds later. The knife clanked on the hard ground as Buri fell onto his back with a thud. Small bursts of dust shot out from under his form and blew away in the dry air.

Dak dropped to his knees, and his lungs finally opened up. He sucked in the air in deep gasps, bracing himself with his palms against the earth. He had enough presence of mind to tilt his head to the left, where he saw the figure still standing with her pistol raised.

Tara's hand remained steady; her eyes unemotional, like a fox after a kill. Then she lowered the weapon and nodded at him.

Dak spun around, his eyes still hazy, and grabbed the wounded man who clutched at the bleeding wound to his collarbone.

Buri grimaced in agony. The hollow point had shattered his clavicle into fragments. He rolled from side to side as if that would alleviate his pain. But it was only about to get worse.

Dak picked up the man's knife, grabbed Buri by the collar, and dragged him to his feet. He wrapped his arm around the man's neck, much as Buri had done to him, and jabbed the point of the knife into his throat, drawing a few droplets of blood that trickled down the shiny metal.

"Hey!" Dak shouted over the firefight across the ruins.

One of the flankers was nearly in position to take out Alex, who remained couched behind a large stone.

Tara fired her weapon in the air three times to draw the gunmen's attention.

"Put down your guns, or I kill this one!" Dak yelled. His voice carried over the mesa and beyond.

The gunmen froze. Two were still hiding behind cover, while the other two were stuck in mid-maneuver.

Dak felt the world settling in his vision. As his heartbeat returned normal, the throbbing in his head also diminished.

The last of the gunmen looked at each other, wondering what they should do next.

Buri tightened his throat, and Dak knew he was about to say

something stupid, like telling his men to never surrender. Dak tightened the knife tip against the man's neck. That shut him up.

Alex watched from behind his rock. Tara, too, risked a look around the gate's rubble.

Reluctantly, the gunmen lowered their weapons and put their hands in the air.

"Down here, please!" Tara shouted at them, satisfied they'd disarmed themselves.

The men hesitated.

"Do what she says!" Dak shouted, the exertion and volume causing his blood pressure to rise painfully again.

The gunmen obeyed and gradually made their way down to where Tara stood at the remnants of the ancient stone portal. Alex emerged from his hiding spot and kept his weapon trained on the gunmen.

The sounds of sirens echoed across the plateau, accompanied by the roars of engines. Then the first of the local police cars skidded around the bend in the road and screamed across the parking area. Five other squad cars followed and formed a protective wall around the perimeter of the ruins.

Dak dropped his captive to the ground with a thump. Buri screamed out in pain as his shoulder hit the ground and shot a new surge of fire through his collarbone. Dak tossed the blade aside as the cops emerged from their cars and began surrounding the area.

Tara and Alex also dropped their weapons to the ground and put their hands up in surrender.

Tara turned to her husband, who returned her gaze. She smirked at him, and he returned the gesture with a smile in his eyes. A galaxy of emotions swirled inside them, but relief was the one they latched on to and gripped tight. They'd won the battle at least, but something told them that behind the events of the last week, there was a larger war raging under the cover of darkness.

30

LA PAZ

Dak sat on the back step of an ambulance. His torn shirt lay on the ground next to him as the dark-haired male paramedic worked on the cut in his side. They'd already bandaged the wounds to his fingers. Another ambulance had already sped away with Dimitris. The paramedics said he'd lost a lot of blood, and as Tara and Alex suspected, was lucky to even be alive. But the men who'd brought him here had done enough to sustain him and even prevent further blood loss, which meant Dimitris was going to be okay with proper medical attention.

The police had taken away the gunmen and had also arrested the bus drivers whom Buri had employed. From the sound of it, the drivers would be released since they apparently had no idea why they were being paid to take visitors away from the ruins.

Tara and Alex meandered up to the ambulance and stopped short of Dak. Alex risked patting him on the shoulder. "How you feeling, man?" he asked.

Dak looked up and nodded. "Dizziness is fading. So is my headache. Gotta love that ibuprofen."

"Those cuts bad?" Tara asked, pointing at the one on his side.

"Nah," Dak shook his head. "Those are nothing. This one," he pointed at a scar on the left side of his abdomen, "was way worse."

"I kinda want to ask, but I'm not going to," Tara said, half laughing.

"Probably best you not know." His response teetered on playful and scary, like a cuddly otter holding an ax.

Alex looked out across the ruins. The grounds crawled with investigators of every kind. Ballistics, forensics, coroners, and ordinary cops all worked busily to figure out exactly what had happened.

A small group of historians from a local museum gathered around the damaged gate. They would rebuild it, as had been done before, though the stones wouldn't be original anymore. Tara and Alex both wondered if that might have any impact on the mysterious power of the portal. They secretly hoped it would render the gate useless. Either way, the people of La Paz were already planning solutions to keep their precious historical monument safe in the future.

"What's next for you two?" Dak asked, his voice cutting through the murmur of the crowd. "You could probably knock off a bank in this town, and no one would know it." He chuckled at his own joke.

"Yeah," Alex said, running fingers through his hair. "Looks like every cop in the region is here. Not that I blame them. I doubt they get much action, not like this." He glanced over at Tara and shrugged. "Guess it's back to Atlanta for us. Always plenty for us to do, and I'm sure that Tommy will have something since he's due to return in a couple of days."

Dak nodded and stuck out his bottom lip in approval. "Sounds good."

"What about you?" Tara asked.

Dak took a deep breath. "Back to babysitting for me. Gotta take care of that kid, make sure he doesn't get into too much trouble."

Tara's lips curled on the right side of her face. "Yeah, we can't have him homing in on your turf, can we?"

Dak laughed a little harder and then winced as the pain tugged at the new stitches in his side. "Definitely not. He causes enough on his own."

"So, back to hunting down relics?" Alex pressed.

"Yeah, probably," Dak grunted. "But I like it. It's usually a lot less dangerous than running a Delta Force day care."

"Usually?"

Dak snorted. "Well, sometimes I have to go to...let's just say... sketchy places."

"Understood."

A new voice scratched their ears from behind a set of police cars. "Well, it looks like you two can't seem to stay out of trouble, can you?"

Todd Brooks stepped out from the back of a black Chevy Tahoe. Two guards escorted him. All of them wore black suits and ties. Their outfits screamed Secret Service or special agents, which should have been the opposite of what they wanted.

"Agent Brooks," Alex muttered. "Great."

"Who?" Dak asked, befuddled.

"He's a fun goalie," Tara hissed before Brooks was within earshot.

"Oh, one of those."

"I see you made quite the mess of a national landmark," Brooks said, smiling as he put his hands out wide. He spun around dramatically to emphasize his point. "I gotta tell you, this is going to make shutting down your little operation in Atlanta a walk in the park."

Dak's forehead wrinkled, then he looked up at Tara. "Does this guy always talk in clichés, or does he eventually come up with something original to say?"

"No, it's pretty much standard fuzz speak."

"Oh, you think this is funny?" Brooks snapped, suddenly not so jovial. He raised a finger and pointed at all three of them. "I've got news for you. This is going to make international news. And it's going to have your names, and your precious IAA written all over it. You're done. You hear me?"

"You used the word news in back-to-back sentences," Alex quipped.

"Fine," Brooks said, nodding deliberately. "Make jokes all you want. By the end of the week, the IAA will be finished. And I will confiscate every artifact and relic you have in your possession."

"I doubt that," Dak said.

"What? Who are you? Their babysitter?"

"Some special agent," Dak huffed. "If you were so special, you'd know exactly who I am."

One of the guards stepped close and whispered in his superior's ear. Brooks's face drew long, his mouth gaping. He immediately collected himself, albeit with red cheeks. "Doesn't matter who he is," Brooks dug. It was the best he could do to save face in front of his men. He straightened his suit and tried to look dignified. "Be that as it may, by the time this story gets even the slightest media attention, you three are going to be—"

"Heroes," a familiar voice said from behind.

Incensed, Brooks spun on his heels to see who'd interrupted them. The truth was, he already knew.

"Hello again, Emily. What are you doing here?"

"Well, I heard a few of my friends were down here in La Paz for one of the local festivals. So," she raised her hands, "I decided to come down for a visit."

"What?" The confused look on Brooks's face was worth her long trip to Bolivia.

"They called me," Emily clarified, indicating Tara and Alex. "They told me what was going on and what they were doing. I tried to get here faster, but I got held up in Atlanta traffic."

"How unfortunate," he seethed.

"Yes, well, it looks like they know how to handle themselves." Emily paused and cocked her head to the left. For a second, the others couldn't tell if she was checking *on* Dak or checking him *out*. Given she was in a relationship with the former president, John Dawkins, it was likely the former. "You okay, Dak?"

Dak nodded lazily. "Yes, ma'am. I'll be all right. Nothin' I haven't seen before."

Brooks's head whipped back and forth as if watching a tennis match. "Wait a second. You know him?"

"You don't?"

He pressed his lips together.

Emily imagined that if he had been a cartoon character, steam would be blowing out of his ears.

"Dak Harper is an elite warrior, Agent Brooks. You'd do well to show him the proper respect."

"Didn't feel too elite today, ma'am," Dak grumbled.

"Things seemed to turn out fine." She realized Brooks was still standing impotently nearby. "Oh, I'm sorry. Todd, you may go now. Run along."

Brooks fumed but said nothing. He turned, motioned to his two men with a twirling finger, and stormed back toward the Chevy Tahoe.

"Let me guess!" Alex shouted at the fleeing agents. "You wanted to say something like, 'This is not over'?"

Brooks froze in midstride, paused, and then stalked faster toward his SUV.

After the laughter subsided, Emily turned her head and surveyed the damage to the ancient stone gate. "Sounds like you three got here just in the nick of time. Although I'm concerned that you could have been killed—multiple times, I might add. I don't feel good about you two doing this kind of work. Dak, you're fine."

"I'm retired."

"Maybe." Emily's lips curled upward. She focused on Tara and Alex. "Regardless of my concerns for your personal safety, you obviously know how to handle yourselves in the field. It's a good thing you were here. I shudder to think of what that lunatic might have pulled out of the gate." Her eyes wandered to the pile of stones once more. "I wonder," she said, pulling her gaze back to the couple, "you two were close to it when it blew, yes?"

"Yes, ma'am," they said together.

"Tell me what happened."

They relayed the story to Emily—the swirling blue light, the humming, and how their young friend had detonated the explosive from a remote location. Upon hearing that part, Dak excused himself to go call and check on the kid.

"That was it?" Emily asked after he limped away. "There was nothing else I should know?"

Tara wanted to relay what she'd felt, what she heard, but she simply shook her head. "No, that's it. Sounds an awful lot like the tech the Nazis were researching around the time of the Foo Fighter reports."

"It does," Emily agreed. "Glowing orbs from nothing. Sorry to say, I have no explanation for that one. It won't be a problem again. You helped make sure of that. I have to talk to a few more people here, make sure that nothing Todd was yammering about gets through to the media. And don't worry, you guys are safe. So is the IAA."

"We weren't," Tara said with a wink.

"Get home. Get some rest. Although I know you won't do the second thing. Knowing you two, you'll be back in the lab first thing tomorrow morning."

Tara and Alex shared a broad grin and nodded.

"You never know. We may call in sick tomorrow," Alex said.

"Yeah. Okay." Emily shook her head and walked away. Her tall black boots glistened in the sun. Her matching black skirt and trench coat fluttered in the breeze, flapping against the backs of her legs.

Dak meandered back over to where Tara and Alex stood. He looked out over the mesa.

"Boston okay?" Tara asked.

"Oh, yeah. He's fine. And I'll never...ever live it down that he was the one who bailed us out."

"That was good planning, though, giving him access to the detonator like that."

"Yeah, I just have to make sure he doesn't think he hurt anyone. Kid doesn't need that kind of baggage hanging in his brain."

"True," Tara said. She hadn't even considered that.

"Easy enough," Dak said. "It'll all be fine. Let's get back to town, maybe grab a bite to eat before we head home?"

"Sounds good to me," Alex said. He and Dak turned and started walking toward the parking area.

They didn't notice Tara linger behind, watching them closely. Her right hand reached into a pocket and then held it in front of her for a moment near her belt. She peeled back her fingers and looked at her palm. The sliver of Quantium had dimmed. It still glowed, but not with the same brightness as before. She swallowed and closed her fingers into a fist just as Alex realized she wasn't with them.

"You okay?" he asked.

She put on a fake half grin and nodded as she hurried to catch up. "Yep. I'm good." When the two men turned away again, she slid the chard back into her pocket, next to the one she'd taken from Buri.

31

LA PAZ

SIX WEEKS LATER

Buri climbed into the back of the prisoner transport truck, ushered in by three armed guards. The shackles on his wrists and ankles clanked and jingled with every move he made.

One of the guards stepped into the cargo hold and shoved the prisoner closer to the front cab. The guard used some choice words in Spanish to express his disdain for the prisoner.

Everyone in La Paz had heard about what this man had done to the ruins of Tiwanaku. The media covered it extensively: the plan to scare away visitors so he and his men could use an explosive to destroy the historical Sun Gate, one of the most important pieces of history in all of Bolivia.

In the weeks after the attack, the local government worked in record time—for a government—to repair the damage to the megalith, even bringing in stone from the nearby mountains to shape and mold the pillar into the exact shape and color as the original.

The authorities had never been able to pin a motive on the man who called himself Buri. It seemed an extravagant stunt, an attack on Bolivian pride perhaps. But why? The only thing the experts could come up with was that the man was insane.

Buri knew better than to expect some kind of mental health institution in his sentencing. He'd been lucky to receive medical care for his collarbone. The thought caused him to wiggle his shoulder around in a tight circle and he winced at the all-too-familiar pain that still radiated from the wound.

He'd been under close watch in a hospital for the first few weeks after surgery removed the bullet and bone fragments between his neck and shoulder. Armed guards watched his room 24/7. Once he'd healed and recovered from surgery, he was moved to the local jail and placed in a cell where he could continue to recover while the trial arrangements were made.

Buri knew how it was going to go down. The media narrative had already been fixed, selling lies about his attack on Tiwanaku, a crazy man bent on destroying historical landmarks due to a personal vendetta against the Bolivian people.

He knew the Americans were behind the lies. Not that it mattered. Now that he was fully recovered, they were moving him to San Pedro, the largest prison in Bolivia.

Most people would be terrified of being sent to such a vast holding facility, but Buri showed no fear.

San Pedro worked much like a self-contained community. Unlike prisons in most of the Western world, inmates were required to purchase their cells and how much they could afford to pay either increased or decreased the comfort level of their quarters. Money could also buy other amenities—if paid to the ruling sect of the prison's internal government. Of course, there were downsides to such a system. Those in charge enforced their laws through violence, usually in the form of stabbings, but occasionally with a strangling. And there were always "accidents" that occurred from time to time.

Buri knew he could manipulate such a system. It was built for a man like him, constructed on a foundation of corruption.

The prison guards cared little about what happened inside the walls so long as no one got out. The facility also contained an area for families of inmates to stay so they wouldn't be separated from husbands and fathers. There was even a prison hotel. In fact, the entire facility—shaped like a giant asterisk—was built to look just like a small, self-contained town. There were fountains, balconies, promenades, and even a few shops where inmates hawked their wares, cocaine being the most profitable.

Prisoners making a profit in jail.

The thought caused Buri to snicker, which caught the ire of the guard next to him.

"*Cállate*," the guard snapped.

Buri spoke enough Spanish to know he'd been told to shut up. Not that he cared. These guards were beneath him. He was descended from the gods. These people were nothing more than sheep to him, a commodity for indulgence or trade, nothing more.

A second guard climbed into the back of the truck and pulled the door shut. The third remained outside and locked up, then proceeded to hurry around to the front to join the driver in the cab.

A moment later, the engine roared, and the transport truck rumbled down the rough street.

It wouldn't be a long ride to San Pedro, maybe fifteen minutes depending on traffic. In a town like La Paz, a variety of factors could impede travel through the crowded streets. Cars, motorcycles, bicycles, pedestrians, and the occasional pack animal all vied for space as they maneuvered through the busy city.

The truck jostled the occupants as it bumped and swerved on the streets. Buri could hear horns honking intermittently. Moped and motorcycle motors could be heard on both sides, their drivers skirting by the truck and through traffic between the lanes to get ahead.

Buri closed his eyes and relaxed his neck, letting the back of his head rest against the wall. He felt the vehicle tilt the other direction when the driver made a sharp right-hand turn onto another street. Within a minute, the sounds of the city faded. Buri didn't think much of it. La Paz was strewn with backstreets and alleys, thoroughfares with far less noise. Many of those side streets hosted a cornucopia of criminal activity, the most prominent being the cocaine trade, though in recent years the cartels had pivoted more heavily toward heroin.

Buri detested the drug trade. He had some contacts in that world, but he loathed to use them. They were untrustworthy filth, and he held no appreciation for what their product did to people. Although, in a strange way, narcotics did help thin a portion of the herd he planned on eliminating. So, they weren't all bad.

The truck continued rolling at a monotonous pace, the engine lulling Buri into a semi-haze of sleep and delirium that was only interrupted by sporadic stabs of pain from his wounded shoulder. He wondered if that would ever go away. The thought of it being permanent angered him, but that was something he'd have to deal with later.

Fifteen minutes into the drive, Buri started wondering what was taking so long. The guards seemed unaffected by the duration of the ride, so he should have been unconcerned. He considered asking the men how much longer it was going to take, but he had a feeling the answer would be curt and rude.

Ten more minutes passed like years. Buri felt the road roughen, indicated by the steady vibrations of the vehicle and the occasional bumps. He wasn't sure, but it felt like they were no longer on a city street. If they were, it needed to be repaved. Perhaps they were on one of those cobblestone streets, one that played home to a litany of potholes.

Buri's concerns grew with every passing minute. Without many stops for traffic lights or signs, they should have already been at the prison by now. The guards appeared oblivious to any issues, which only heightened Buri's paranoia. Another five minutes dragged by, and a new thought racked his head. He'd heard of this sort of thing happening, though usually with a low-level functionary in a cartel.

Hit men would dress as cops, show up to transport a prisoner who was also a potential witness, and then they would drive them out to the middle of nowhere to be executed.

Why would these men want to kill him? It didn't make any sense.

The truck suddenly lurched forward, nearly throwing the three occupants against the front wall. The tires skidded on the earth beneath until the vehicle stopped. If they were on pavement, there would have been screeching of rubber on asphalt. They were out of the city on an unscheduled stop.

Dread flooded Buri's chest, and he felt his breath catch in a lump in his throat. This was how it ended? On the prairies of Bolivia where no one would ever find his body? He would vanish like an insect plucked up by a bird, the husk dropped in the wilderness to rot.

The seconds ticked by and Buri found himself breathing quickly as panic took hold.

The guards, for their part, also looked confused. One of them asked the other what was going on. The second merely shrugged.

Then the latch on the door unlocked and turned. Daylight poured into the cargo hold, momentarily blinding everyone inside. Buri shielded his eyes against the light of the sun, as did the two cops.

Six muffled pops cut the air, and for a moment Buri wondered when the pain would stab though his nerves. That stinging pain never came.

"You'd better hurry, sir," a familiar voice interrupted the silence. "It will only be a matter of time before the authorities figure out this truck didn't make it to its destination."

Buri lowered his hands and let his eyes adjust to the daylight.

The two guards were dead; one slumped against the wall of the truck, the other in a heap on the floor.

Buri raised his eyes and squinted. The man's American accent surprised him at first, but when he saw the face, he knew everything was going to be fine.

The prisoner stood, hunched over, and shuffled to the back of the truck. Todd Brooks extended a hand to help the man down. Once Buri was on the ground, he took in the surroundings. The city stood in the valley several miles away. They were near the foot of the mountains on an old dirt-and-gravel road.

Brooks motioned to one of his gunmen to release the shackles from the prisoner.

Buri felt blood return to his fingers and toes. The bitter smell of burned gunpowder lingered in the air, hanging in the cargo hold.

"Thank you," Buri said with a nod to Brooks.

"My pleasure, sir. We thought we lost you for a minute back at the ruins. Glad to hear it wasn't a mortal wound. How's your shoulder?"

Buri rolled the arm a few times and grimaced, then shrugged. "Still hurts, but nothing I can't manage. The surgeons were... adequate, but I may still need further attention in a better facility."

"We can arrange that once we're out of the country," Brooks assured him.

"Excellent." Buri looked around the corner of the transport vehicle and saw two Chevy Tahoes blocking the road. "I see you've taken care of everything, Agent Brooks. You and your men will be rewarded for this."

"Not necessary, sir. Just doing our job for the cause."

"Indeed." He paused, then asked, "What of the troublesome couple and their friend who caused all this?"

"Alex Simms and Tara Watson. They work for the International Archaeological Agency in Atlanta."

"That's a mouthful. What were they doing here? And their friend?"

"Dak Harper, sir. I had to do some additional research to dig up anything about him. He's former Delta Force. Not sure how he got roped into this."

"Ah. Well, it seems our adversaries may have won this round." Irritation sizzled on his tongue.

"All due respect, sir, we need to get you out of here. We can handle eliminating those pests later."

"Yes, Agent Brooks. Very good. Besides, this isn't the only site with a portal into the other realm."

"It's not?"

One of the men trotted up and informed Brooks the charges had been set.

"Good. Get the others back in the trucks. It's time to go." Brooks looked back to Buri. "You said this isn't the only site with a portal?"

Buri's head turned side to side, and he bared his teeth like a wolf. "No. There are others."

THANK YOU

Thank you for taking the time to read this story. We can always make more money, but time is a finite resource for all of us, so the fact you took the time to read my work means the world to me and I truly appreciate it. I hope you enjoyed it as much as I enjoyed sharing it, and I look forward to bringing you more fun adventures in the future. Also, if this story made you laugh, swing by Amazon and leave a review. I'd appreciate it and so would potential readers.

Ernest

OTHER BOOKS BY ERNEST DEMPSEY

Sean Wyatt Adventures:

The Secret of the Stones

The Cleric's Vault

The Last Chamber

The Grecian Manifesto

The Norse Directive

Game of Shadows

The Jerusalem Creed

The Samurai Cipher

The Cairo Vendetta

The Uluru Code

The Excalibur Key

The Denali Deception

The Sahara Legacy

The Fourth Prophecy

The Templar Curse

The Forbidden Temple

The Omega Project

The Napoleon Affair

Adriana Villa Adventures:

War of Thieves Box Set

When Shadows Call

Shadows Rising

Shadow Hour

The Adventure Guild:

The Caesar Secret: Books 1-3

The Carolina Caper

Beta Force:

Operation Zulu

London Calling

The Relic Runner:

Out of the Fire

For my editor Jason. Thanks for helping me push the limits of my imagination.

ACKNOWLEDGEMENT

As always, I would like to thank my terrific editors for their hard work. What they do makes my stories so much better for readers all over the world. Anne Storer and Jason Whited are the best editorial team a writer could hope for and I appreciate everything they do.

I also want to thank Elena at LI Graphics for her tremendous work on my book covers and for always overdelivering. Elena is amazing.

Last but not least, I need to thank all my wonderful fans and especially the advance reader team. Their feedback and reviews are always so helpful and I can't say enough good things about all of them.

See you next time,

Ernest

All places, people, and events in this book are fictional or used in a fictional way concocted from the author's imagination. Any correlation between those things and real people, places, things, or events is purely coincidence.

Printed in Great Britain
by Amazon

40939047R00151